AGATHA CHRISTIE

HALLOWE'EN PARTY

HarperCollins*Publishers*

To P.G. Wodehouse
whose books and stories have brightened my life for
many years. Also to show my pleasure in his having
been kind enough to tell me that he enjoys *my* books

HarperCollins*Publishers*
77-85 Fulham Palace Road,
Hammersmith, London W6 8JB
www.**fire**and**water**.com

This paperback edition 1994
9

Previously published in paperback by Fontana 1972
Reprinted twenty-three times

First published in Great Britain by
Collins 1969

Copyright Agatha Christie Mallowan 1969

ISBN 0 00 765949 0

Set in Plantin

Printed and bound in Great Britain by
Mackays of Chatham plc, Chatham, Kent

Hallowe'en Party

Agatha Christie is known throughout the world as the Queen of Crime. Her books have sold over a billion copies in English with another billion in 44 foreign languages. She is the most widely published author of all time and in any language, outsold only by the Bible and Shakespeare. She is the author of 80 crime novels and short story collections, 19 plays, and six novels written under the name of Mary Westmacott.

Agatha Christie's first novel, *The Mysterious Affair at Styles*, was written towards the end of the First World War, in which she served as a VAD. In it she created Hercule Poirot, the little Belgian detective who was destined to become the most popular detective in crime fiction since Sherlock Holmes. It was eventually published by The Bodley Head in 1920.

In 1926, after averaging a book a year, Agatha Christie wrote her masterpiece. *The Murder of Roger Ackroyd* was the first of her books to be published by Collins and marked the beginning of an author-publisher relationship which lasted for 50 years and well over 70 books. *The Murder of Roger Ackroyd* was also the first of Agatha Christie's books to be dramatised – under the name *Alibi* – and to have a successful run in London's West End. *The Mousetrap*, her most famous play of all, opened in 1952 and is the longest-running play in history.

Agatha Christie was made a Dame in 1971. She died in 1976, since when a number of books have been published posthumously: the bestselling novel *Sleeping Murder* appeared later that year, followed by her autobiography and the short story collections *Miss Marple's Final Cases*, *Problem at Pollensa Bay* and *While the Light Lasts*. In 1998 *Black Coffee* was the first of her plays to be novelised by another author, Charles Osborne.

BY THE SAME AUTHOR

CHAPTER 1

Mrs Ariadne Oliver had gone with the friend with whom she was staying, Judith Butler, to help with the preparations for a children's party which was to take place that same evening.

At the moment it was a scene of chaotic activity. Energetic women came in and out of doors moving chairs, small tables, flower vases, and carrying large quantities of yellow pumpkins which they disposed strategically in selected spots.

It was to be a Hallowe'en party for invited guests of an age group between ten and seventeen years old.

Mrs Oliver, removing herself from the main group, leant against a vacant background of wall and held up a large yellow pumpkin, looking at it critically – 'The last time I saw one of these,' she said, sweeping back her grey hair from her prominent forehead, 'was in the United States last year – hundreds of them. All over the house. I've never seen so many pumpkins. As a matter of fact,' she added thoughtfully, 'I've never really known the difference between a pumpkin and a vegetable marrow. What's this one?'

'Sorry, dear,' said Mrs Butler, as she fell over her friend's feet.

Mrs Oliver pressed herself closer against the wall.

'My fault,' she said. 'I'm standing about and getting in the way. But it *was* rather remarkable, seeing so many pumpkins or vegetable marrows, whatever they are. They were everywhere, in the shops, and in people's houses, with candles or nightlights inside them or strung up. Very interesting really. But it wasn't for a Hallowe'en party, it was Thanksgiving. Now I've always associated pumpkins with Hallowe'en and that's the end of October. Thanksgiving comes much later, doesn't it? Isn't it November, about the third week in November? Anyway, here, Hallowe'en is definitely the 31st of October, isn't it? First Hallowe'en and then, what comes next? All Souls' Day? That's when in Paris you go to cemeteries and put flowers on graves. Not a sad sort of feast. I mean, all the children go too, and enjoy themselves. You go to flower markets first and buy lots and lots of lovely flowers. Flowers never look so lovely as they do in Paris in the market there.'

A lot of busy women were falling over Mrs Oliver occasionally, but they were not listening to her. They were all too busy with what they were doing.

They consisted for the most part of mothers, one or two competent spinsters; there were useful teenagers, boys of sixteen and seventeen climbing up ladders or standing on chairs to put decorations, pumpkins or vegetable marrows or brightly coloured witchballs at a suitable elevation; girls from eleven to fifteen hung about in groups and giggled.

'And after All Souls' Day and cemeteries,' went on Mrs Oliver, lowering her bulk on to the arm of a settee, 'you have All Saints' Day. I think I'm right?'

Nobody responded to this question. Mrs Drake, a handsome middle-aged woman who was giving the party, made a pronouncement.

'I'm not calling this a Hallowe'en party, although of course it is one really. I'm calling it the Eleven Plus party. It's that sort of age group. Mostly people who are leaving the Elms and going on to other schools.'

'But that's not very accurate, Rowena, is it?' said Miss Whittaker, resetting her pince-nez on her nose disapprovingly.

Miss Whittaker as a local school-teacher was always firm on accuracy.

'Because we've abolished the eleven-plus some time ago.'

Mrs Oliver rose from the settee apologetically. 'I haven't been making myself useful. I've just been sitting here saying silly things about pumpkins and vegetable marrows' – And resting my feet, she thought, with a slight pang of conscience, but without sufficient feeling of guilt to say it aloud.

'Now what can I do next?' she asked, and added, 'What lovely apples!'

Someone had just brought a large bowl of apples into the room. Mrs Oliver was partial to apples.

'Lovely red ones,' she added.

'They're not really very good,' said Rowena Drake. 'But they look nice and partified. That's for bobbing for apples. They're rather soft apples, so people will be able to get their teeth into them better. Take them into the library, will you, Beatrice? Bobbing for apples always makes a mess with the water slopping over, but that doesn't matter with the library carpet, it's so old. Oh! Thank you, Joyce.'

Joyce, a sturdy thirteen-year-old, seized the bowl of apples. Two rolled off it and stopped, as though arrested by a witch's wand, at Mrs Oliver's feet.

'You like apples, don't you,' said Joyce. 'I read you did, or perhaps I heard it on the telly. You're the one who writes murder stories, aren't you?'

'Yes,' said Mrs Oliver.

'We ought to have made you do something connected with murders. Have a murder at the party tonight and make people solve it.'

'No, thank you,' said Mrs Oliver. 'Never again.'

'What do you mean, never again?'

'Well, I did once, and it didn't turn out much of a success,' said Mrs Oliver.

'But you've written lots of books,' said Joyce, 'you make a lot of money out of them, don't you?'

'In a way,' said Mrs Oliver, her thoughts flying to the Inland Revenue.

'And you've got a detective who's a Finn.'

Mrs Oliver admitted the fact. A small stolid boy not yet, Mrs Oliver would have thought, arrived at the seniority of the eleven-plus, said sternly, 'Why a Finn?'

'I've often wondered,' said Mrs Oliver truthfully.

Mrs Hargreaves, the organist's wife, came into the room breathing heavily, and bearing a large green plastic pail.

'What about this,' she said, 'for the apple bobbing? Kind of gay, I thought.'

Miss Lee, the doctor's dispenser, said, 'Galvanized bucket's better. Won't tip over so easily. Where are you going to have it, Mrs Drake?'

'I thought the bobbing for apples had better be in the library. The carpet's old there and a lot of water always gets spilt, anyway.'

'All right. We'll take them along. Rowena, here's another basket of apples.'

'Let me help,' said Mrs Oliver.

She picked up the two apples at her feet. Almost without noticing what she was doing, she sank her teeth into one of them and began to crunch it. Mrs Drake abstracted the second apple from her firmly and restored it to the basket. A buzz of conversation broke out.

'Yes, but where are we going to have the Snapdragon?'

'You ought to have the Snapdragon in the library, it's much the darkest room.'

'No, we're going to have that in the dining-room.'

'We'll have to put something on the table first.'

'There's a green baize to put on that and then the rubber sheet over it.'

'What about the looking-glasses? Shall we really see our husbands in them?'

Surreptitiously removing her shoes and still quietly champing at her apple, Mrs Oliver lowered herself once more on to the settee and surveyed the room full of people critically. She was thinking in her authoress's mind: 'Now, if I was going to make a book about all these people, how should I do it? They're nice people, I should think, on the whole, but who knows?'

In a way, she felt, it was rather fascinating *not* to know anything about them. They all lived in Woodleigh Common, some of them had faint tags attached to them in her memory because of what Judith had told her. Miss Johnson – something to do with the church, not the vicar's sister. Oh no, it was the organist's sister, of course. Rowena Drake, who seemed to run things in Woodleigh Common. The puffing woman who had brought in the pail, a particularly hideous plastic pail. But then Mrs Oliver had never been fond of plastic things. And then the children, the teenage girls and boys.

So far they were really only names to Mrs Oliver. There was a Nan and a Beatrice and a Cathie, a Diana and a Joyce, who was boastful and asked questions. I don't like Joyce much, thought Mrs Oliver. A girl called Ann, who looked tall and superior. There were two adolescent boys who appeared to have just got used to trying out different hair styles, with rather unfortunate results.

A smallish boy entered in some condition of shyness.

'Mummy sent these mirrors to see if they'd do,' he said in a slightly breathless voice.

Mrs Drake took them from him.

'Thank you so much, Eddy,' she said.

'They're just ordinary looking hand-mirrors,' said the girl called Ann. 'Shall we really see our future husbands' faces in them?'

'Some of you may and some may not,' said Judith Butler.

'Did you ever see your husband's face when you went to a party – I mean this kind of a party?'

'Of course she didn't,' said Joyce.

'She might have,' said the superior Beatrice. 'E.S.P. they call it. Extra sensory perception,' she added in the tone of one pleased with being thoroughly conversant with the terms of the times.

'I read one of your books,' said Ann to Mrs Oliver. '*The Dying Goldfish*. It was quite good,' she said kindly.

'I didn't like that one,' said Joyce. 'There wasn't enough blood in it. I like murders to have lots of blood.'

'A bit messy,' said Mrs Oliver, 'don't you think?'

'But exciting,' said Joyce.

'Not necessarily,' said Mrs Oliver.

'I *saw* a murder once,' said Joyce.

'Don't be silly, Joyce,' said Miss Whittaker, the school-teacher.

'I did,' said Joyce.

'Did you really?' asked Cathie, gazing at Joyce with wide eyes, 'really and truly see a murder?'

'Of course she didn't,' said Mrs Drake. 'Don't say silly things, Joyce.'

'I did see a murder,' said Joyce. 'I did. I did. I did.'

A seventeen-year-old boy poised on a ladder looked down interestedly.

'What kind of a murder?' he asked.

'I don't believe it,' said Beatrice.

'Of course not,' said Cathie's mother. 'She's just making it up.'

'I'm *not*. I *saw* it.'

'Why didn't you go to the police about it?' asked Cathie.

'Because I didn't know it *was* a murder when I saw it. It wasn't really till a long time afterwards, I mean, that I began to know that it was a murder. Something that somebody said only about a month or two ago suddenly made me think: Of course, that was a *murder* I saw.'

'You see,' said Ann, 'she's making it all up. It's nonsense.'

'When did it happen?' asked Beatrice.

'Years ago,' said Joyce. 'I was quite young at the time,' she added.

'Who murdered who?' said Beatrice.

'I shan't tell any of you,' said Joyce. 'You're all so horrid about it.'

Miss Lee came in with another kind of bucket. Conversation shifted to a comparison of buckets or plastic pails as most suitable for the sport of bobbing for apples. The majority of the helpers repaired to the library for an appraisal on the spot. Some of the younger members, it may be said, were anxious to demonstrate, by a rehearsal of the difficulties and their own accomplishment in the sport. Hair got wet, water got spilt, towels were sent for to mop it up. In the end it was decided that a galvanized bucket was preferable to the more meretricious charms of a plastic pail which overturned rather too easily.

Mrs Oliver, setting down a bowl of apples which she had carried in to replenish the store required for tomorrow, once more helped herself to one.

'I read in the paper that you were fond of eating apples,' the accusing voice of Ann or Susan – she was not quite sure which – spoke to her.

'It's my besetting sin,' said Mrs Oliver.

'It would be more fun if it was melons,' objected one of the boys. 'They're so juicy. Think of the mess it would make,' he said, surveying the carpet with pleasurable anticipation.

'Mrs Oliver, feeling a little guilty at the public arraignment of greediness, left the room in search of a particular apartment, the geography of which is usually fairly easily identified. She went up the staircase and, turning the corner on the half landing, cannoned into a pair, a girl and a boy, clasped in each other's arms and leaning against the door which Mrs Oliver felt fairly certain was the door to the room to which she herself was anxious to gain access. The couple paid no attention to her. They sighed and they snuggled. Mrs Oliver wondered how old they were. The boy was fifteen, perhaps, the girl little more than twelve, although the development of her chest seemed certainly on the mature side.

Apple Trees was a house of fair size. It had, she thought, several agreeable nooks and corners. How selfish people are, thought Mrs Oliver. No consideration for others. That well-known tag from the past came into her mind. It had been said to her in succession by a nursemaid, a nanny, a governess, her grandmother, two great-aunts, her mother and a few others.

'Excuse me,' said Mrs Oliver in a loud, clear voice.

The boy and the girl clung closer than ever, their lips fastened on each other's.

'Excuse me,' said Mrs Oliver again, 'do you *mind* letting me pass? I want to get in at this door.'

Unwillingly the couple fell apart. They looked at her in an aggrieved fashion. Mrs Oliver went in, banged the door and shot the bolt.

It was not a very close fitting door. The faint sound of words came to her from outside.

'Isn't that like people?' one voice said in a somewhat uncertain tenor. 'They might *see* we didn't want to be disturbed.'

'People are so selfish,' piped a girl's voice. 'They never think of anyone but themselves.'

'No consideration for others,' said the boy's voice.

CHAPTER 2

Preparations for a children's party usually give far more trouble to the organizers than an entertainment devised for those of adult years. Food of good quality and suitable alcoholic refreshment – with lemonade on the side, that, to the right people, is quite enough to make a party go. It may cost more but the trouble is infinitely less. So Ariadne Oliver and her friend Judith Butler agreed together.

'What about teenage parties?' said Judith.

'I don't know much about them,' said Mrs Oliver.

'In one way,' said Judith, 'I think they're probably least trouble of all. I mean, they just throw all of us adults out. And say they'll do it all themselves.'

'And do they?'

'Well, not in our sense of the word,' said Judith. 'They forget to order some of the things, and order a lot of other things that nobody likes. Having turfed us out, then they say there were things we ought to have provided for them to find. They break a lot of glasses, and other things, and there's always somebody undesirable or who brings an undesirable friend. You know the sort of thing. Peculiar drugs and – what do they call it? – Flower Pot or Purple Hemp or L.S.D., which I always have thought just meant money, but apparently it doesn't.'

'I suppose it costs it,' suggested Ariadne Oliver.

'It's very unpleasant, and Hemp has a nasty smell.'

'It all sounds very depressing,' said Mrs Oliver.

'Anyway, this party will go all right. Trust Rowena Drake for that. She's a wonderful organizer. You'll see.'

'I don't feel I even want to go to a party,' sighed Mrs Oliver.

'You go up and lie down for an hour or so. You'll see.

You'll enjoy it when you get there. I wish Miranda hadn't got a temperature – she's so disappointed at not being able to go, poor child.'

The party came into being at half past seven. Ariadne Oliver had to admit that her friend was right. Arrivals were punctual. Everything went splendidly. It was well imagined, well run and ran like clockwork. There were red and blue lights on the stairs and yellow pumpkins in profusion. The girls and boys arrived holding decorated broomsticks for a competition. After greetings, Rowena Drake announced the programme for the evening. 'First, judging of the broomstick competition,' she said, 'three prizes, first, second and third. Then comes cutting the flour cake. That'll be in the small conservatory. Then bobbing for apples – there's a list pinned upon the wall over there of the partners for that event – then there'll be dancing. Every time the lights go out you change partners. Then girls to the small study where they'll be given their mirrors. After that, supper, Snapdragon and then prize-giving.'

Like all parties, it went slightly stickily at first. The brooms were admired, they were very small miniature brooms, and on the whole the decorating of them had not reached a very high standard of merit, 'which makes it easier,' said Mrs Drake in an aside to one of her friends. 'And it's a very useful thing because I mean there are always one or two children one knows only too well won't win a prize at anything else, so one can cheat a little over this.'

'So unscrupulous, Rowena.'

'I'm not really. I just arrange so that things should be fair and evenly divided. The whole point is that everyone wants to win *something*.'

'What's the Flour Game?' asked Ariadne Oliver.

'Oh yes, of course, you weren't here when we were doing it. Well, you just fill a tumbler with flour, press it in well, then you turn it out in a tray and place a sixpence on top of it. Then everyone slices a slice off it very carefully so as not to tumble the sixpence off. As soon as someone tumbles the sixpence off, that person goes out. It's a sort of elimination. The last one left in gets the sixpence of course. Now then, away we go.'

And away they went. Squeals of excitement were heard coming from the library where bobbing for apples went on, and competitors returned from there with wet locks and having disposed a good deal of water about their persons.

One of the most popular contests, at any rate among the girls, was the arrival of the Hallowe'en witch played by Mrs Goodbody, a local cleaning woman who, not only having the necessary hooked nose and chin which almost met, was admirably proficient in producing a semi-cooing voice which had definitely sinister undertones and also produced magical doggerel rhymes.

'Now then, come along, Beatrice, is it? Ah, Beatrice. A very interesting name. Now you want to know what your husband is going to look like. Now, my dear, sit here. Yes, yes, under this light here. Sit here and hold this little mirror in your hand, and presently when the lights go out you'll see him appear. You'll see him looking over your shoulder. Now hold the mirror steady. *Abracadabra, who shall see? The face of the man who will marry me. Beatrice, Beatrice, you shall find, the face of the man who shall please your mind.*'

A sudden shaft of light shot across the room from a stepladder, placed behind a screen. It hit the right spot in the room, which was reflected in the mirror grasped in Beatrice's excited hand.

'Oh!' cried Beatrice. 'I've seen him. I've seen him! I can see him in my mirror!'

The beam was shut off, the lights came on and a coloured photograph pasted on a card floated down from the ceiling. Beatrice danced about excitedly.

'That was him! That was him! I saw him,' she cried. 'Oh, he's got a *lovely* ginger beard.'

She rushed to Mrs Oliver, who was the nearest person.

'Do look, do look. Don't you think he's rather wonderful? He's like Eddie Presweight, the pop singer. Don't you think so?'

Mrs Oliver did think he looked like one of the faces she daily deplored having to see in her morning paper. The beard, she thought, had been an after-thought of genius.

'Where do all these things come from?' she asked.

'Oh, Rowena gets Nicky to make them. And his friend Desmond helps. He experiments a good deal with photography. He and a couple of pals of his made themselves up, with a great deal of hair or side-burns or beards and things. And then with the light on him and everything, of course it sends the girls wild with delight.'

'I can't help thinking,' said Ariadne Oliver, 'that girls are really very silly nowadays.'

'Don't you think they always were?' asked Rowena Drake.

Mrs Oliver considered.

'I suppose you're right,' she admitted.

'Now then,' cried Mrs Drake – 'supper.'

Supper went off well. Rich iced cakes, savouries, prawns, cheese and nut confections. The eleven-pluses stuffed themselves.

'And now,' said Rowena, 'the last one for the evening. Snapdragon. Across there, through the pantry. That's right. Now then. Prizes first.'

The prizes were presented, and then there was a wailing, banshee call. The children rushed across the hall back to the dining-room.

The food had been cleared away. A green baize cloth was laid across the table and here was borne a great dish of flaming raisins. Everybody shrieked, rushing forward, snatching the blazing raisins, with cries of 'Ow, I'm burned! Isn't it lovely?' Little by little the Snapdragon flickered and died down. The lights went up. The party was over.

'It's been a great success,' said Rowena.

'So it should be with all the trouble you've taken.'

'It was lovely,' said Judith quietly. 'Lovely.'

'And now,' she added ruefully, 'we'll have to clear up a bit. We can't leave everything for those poor women tomorrow morning.'

CHAPTER 3

In a flat in London the telephone bell rang. The owner of the flat, Hercule Poirot, stirred in his chair. Disappointment attacked him. He knew before he answered it what it meant. His friend Solly, with whom he had been going to spend the evening, reviving their never-ending controversy about the real culprit in the Canning Road Municipal Baths murder, was about to say that he could not come. Poirot, who had collected certain bits of evidence in favour of his own somewhat far-fetched theory, was deeply disappointed. He did not think his friend Solly would accept his suggestions, but he had no doubt that when Solly in his turn produced his own fantastic beliefs, he himself, Hercule Poirot, would just as easily be able to demolish them in the name of sanity, logic, order and method. It was annoying, to say the least of it, if Solly did not come this evening. But it is true that when they had met earlier in the day, Solly had been racked with a chesty cough and was in a state of highly infectious catarrh.

'He had a nasty cold,' said Hercule Poirot, 'and no doubt, in spite of the remedies that I have handy here, he would probably have given it to me. It is better that he should not come. *Tout de même*,' he added, with a sigh, 'it will mean that now I shall pass a dull evening.'

Many of the evenings were dull now, Hercule Poirot thought. His mind, magnificent as it was (for he had never doubted that fact) required stimulation from outside sources. He had never been of a philosophic cast of mind. There were times when he almost regretted that he had not taken to the study of theology instead of going into the police force in his early days. The number of angels who could dance on the point of a needle; it would be interesting

17

to feel that that mattered and to argue passionately on the point with one's colleagues.

His manservant, George, entered the room.

'It was Mr Solomon Levy, sir.'

'Ah yes,' said Hercule Poirot.

'He very much regrets that he will not be able to join you this evening. He is in bed with a serious bout of 'flu.'

'He has not got 'flu,' said Hercule Poirot. 'He has only a nasty cold. Everyone always thinks they have 'flu. It sounds more important. One gets more sympathy. The trouble with a catarrhal cold is that it is hard to glean the proper amount of sympathetic consideration from one's friends.'

'Just as well he isn't coming here, sir, really,' said George. 'Those colds in the head are very infectious. Wouldn't be good for you to go down with one of those.'

'It would be extremely tedious,' Poirot agreed.

The telephone bell rang again.

'And now who has a cold?' he demanded. 'I have not asked anyone else.'

George crossed towards the telephone.

'I will take the call here,' said Poirot. 'I have no doubt that it is nothing of interest. But at any rate –' he shrugged his shoulders ' – it will perhaps pass the time. Who knows?'

George said, 'Very good, sir,' and left the room.

Poirot stretched out a hand, raised the receiver, thus stilling the clamour of the bell.

'Hercule Poirot speaks,' he said, with a certain grandeur of manner designed to impress whoever was at the other end of the line.

'That's wonderful,' said an eager voice. A female voice, slightly impaired with breathlessness. 'I thought you'd be sure to be out, that you wouldn't be there.'

'Why should you think that?' inquired Poirot.

'Because I can't help feeling that nowadays things always happen to frustrate one. You want someone in a terrible hurry, you feel you can't wait, and you *have* to wait. I wanted to get hold of you urgently – absolutely urgently.'

'And who are you?' asked Hercule Poirot.

The voice, a female one, seemed surprised.

'Don't you *know?*' it said incredulously.

'Yes, I know,' said Hercule Poirot. 'You are my friend, Ariadne.'

'And I'm in a terrible state,' said Ariadne.

'Yes, yes, I can hear that. Have you also been running? You are very breathless, are you not?'

'I haven't exactly been running. It's emotion. Can I come and see you *at once?*'

Poirot let a few moments elapse before he answered. His friend, Mrs Oliver, sounded in a highly excitable condition. Whatever was the matter with her, she would no doubt spend a very long time pouring out her grievances, her woes, her frustrations or whatever was ailing her. Once having established herself within Poirot's sanctum, it might be hard to induce her to go home without a certain amount of impoliteness. The things that excited Mrs Oliver were so numerous and frequently so unexpected that one had to be careful how one embarked upon a discussion of them.

'Something has upset you?'

'Yes. Of course I'm upset. I don't know what to do. I don't know – oh, I don't know anything. What I feel is that I've got to come and tell you – tell you just what's happened, for you're the only person who might know what to do. Who might tell me what I ought to do. So can I come?'

'But certainly, but certainly. I shall be delighted to receive you.'

The receiver was thrown down heavily at the other end and Poirot summoned George, reflected a few minutes, then ordered lemon barley water, bitter lemon and a glass of brandy for himself.

'Mrs Oliver will be here in about ten minutes,' he said.

George withdrew. He returned with the brandy for Poirot, who accepted it with a nod of satisfaction, and George then proceeded to provide the teetotal refreshment that was the only thing likely to appeal to Mrs Oliver. Poirot took a sip of brandy delicately, fortifying himself for the ordeal which was about to descend upon him.

'It's a pity,' he murmured to himself, 'that she is so scatty. And yet, she has originality of mind. It could be that I am going to enjoy what she is coming to tell me. It could be –' he reflected a minute ' – that it may take a great deal of the evening and that it will all be excessively foolish. *Eh bien*, one must take one's risks in life.'

A bell sounded. A bell on the outside door of the flat this time. It was not a single pressure of the button. It lasted for a long time with a kind of steady action that was very effective, the sheer making of noise.

'Assuredly, she has excited herself,' said Poirot.

He heard George go to the door, open it, and before any decorous announcement could be made the door of his sitting-room opened and Ariadne Oliver charged through it, with George in tow behind her, hanging on to something that looked like a fisherman's sou'wester and oilskins.

'What on earth are you wearing?' said Hercule Poirot. 'Let George take it from you. It's very wet.'

'Of course it's wet,' said Mrs Oliver. 'It's very wet out. I never thought about water before. It's a terrible thing to think of.

Poirot looked at her with interest.

'Will you have some lemon barley water,' he said, 'or could I persuade you to a small glass of *eau de vie*?'

'I hate water,' said Mrs Oliver.

Poirot looked surprised.

'I hate it. I've never thought about it before. What it can do, and everything.'

'My dear friend,' said Hercule Poirot, as George extricated her from the flapping folds of watery oilskin. 'Come and sit down here. Let George finally relieve you of – what is it you are wearing?'

'I got it in Cornwall,' said Mrs Oliver. 'Oilskins. A real, proper fisherman's oilskin.'

'Very useful to him, no doubt,' said Poirot, 'but not, I think, so suitable for you. Heavy to wear. But come – sit down and tell me.'

'I don't know how,' said Mrs Oliver, sinking into a chair. 'Sometimes, you know, I can't feel it's really true. But it happened. It really happened.'

'Tell me,' said Poirot.

'That's what I've come for. But now I've got here, it's so difficult because I don't know where to begin.'

'At the beginning?' suggested Poirot, 'or is that too conventional a way of acting?'

'I don't know when the beginning was. Not really. It could have been a long time ago, you know.'

'Calm yourself,' said Poirot. 'Gather together the various threads of this matter in your mind and tell me. What is it that has so upset you?'

'It would have upset you, too,' said Mrs Oliver. 'At least, I suppose it would.' She looked rather doubtful. 'One doesn't know, really, what does upset you. You take so many things with a lot of calm.'

'It is often the best way,' said Poirot.

'All right,' said Mrs Oliver. 'It began with a party.'

'Ah yes,' said Poirot, relieved to have something as ordinary and sane as a party presented to him. 'A party. You went to a party and something happened.'

'Do you know what a Hallowe'en party is?' said Mrs Oliver.

'I know what Hallowe'en is,' said Poirot. 'The 31st of October.' He twinkled slightly as he said, 'When witches ride on broomsticks.'

'There *were* broomsticks,' said Mrs Oliver. 'They gave prizes for them.'

'Prizes?'

'Yes, for who brought the best decorated ones.'

Poirot looked at her rather doubtfully. Originally relieved at the mention of a party, he now again felt slightly doubtful. Since he knew that Mrs Oliver did not partake of spirituous liquor, he could not make one of the assumptions that he might have made in any other case.

'A children's party,' said Mrs Oliver. 'Or rather, an eleven-plus party.'

'Eleven-plus?'

'Well, that's what they used to call it, you know, in schools. I mean they see how bright you are, and if you're bright enough to pass your eleven-plus, you go on to a grammar school or something. But if you're not bright enough, you go to something called a Secondary Modern. A silly name. It doesn't seem to mean anything.'

'I do not, I confess, really understand what you are talking about,' said Poirot. They seemed to have got away from parties and entered into the realms of education.

Mrs Oliver took a deep breath and began again.

'It started really,' she said, 'with the apples.'

'Ah yes,' said Poirot, 'it would. It always might with you, mightn't it?'.

He was thinking to himself of a small car on a hill and a large woman getting out of it, and a bag of apples breaking, and the apples running and cascading down the hill.

'Yes,' he said encouragingly, 'apples.'

'Bobbing for apples,' said Mrs Oliver. 'That's one of the things you do at a Hallowe'en party.'

'Ah yes, I think I have heard of that, yes.'

'You see, all sorts of things were being done. There was bobbing for apples, and cutting sixpence off a tumblerful of flour, and looking in a looking-glass –'

'To see your true love's face?' suggested Poirot knowledgeably.

'Ah,' said Mrs Oliver, 'you're beginning to understand at last.'

'A lot of old folklore, in fact,' said Poirot, 'and this all took place at your party.'

'Yes, it was all a great success. It finished up with Snapdragon. You know, burning raisins in a great dish. I suppose – ' her voice faltered, ' – I suppose that must be the actual time when it was done.'

'When what was done?'

'A murder. After the Snapdragon everyone went home,' said Mrs Oliver. 'That, you see, was when they couldn't find her.'

'Find whom?'

'A girl. A girl called Joyce. Everyone called her name and looked around and asked if she'd gone home with anyone else, and her mother got rather annoyed and said that Joyce must have felt tired or ill or something and gone off by herself, and that it was very thoughtless of her not to leave word. All the sort of things that mothers say when things like that happen. But anyway, we couldn't find Joyce.'

'And had she gone home by herself?'

'No,' said Mrs Oliver, 'she hadn't gone home . . .' Her voice faltered. 'We found her in the end – in the library. That's where – where someone did it, you know. Bobbing for apples. The bucket was there. A big, galvanized bucket. They wouldn't have the plastic one. Perhaps if they'd had the plastic one it wouldn't have happened. It wouldn't have been heavy enough. It might have tipped over –'

'What happened?' said Poirot. His voice was sharp.

'That's where she was found,' said Mrs Oliver. 'Someone, you know, someone had shoved her head down into the water with the apples. Shoved her down and held her there so that she was dead, of course. Drowned. *Drowned*. Just in a galvanized iron bucket nearly full of water. Kneeling there, sticking her head down to bob at an apple. I hate apples,' said Mrs Oliver. 'I never want to see an apple again.'

Poirot looked at her. He stretched out a hand and filled a small glass with cognac.

'Drink this,' he said. 'It will do you good.'

CHAPTER 4

Mrs Oliver put down the glass and wiped her lips.

'You were right,' she said. 'That – that helped. I was getting hysterical.'

'You have had a great shock, I see now. When did this happen?'

'Last night. Was it only last night? Yes, yes, of course.'

'And you came to me.'

It was not a quite a question, but it displayed a desire for more information than Poirot had yet had.

'You came to me – why?'

'I thought you could help,' said Mrs Oliver. 'You see, it's – it's not simple.'

'It could be and it could not,' said Poirot. 'A lot depends. You must tell me more, you know. The police, I presume, are in charge. A doctor was, no doubt, called. What did he say?'

'There's to be an inquest,' said Mrs Oliver.

'Naturally.'

'Tomorrow or the next day.'

'This girl, Joyce, how old was she?'

'I don't know exactly. I should think perhaps twelve or thirteen.'

'Small for her age?'

'No, no, I should think rather mature, perhaps. Lumpy,' said Mrs Oliver.

'Well developed? You mean sexy-looking?'

'Yes, that is what I mean. But I don't think that was the kind of crime it was – I mean that would have been more simple, wouldn't it?'

'It is the kind of crime,' said Poirot, 'of which one reads every day in the paper. A girl who is attacked, a school child who is assaulted – yes, every day. This happened in a private house which makes it different, but perhaps not so different as all that. But all the same, I'm not sure yet that you've told me everything.'

'No, I don't suppose I have,' said Mrs Oliver. 'I haven't told you the reason, I mean, why I came to you.'

'You knew this Joyce, you knew her well?'

'I didn't know her at all. I'd better explain to you, I think, just how I came to be there.'

'There is *where?*'

'Oh, a place called Woodleigh Common.'

'Woodleigh Common,' said Poirot thoughtfully. 'Now where lately –' he broke off.

'It's not very far from London. About – oh, thirty to forty miles, I think. It's near Medchester. It's one of those places where there are a few nice houses, but where a certain amount of new building has been done. Residential. A good school nearby, and people can commute from there to London or into Medchester. It's quite an ordinary sort of place where people with what you might call everyday reasonable incomes live.'

'Woodleigh Common,' said Poirot again, thoughtfully.

'I was staying with a friend there. Judith Butler. She's a widow. I went on a Hellenic cruise this year and Judith was on the cruise and we became friends. She's got a daughter. A girl called Miranda who is twelve or thirteen. Anyway, she asked me to come and stay and she said friends of hers were giving this party for children, and it was to be a Hallowe'en party. She said perhaps I had some interesting ideas.'

'Ah,' said Poirot, 'she did not suggest this time that you should arrange a murder hunt or anything of that kind?'

'Good gracious, no,' said Mrs Oliver. 'Do you think I should ever consider such a thing again?'

'I should think it unlikely.'

'But it happened, that's what's so awful,' said Mrs Oliver. 'I mean, it couldn't have happened just because *I* was there, could it?'

'I do not think so. At least – Did any of the people at the party know who you were?'

'Yes,' said Mrs Oliver. 'One of the children said something about my writing books and that they liked murders. That's how it – well – that's what led to the thing – I mean to the thing that made me come to you.'

'Which you still haven't told me.'

'Well, you see, at first I didn't think of it. Not straight away. I mean, children do queer things sometimes. I mean there are queer children about, children who – well, once I suppose they would have been in mental homes and things, but they send them home now and tell them to lead ordinary lives or something, and then they go and do something like this.'

'There were some young adolescents there?'

'There were two boys, or youths as they always seem to call them in police reports. About sixteen to eighteen.'

'I suppose one of them might have done it. Is that what the police think?'

'They don't say what they think,' said Mrs Oliver, 'but they looked as though they might think so.'

'Was this Joyce an attractive girl?'

'I don't think so,' said Mrs Oliver. 'You mean attractive to boys, do you?'

'No,' said Poirot, 'I think I meant – well, just the plain simple meaning of the word.'

'I don't think she was a very nice girl,' said Mrs Oliver, 'not one you'd want to talk to much. She was the sort of girl who shows off and boasts. It's a rather tiresome age, I think. It sounds unkind what I'm saying, but –'

'It is not unkind in murder to say what the victim was like,' said Poirot. It is very, very necessary. The personality of the victim is the cause of many a murder. How many people were there in the house at the time?'

'You mean for the party and so on? Well, I suppose there were five or six women, some mothers, a schoolteacher, a doctor's wife, or sister, I think, a couple of middle-aged married people, the two boys of sixteen to eighteen, a girl of fifteen, two or three of eleven or twelve – well that sort of thing. About twenty-five or thirty in all, perhaps.'

'Any strangers?'

'They all knew each other, I think. Some better than others. I think the girls were mostly in the same school. There were a couple of women who had come in to help with the food and the supper and things like that. When the party ended, most of the mothers went home with their children. I stayed behind with Judith and a couple of others to help Rowena Drake, the woman who gave the party, to clear up a bit, so the cleaning women who came in the morning wouldn't have so much mess to deal with. You know, there was a lot of flour about, and paper caps out of crackers and different things. So we swept up a bit, and we got to the library last of all. And that's when – when we found her. And then I remembered what she'd said.'

'What who had said?'

'Joyce.'

'What did she say? We are coming to it now, are we not? We are coming to the reason why you are here?'

'Yes. I thought it wouldn't mean anything to – oh, to a doctor or the police or anyone, but I thought it might mean something to you.'

'*Eh bien*,' said Poirot, 'tell me. Was this something Joyce said at the party?'

'No – earlier in the day. That afternoon when we were fixing things up. It was after they'd talked about my writing murder stories and Joyce said "I *saw* a murder once" and her mother or somebody said "Don't be silly, Joyce, saying things like that" and one of the older girls said "You're just making it up" and Joyce said "I did. I *saw* it I tell you. I did. I saw someone do a murder," but no one believed her. They just laughed and she got very angry.'

'Did *you* believe her?'

'No, of course not.'

'I see,' said Poirot, 'yes, I see.' He was silent for some

moments, tapping a finger on the table. Then he said: 'I wonder – she gave no details – no names?'

'No. She went on boasting and shouting a bit and being angry because most of the other girls were laughing at her. The mothers, I think, and the older people, were rather cross with her. But the girls and the younger boys just laughed at her! They said things like "Go on, Joyce, when was this? Why did you never tell us about it?" And Joyce said, "I'd forgotten all about it, it was so long ago".'

'Aha! Did she say how long ago?'

'Years ago,' she said. 'You know, in rather a would-be grown-up way.'

'"Why didn't you go and tell the police then?" one of the girls said. Ann, I think, or Beatrice. Rather a smug, superior girl.'

'Aha, and what did she say to *that*?'

'She said: "Because I didn't know at the time it *was* a murder".'

'A very interesting remark,' said Poirot, sitting up rather straighter in his chair.

'She'd got a bit mixed up by then, I think,' said Mrs Oliver. 'You know, trying to explain herself and getting angry because they were all teasing her.

'They kept asking her why she hadn't gone to the police, and she kept on saying "Because I didn't know then that it was a murder. It wasn't until afterwards that it came to me quite suddenly that that was what I had seen".'

'But nobody showed any signs of believing her – and you yourself did not believe her – but when you came across her dead you suddenly felt that she might have been speaking the truth?'

'Yes, just that. I didn't know what I ought to do, or what I could do. But then, later, I thought of you.'

Poirot bowed his head gravely in acknowledgement. He was silent for a moment or two, then he said:

'I must pose to you a serious question, and reflect before you answer it. Do you think that this girl had *really* seen a murder? Or do you think that she merely *believed* that she had seen a murder?'

'The first, I think,' said Mrs Oliver. 'I didn't at the time. I just thought that she was vaguely remembering something she had once seen and was working it up to make it sound important and exciting. She became very vehement, saying, "I *did* see it, I tell you. I *did* see it happen".'

'And so.'

'And so I've come along to you,' said Mrs Oliver, 'because the only way her death makes sense is that there really *was* a murder and that she was a witness to it.'

'That would involve certain things. It would involve that one of the people who were at the party committed the murder, and that that same person must also have been there earlier that day and have heard what Joyce said.'

'You don't think I'm just imagining things, do you?' said Mrs Oliver. 'Do you think that it is all just my very far-fetched imagination?'

'A girl was murdered,' said Poirot. 'Murdered by someone who had strength enough to hold her head down in a bucket of water. An ugly murder and a murder that was committed with what we might call, no time to lose. Somebody was threatened, and whoever it was struck as soon as it was humanly possible.'

'Joyce could not have known who it was who did the murder she saw,' said Mrs Oliver. 'I mean she wouldn't have said what she did if there was someone actually in the room who was concerned.'

'No,' said Poirot, 'I think you are right there. She saw a murder, but she did not see the murderer's face. We have to go beyond that.'

'I don't understand exactly what you mean.'

'It could be that someone who was there earlier in the day and heard Joyce's accusation knew about the murder, knew who committed the murder, perhaps was closely involved with that person. It may have been that someone thought he was the only person who knew what his wife had done, or

29

his mother or his daughter or his son. Or it might have been a woman who knew what her husband or mother or daughter or son had done. Someone who thought that no one else knew. And then Joyce began talking . . .'

'And so –'

'Joyce had to die?'

'Yes. What are you going to do?'

'I have just remembered,' said Hercule Poirot, 'why the name of Woodleigh Common was familiar to me.'

CHAPTER 5

Hercule Poirot looked over the small gate which gave admission to Pine Crest. It was a modern, perky little house, nicely built. Hercule Poirot was slightly out of breath. The small, neat house in front of him was very suitably named. It was on a hill top, and the hill top was planted with a few sparse pines. It had a small neat garden and a large elderly man was trundling along a path a big tin galvanized waterer.

Superintendent Spence's hair was now grey all over instead of having a neat touch of grey hair at the temples. He had not shrunk much in girth. He stopped trundling his can and looked at the visitor at the gate. Hercule Poirot stood there without moving.

'God bless my soul,' said Superintendent Spence. 'It must be. It can't be but it is. Yes, it must be. Hercule Poirot, as I live.'

'Aha,' said Hercule Poirot, 'you know me. That is gratifying.'

'May your moustaches never grow less,' said Spence.

He abandoned the watering can and came down to the gate.

'Diabolical weeds,' he said. 'And what brings you down here?'

'What has brought me to many places in my time,' said Hercule Poirot, 'and what once a good many years ago brought *you* to see *me*. Murder.'

'I've done with murder,' said Spence, 'except in the case of weeds. That's what I'm doing now. Applying weed killer. Never so easy as you think, something's always wrong, usually the weather. Mustn't be too wet, mustn't be too dry and all the rest of it. How did you know where to find me?'

he asked as he unlatched the gate and Poirot passed through.

'You sent me a Christmas card. It had your new address notified on it.'

'Ah yes, so I did. I'm old-fashioned, you know. I like to send round cards at Christmas time to a few old friends.'

'I appreciate that,' said Poirot.

Spence said, 'I'm an old man now.'

'We are both old men.'

'Not much grey in your hair,' said Spence.

'I attend to that with a bottle,' said Hercule Poirot. 'There is no need to appear in public with grey hair unless you wish to do so.'

'Well, I don't think jet black would suit me,' said Spence.

'I agree,' said Poirot. 'You look most distinguished with grey hair.'

'I should never think of myself as a distinguished man.'

'I think of you as such. Why have you come to live in Woodleigh Common?'

'As a matter of fact, I came here to join forces with a sister of mine. She lost her husband, her children are married and living abroad, one in Australia and the other in South Africa. So I moved in here. Pensions don't go far nowadays, but we do pretty comfortably living together. Come and sit down.'

He led the way on to the small glazed-in verandah where there were chairs and a table or two. The autumn sun fell pleasantly upon this retreat.

'What shall I get you?' said Spence. 'No fancy stuff here, I'm afraid. No blackcurrant or rose hip syrup or any of your patent things. Beer? Or shall I get Elspeth to make you a cup of tea? Or I can do you a shandy or Coca-Cola or some cocoa if you like it. My sister, Elspeth, is a cocoa drinker.'

'You are very kind. For me, I think a shandy. The ginger beer and the beer? That is right, is it not?'

'Absolutely so.'

He went into the house and returned shortly afterwards carrying two large glass mugs. 'I'm joining you,' he said.

He drew a chair up to the table and sat down, placing the two glasses in front of himself and Poirot.

'What was it you said just now?' he said, raising his glass. 'We won't say "Here's to crime." I've done with crime, and if you mean the crime I think you do, in fact which I think you have to do, because I don't recall any other crime just lately. I don't like the particular form of murder we've just had.'

'No. I do not think you would do so.'

'We *are* talking about the child who had her head shoved into a bucket?'

'Yes,' said Poirot, 'that is what I am talking about.'

'I don't know why you come to me,' said Spence. 'I'm nothing to do with the police nowadays. All that's over many years ago.'

'Once a policeman,' said Hercule Poirot, 'always a policeman. That is to say, there is always the point of view of the policeman behind the point of view of the ordinary man. I know, I who talk to you. I, too, started in the police force in my country.'

'Yes, so you did. I remember now your telling me. Well, I suppose one's outlook is a bit slanted, but it's a long time since I've had any active connection.'

'But you hear the gossip,' said Poirot. 'You have friends of your own trade. You will hear what they think or suspect or what they know.'

Spence sighed.

'One knows too much,' he said, 'that is one of the troubles nowadays. There is a crime, a crime of which the pattern is familiar, and you know, that is to say the active police officers know, pretty well who's probably done that crime. They don't tell the newspapers but they make their inquiries, and *they know*. But whether they're going to get any further than that – well, things have their difficulties.'

'You mean the wives and the girl friends and the rest of it?'

'Partly that, yes. In the end, perhaps, one gets one's man. Sometimes a year or two passes. I'd say, you know, roughly, Poirot, that more girls nowadays marry wrong 'uns than they ever used to in my time.'

Hercule Poirot considered, pulling his moustaches.

'Yes,' he said, 'I can see that that might be so. I suspect that girls have always been partial to the bad lots, as you say, but in the past there were safeguards.'

'That's right. People were looking after them. Their mothers looked after them. Their aunts and their older sisters looked after them. Their younger sisters and brothers knew what was going on. Their fathers were not averse to kicking the wrong young men out of the house. Sometimes, of course, the girls used to run away with one of the bad lots. Nowadays there's no need even to do that. Mother doesn't know who the girl's out with, father's not told who the girl is out with, brothers know who the girl is out with but they think "more fool her". If the parents refuse consent, the couple go before a magistrate and manage to get permission to marry, and then when the young man who everyone knows is a bad lot proceeds to prove to everybody, including his wife, that he *is* a bad lot, the fat's in the fire! But love's love; the girl doesn't want to think that her Henry has these revolting habits, these criminal tendencies, and all the rest of it. She'll lie for him, swear black's white for him and everything else. Yes, it's difficult. Difficult for us, I mean. Well, there's no good going on saying things were better in the old days. Perhaps we only thought so. Anyway, Poirot, how did you get yourself mixed up in all this? This isn't your part of the country, is it? Always thought you lived in London. You used to when I knew you.'

'I still live in London. I involved myself here at the request of a friend, Mrs Oliver. You remember Mrs Oliver?'

Spence raised his head, closed his eyes and appeared to reflect.

'Mrs Oliver? Can't say that I do.'

'She writes books. Detective stories. You met her, if you will throw your mind back, during the time that you persuaded me to investigate the murder of Mrs McGinty. You will not have forgotten Mrs McGinty?'

'Good lord, no. But it was a long time ago. You did me a good turn there, Poirot, a very good turn. I went to you for help and you didn't let me down.'

'I was honoured – flattered – that you should come to consult me,' said Poirot. 'I must say that I despaired once or twice. The man we had to save – to save his neck in those days I believe, it is long ago enough for that – was a man who was excessively difficult to do anything for. The kind of standard example of how not to do anything useful for himself.'

'Married that girl, didn't he? The wet one. Not the bright one with the peroxide hair. Wonder how they got on together. Have you ever heard about it?'

'No,' said Poirot. 'I presume all goes well with them.'

'Can't see what she saw in him.'

'It is difficult,' said Poirot, 'but it is one of the great consolations in nature that a man, however unattractive, will find that he is attractive – to some woman. One can only say or hope that they married and lived happily ever afterwards.'

'Shouldn't think they lived happily ever afterwards if they had to have Mother to live with them.'

'No, indeed,' said Poirot. 'Or Step-father,' he added.

'Well,' said Spence, 'here we are talking of old days again. All that's over. I always thought that man, can't remember his name now, ought to have run an undertaking parlour. Had just the face and manner for it. Perhaps he did. The girl had some money, didn't she? Yes, he'd have made a very good undertaker. I can see him, all in black, calling for orders for the funeral. Perhaps he can even have been enthusiastic over the right kind of elm or teak or whatever they use for coffins. But he'd never have made good selling insurance or real estate. Anyway, don't let's harp back.' Then he said suddenly, 'Mrs Oliver. Ariadne Oliver. *Apples.* Is that how she's got herself mixed up in this? That poor child got her head shoved under water in a bucket of floating apples, didn't she, at a party? Is that what interested Mrs Oliver?'

'I don't think she was particularly attracted because of the apples,' said Poirot, 'but she was at the party.'

'Do you say she lived here?'

'No, she does not live here. She was staying with a friend, a Mrs Butler.'

'Butler?' Yes, I know her. Lives down not far from the church. Widow. Husband was an airline pilot. Has a daughter. Rather nice-looking girl. Pretty manners. Mrs Butler's rather an attractive woman, don't you think so?'

'I have as yet barely met her, but, yes, I thought she was very attractive.'

'And how does this concern you, Poirot? You weren't here when it happened?'

'No. Mrs Oliver came to me in London. She was upset, very upset. She wanted me to do something.'

A faint smile showed on Superintendent Spence's face.

'I see. Same old story. I came up to you, too, because I wanted you to do something.'

'And I have carried things one step further,' said Poirot. '*I* have come to *you*.'

'Because you want me to do something? I tell you, there's nothing I can do.'

'Oh yes there is. You can tell me all about the people. The people who live here. The people who went to that party. The fathers and mothers of the children who were at the party. The school, the teachers, the lawyers, the doctors. Somebody, during a party, induced a child to kneel down, and perhaps, laughing, saying: "I'll show you the best way to get hold of an apple with your teeth. I know the trick of

36

it." And then he or she – whoever it was – put a hand on that girl's head. There wouldn't have been much struggle or noise or anything of that kind.'

'A nasty business,' said Spence. 'I thought so when I heard about it. What do you want to know? I've been here a year. My sister's been here longer – two or three years. It's not a big community. It's not a particularly settled one either. People come and go. The husband has a job in either Medchester or Great Canning, or one of the other places round about. Their children go to school here. Then perhaps the husband changes his job and they go somewhere else. It's not a fixed community. Some of the people have been here a long time, Miss Emlyn, the school-mistress, has, Dr Ferguson has. But on the whole, it fluctuates a bit.'

'One supposes,' said Hercule Poirot, 'that having agreed with you that this was a nasty business, I might hope that you would know who are the nasty people here.'

'Yes,' said Spence. 'It's the first thing one looks for, isn't it? And the next thing one looks for is a nasty adolescent in a thing of this kind. Who wants to strangle or drown or get rid of a lump of a girl of thirteen? There doesn't seem to have been any evidence of a sexual assault or anything of that kind, which would be the first thing one looks for. Plenty of that sort of thing in every small town or village nowadays. There again, I think there's more of it than there used to be in my young day. We had our mentally disturbed, or whatever they call them, but not so many as we have now. I expect there are more of them let out of the place they ought to be kept safe in. All our mental homes are too full; over-crowded, so doctors say "Let him or her lead a normal life. Go back and live with his relatives," etc. And then the nasty bit of goods, or the poor afflicted fellow, whichever way you like to look at it, gets the urge again and another young woman goes out walking and is found in a gravel pit, or is silly enough to take lifts in a car. Children don't come home from school because they've accepted a lift from a stranger, although they've been warned not to. Yes, there's a lot of that nowadays.'

'Does that quite fit the pattern we have here?'

'Well, it's the first thing one thinks of,' said Spence. 'Somebody was at the party who had the urge, shall we say. Perhaps he'd done it before, perhaps he'd only wanted to do it. I'd say roughly that there might be some past history of assaulting a child somewhere. As far as I know, nobody's come up with anything of that kind. Not officially, I mean. There were two in the right age group at the party. Nicholas Ransom, nice-looking lad, seventeen or eighteen. He'd be the right age. Comes from the East Coast or somewhere like that, I think. Seems all right. Looks normal enough, but who knows? And there's Desmond, remanded once for a psychiatric report, but I wouldn't say there was much to it. It's got to be someone at the party, though of course I suppose anyone *could* have come in from outside. A house isn't usually locked up during a party. There's a side door open, or a side window. One of our half-baked people, I suppose could have come along to see what was on and sneaked in. A pretty big risk to take. Would a child agree, a child who'd gone to a party, to go playing apple games with anyone she *didn't* know? Anyway, you haven't explained yet, Poirot, what brings you into it. You said it was Mrs Oliver. Some wild idea of hers?'

'Not exactly a wild idea,' said Poirot. 'It is true that writers are prone to wild ideas. Ideas, perhaps, which are on the far side of probability. But this was simply something that she heard the girl say.'

'What, the child Joyce?'

'Yes.'

Spence leant forward and looked at Poirot inquiringly.

'I will tell you,' said Poirot.

Quietly and succinctly he recounted the story as Mrs Oliver had told it to him.

'I see,' said Spence. He rubbed his moustache. 'The girl said that, did she? Said she'd seen a murder committed. Did she say when or how?'

'No,' said Poirot.

'What led up to it?'

'Some remark, I think, about the murders in Mrs Oliver's books. Somebody said something about it to Mrs Oliver. One of the children, I think, to the effect that there wasn't enough blood in her books or enough bodies. And then Joyce spoke up and said *she*'d seen a murder once.'

'Boasted of it? That's the impression you're giving me.'

'That's the impression Mrs Oliver got. Yes, she boasted of it.'

'It mightn't have been true.'

'No, it might not have been true at all,' said Poirot.

'Children often make these extravagant statements when they wish to call attention to themselves or to make an effect. On the other hand, it might have been true. Is that what you think?'

'I do not know,' said Poirot. 'A child boasts of having witnessed a murder. Only a few hours later, that child is dead. You must admit that there are grounds for believing that it might – it's a far-fetched idea perhaps – but it might have been cause and effect. If so, somebody lost no time.'

'Definitely,' said Spence. 'How many were present at the time the girl made her statement re murder, do you know exactly?'

'All that Mrs Oliver said was that she thought there were about fourteen or fifteen people, perhaps more. Five or six children, five or six grown-ups who were running the show. But for exact information I must rely on you.'

'Well, that will be easy enough,' said Spence. 'I don't say I know off-hand at the moment, but it's easily obtained from the locals. As to the party itself, I know pretty well already. A preponderance of women, on the whole. Fathers don't turn up much at children's parties. But they look in, sometimes, or come to take their children home. Dr Ferguson was there, the vicar was there. Otherwise, mothers, aunts, social workers, two teachers from the school. Oh, I can give you a list – and roughly about fourteen children. The youngest not more than ten – running on into teenagers.'

'And I suppose you would know the list of probables amongst them?' said Poirot.

'Well, it won't be so easy now if what you think is true.'

'You mean you are no longer looking for a sexually disturbed personality. You are looking instead for somebody who has committed a murder and got away with it, someone who never expected it to be found out and who suddenly got a nasty shock.'

'Blest if I can think who it could have been, all the same,' said Spence. 'I shouldn't have said we had any likely murderers round here. And certainly nothing spectacular in the way of murders.'

'One can have likely murderers anywhere,' said Poirot, 'or shall I say unlikely murderers, but nevertheless murderers. Because unlikely murderers are not so prone to be suspected. There is probably not very much evidence against them, and it would be a rude shock to such a murderer to find that there had actually been an eye-witness to his or her crime.'

'Why didn't Joyce say anything at the time? That's what I'd like to know. Was she bribed to silence by someone, do you think? Too risky surely.'

'No,' said Poirot. 'I gather from what Mrs Oliver mentioned that she didn't recognize that it *was* a murder she was looking at at the time.'

'Oh, surely that's most unlikely,' said Spence.

'Not necessarily,' said Poirot. 'A child of thirteen was speaking. She was remembering something she'd seen in the past. We don't know exactly when. It might have been three or even four years previously. She saw something but she didn't realize its true significance. That might apply to a lot of things you know, *mon cher*. Some rather peculiar car accident. A car where it appeared that the driver drove straight at the person who was injured or perhaps killed. A child might not realize it *was* deliberate *at the time*. But something someone said, or something she saw or heard a year or two later might awaken her memory and she'd think perhaps: "A or B or X did it *on purpose*." "Perhaps it was really a murder, not just an accident." And there are plenty of other possibilities. Some of them I will admit suggested by my friend, Mrs Oliver, who can easily come up with about twelve different solutions to everything, most of them not very probable but all of them faintly possible. Tablets added to a cup of tea administered to someone. Roughly that sort of thing. A push perhaps on a dangerous spot. You have no cliffs here, which is rather a pity from the point of view of likely theories. Yes, I think there could be plenty of possibilities. Perhaps it is some murder story that the girl reads which recalls to her an incident. It may have been an incident that puzzled her at the time, and she might, when she reads the story, say: "Well, *that* might have been so-and-so and so-and-so. I wonder if he or she did it on purpose?" Yes, there are a lot of possibilities.'

'And you have come here to inquire into them?'

'It would be in the public interest, I think, don't you?' said Poirot.

'Ah, we're to be public spirited, are we, you and I?'

'You can at least give me information,' said Poirot. 'You know the people here.'

'I'll do what I can,' said Spence. 'And I'll rope in Elspeth. There's not much about people she doesn't know.'

CHAPTER 6

Satisfied with what he had achieved, Poirot took leave of his friend.

The information he wanted would be forthcoming – he had no doubt as to that. He had got Spence interested. And Spence, once set upon a trail, was not one to relinquish it. His reputation as a retired high-ranking officer of the C.I.D. would have won him friends in the local police departments concerned.

And next – Poirot consulted his watch – he was to meet Mrs Oliver in exactly ten minutes' time outside a house called Apple Trees. Really, the name seemed uncannily appropriate.

Really, thought Poirot, one didn't seem able to get away from apples. Nothing could be more agreeable than a juicy English apple – And yet here were apples mixed up with broomsticks, and witches, and old-fashioned folklore, and a murdered child.

Following the route indicated to him, Poirot arrived to the minute outside a red brick Georgian style house with a neat beech hedge enclosing it, and a pleasant garden showing beyond.

He put his hand out, raised the latch and entered through the wrought iron gate which bore a painted board labelled 'Apple Trees'. A path led up to the front door. Looking rather like one of those Swiss clocks where figures come out automatically of a door above the clock face, the front door opened and Mrs Oliver emerged on the steps.

'You're absolutely punctual,' she said breathlessly. 'I was watching for you from the window.'

Poirot turned and closed the gate carefully behind him. Practically on every occasion that he had met Mrs Oliver, whether by appointment or by accident, a motif of apples seemed to be introduced almost immediately. She was either eating an apple or *had* been eating an apple – witness an apple core nestling on her broad chest – or was carrying a bag of apples. But today there was no apple in evidence at all. Very correct, Poirot thought approvingly. It would have been in very bad taste to be gnawing an apple here, on the scene of what had been not only a crime but a tragedy. For what else can it be but that? thought Poirot. The sudden death of a child of only thirteen years old. He did not like to think of it, and because he did not like to think of it he was all the more decided in his mind that that was exactly what he was going to think of until by some means or other, light should shine out of the darkness and he should see clearly what he had come here to see.

'I can't think why you wouldn't come and stay with Judith Butler,' said Mrs Oliver. 'Instead of going to a fifth-class guest house.'

'Because it is better that I should survey things with a certain degree of aloofness,' said Poirot. 'One must not get involved, you comprehend.'

'I don't see how you can avoid getting involved,' said Mrs Oliver. 'You've got to see everyone and talk to them, haven't you?'

'That most decidedly,' said Poirot.

'Who have you seen so far?'

'My friend, Superintendent Spence.'

'What's he like nowadays?' said Mrs Oliver.

'A good deal older than he was,' said Poirot.

'Naturally,' said Mrs Oliver, 'what else would you expect? Is he deafer or blinder or fatter or thinner?'

Poirot considered.

'He has lost a little weight. He wears spectacles for reading the paper. I do not think he is deaf, not to any noticeable extent.'

'And what does he think about it all?'

'You go too quickly,' said Poirot.

'And what exactly are you and he going to do?'

'I have planned my programme,' said Poirot. 'First I have seen and consulted with my old friend. I asked him to get me, perhaps, some information that would not be easy to get otherwise.'

'You mean the police here will be his buddies and he'll get a lot of inside stuff from them?'

'Well, I should not put it exactly like that, but yes, those are the lines along which I have been thinking.'

'And after that?'

'I come to meet you here, Madame. I have to see just where this thing happened.'

Mrs Oliver turned her head and looked up at the house.

'It doesn't look the sort of house there'd be a murder in, does it?' she said.

Poirot thought again: What an unerring instinct she has!

'No,' he said, 'it does not look at all that sort of a house. After I have seen *where*, then I go with you to see the mother of the dead child. I hear what she can tell me. This afternoon my friend Spence is making an appointment for me to talk with the local inspector at a suitable hour. I should also like a talk with the doctor here. And possibly the head-mistress at the school. At six o'clock I drink tea and eat sausages with my friend Spence and his sister again in their house and we discuss.'

'What more do you think he'll be able to tell you?'

'I want to meet his sister. She has lived here longer than he has. He came here to join her when her husband died. She will know, perhaps, the people here fairly well.'

'Do you know what you sound like?' said Mrs Oliver. 'A computer. You know. You're programming yourself. That's what they call it, isn't it? I mean you're feeding all these things into yourself all day and then you're going to see what comes out.'

'It is certainly an idea you have there,' said Poirot, with some interest. 'Yes, yes, I play the part of the computer. One feeds in the information –'

'And supposing you come up with all the wrong answers?' said Mrs Oliver.

'That would be impossible,' said Hercule Poirot. 'Computers do not do that sort of a thing.'

'They're not supposed to,' said Mrs Oliver, 'but you'd be surprised at the things that happen sometimes. My last electric light bill, for instance. I know there's a proverb which says "To err is human," but a human error is nothing to what a computer can do if it tries. Come on in and meet Mrs Drake.'

Mrs Drake was certainly something, Poirot thought. She was a tall, handsome woman of forty-odd, her golden hair was lightly tinged with grey, her eyes were brilliantly blue, she oozed competence from the fingertips downwards. Any party she had arranged would have been a successful one. In the drawing-room a tray of morning coffee with two sugared biscuits was awaiting them.

Apple Trees, he saw, was a most admirably kept house. It was well furnished, it had carpets of excellent quality, everything was scrupulously polished and cleaned, and the fact that it had hardly any outstanding object of interest in it was not readily noticeable. One would not have expected it. The colours of the curtains and the covers were pleasant but conventional. It could have been let furnished at any moment for a high rent to a desirable tenant, without having to put away any treasures or make any alterations to the arrangement of the furniture.

Mrs Drake greeted Mrs Oliver and Poirot and concealed almost entirely what Poirot could not help suspecting was a feeling of vigorously suppressed annoyance at the position in which she found herself as the hostess at a social occasion at which something as anti-social as murder had occurred. As a prominent member of the community of Woodleigh Common, he suspected that she felt an unhappy sense of having herself in some way proved inadequate. What had occurred should *not* have occurred. To someone else in someone else's house – yes. But at a party for children, arranged by her, given by her, organized by her, nothing like this ought to have happened. Somehow or other she ought to have seen to it that it did *not* happen. And Poirot also had a suspicion that she was seeking round irritably in the back of her mind for a reason. Not so much a reason for murder having taken place, but to find out and pin down some inadequacy on the part of someone who had been helping her and who had by some mismanagement or some lack of perception failed to realize that something like this *could* happen.

'Monsieur Poirot,' said Mrs Drake, in her fine speaking voice, which Poirot thought would come over excellently in a small lecture room or the village hall, 'I am so pleased you could come down here. Mrs Oliver has been telling me how invaluable your help will be to us in this terrible crisis.'

'Rest assured, Madame, I shall do what I can, but as you no doubt realize from your experience of life, it is going to be a difficult business.'

'Difficult?' said Mrs Drake. 'Of course it's going to be difficult. It seems incredible, absolutely *incredible*, that such an awful thing should have happened. I suppose,' she added, 'the police *may* know something? Inspector Raglan has a very good reputation locally, I believe. Whether or not they ought to call Scotland Yard in, I don't know. The idea seems to be that this poor child's death must have had a local significance. I needn't tell you, Monsieur Poirot – after all, you read the papers as much as I do – that there have been very many sad fatalities with children all over the countryside. They seem to be getting more and more frequent. Mental instability seems to be on the increase, though I must say that mothers and families generally are not looking after their children properly, as they used to do. Children are sent home from school alone, on dark evenings, go alone on dark early mornings. And children, however much you warn them, are unfortunately very foolish when it comes to being offered a lift in a smart-looking car. They believe what they're told. I suppose one cannot help that.'

'But what happened here, Madame, was of an entirely different nature.'

'Oh, I know – I know. That is why I used the term incredible. I still cannot quite believe it,' said Mrs Drake. 'Everything was entirely under control. All the arrangements were made. Everything was going perfectly, all according to plan. It just seems – seems incredible. Personally I consider myself that there *must* be what I call an *outside* significance to this. *Someone* walked into the house – not a difficult thing to do under the circumstances – someone of highly disturbed mentality, I suppose, the kind of people who are let out of mental homes simply because there is no room for them there, as far as I can see. Nowadays, room has to be made for fresh patients all the time. Anyone peeping in through a window could see a children's party was going on, and this poor wretch – if one can really feel pity for these people, which I really must say I find it very hard to do myself sometimes – enticed this child away somehow and killed her. You can't think such a thing could happen, but it *did* happen.'

'Perhaps you would show me where –'

'Of course. No more coffee?'

'I thank you, no.'

Mrs Drake got up. 'The police seem to think it took place while the Snapdragon was going on. That was taking place in the dining-room.'

She walked across the hall, opened the door and, rather in the manner of someone doing the honours of a stately home to a party of charabanc goers, indicated the large dining-table and the heavy velvet curtains.

'It was dark here, of course, except for the blazing dish. And now –'

She led them across the hall and opened the door of a small room with arm-chairs, sporting prints and bookshelves.

'The library,' said Mrs Drake, and shivered a little. 'The bucket was *here*. On a plastic sheet, of course –'

Mrs Oliver had not accompanied them into the room. She was standing outside in the hall –

'I can't come in,' she said to Poirot. 'It makes me think of it too much.'

'There's nothing to see now,' said Mrs Drake. 'I mean, I'm just showing you *where*, as you asked.'

'I suppose,' said Poirot, 'there was water – a good deal of water.'

'There was water in the bucket, of course,' said Mrs Drake.

She looked at Poirot as though she thought that he was not quite all there.'

'And there was water on the sheet. I mean, if the child's head was pushed under water, there would be a lot of water splashed about.'

'Oh yes. Even while the bobbing was going on, the bucket had to be filled up once or twice.'

'So the person who did it? That person also would have got wet, one would think.'

'Yes, yes, I suppose so.'

'That was not specially noticed?'

'No, no, the Inspector asked me about that. You see, by the end of the evening nearly everyone was a bit dishevelled or damp or floury. There doesn't seem to be any useful clues there at all. I mean, the police didn't think so.'

'No,' said Poirot. 'I suppose the only clue was the child herself. I hope you will tell me all you know about her.'

'About Joyce?'

Mrs Drake looked slightly taken aback. It was as though Joyce in her mind had by now retreated so far out of things that she was quite surprised to be reminded of her.

'The victim is always important,' said Poirot. 'The victim, you see, is so often the *cause* of the crime.'

'Well, I suppose, yes, I see what you mean,' said Mrs Drake, who quite plainly did not. 'Shall we come back to the drawing-room?'

'And then you will tell me about Joyce,' said Poirot.

They settled themselves once more in the drawing-room. Mrs Drake was looking uncomfortable.

'I don't know really what you expect me to say, Monsieur Poirot,' she said. 'Surely all information can be obtained quite easily from the police or from Joyce's mother. Poor woman, it will be painful for her, no doubt, but –'

'But what I want,' said Poirot, 'is not a mother's estimate of a dead daughter. It is a clear, unbiased opinion from someone who has a good knowledge of human nature. I should say, Madame, that you yourself have been an active worker in many welfare and social fields here. Nobody, I am sure, could sum up more aptly the character and disposition of someone whom you know.'

'Well – it is a little difficult. I mean, children of that age – she was thirteen, I think, twelve or thirteen – are very much alike at a certain age.'

'Ah no, surely not,' said Poirot. 'There are very great differences in character, in disposition. Did you like her?'

Mrs Drake seemed to find the question embarrassing.

'Well, of course I – I liked her. I mean, well, I like all children. Most people do.'

'Ah, there I do not agree with you,' said Poirot. 'Some children I consider are *most* unattractive.'

'Well, I agree, they're not brought up very well nowadays. Everything seems left to the school, and of course they lead very permissive lives. Have their own choice of friends and – er – oh, really, Monsieur Poirot.'

'Was she a nice child or not a nice child?' said Poirot insistently.

Mrs Drake looked at him and registered censure.

'You must realize, Monsieur Poirot, that the poor child is *dead*.'

'Dead or alive, it matters. Perhaps if she was a nice child, nobody would have wanted to kill her, but if she was not a nice child, somebody might have wanted to kill her, and did so –'

'Well, I suppose – Surely it isn't a question of niceness, is it?'

'It could be. I also understand that she claimed to have seen a murder committed.'

'Oh *that*,' said Mrs Drake contemptuously.

'You did not take that statement seriously?'

'Well, of course I didn't. It was a very silly thing to say.'

'How did she come to say it?'

'Well, I think really they were all rather excited about Mrs Oliver being here. You are a very famous person, you must remember, dear,' said Mrs Drake, addressing Mrs Oliver.

'The word 'dear' seemed included in her speech without any accompanying enthusiasm.

'I don't suppose the subject would ever have arisen otherwise, but the children were excited by meeting a famous authoress –'

'So Joyce said that she had seen a murder committed,' said Poirot thoughtfully.

'Yes, she said something of the kind. I wasn't really listening.'

'But you do remember that she said it?'

'Oh yes, she said it. But I didn't believe it,' said Mrs Drake. 'Her sister hushed her up at once, very properly.'

'And she was annoyed about that, was she?'

'Yes, she went on saying that it was true.'

'In fact, she boasted about it.'

'When you put it that way, yes.'

'It *might* have been true, I suppose,' said Poirot.

'Nonsense! I don't believe it for one minute,' said Mrs Drake. 'It's the sort of stupid thing Joyce would say.'

'She was a stupid girl?'

'Well, she was the kind, I think, who liked to show off.' said Mrs Drake. 'You know, she always wanted to have seen more or done more than other girls.'

'Not a very lovable character,' said Poirot.

'No indeed,' said Mrs Drake. 'Really the kind that you have to be shutting up all the time.'

'What did the other children who were here have to say about it? Were they impressed?'

'They laughed at her,' said Mrs Drake. 'So, of course, that made her worse.'

'Well,' said Poirot, as he rose, 'I am glad to have your positive assurance on that point.' He bowed politely over her hand. 'Good-bye, Madame, thank you so much for allowing me to view the scene of this very unpleasant occurrence. I hope it has not recalled unpleasant memories too definitely to you.'

'Of course,' said Mrs Drake, 'it *is* very painful to recall anything of this kind. I had so hoped our little party would go off well. Indeed, it *was* going off well and everyone seemed to be enjoying it so much till this terrible thing happened. However, the only thing one can do is to try and forget it all. Of course, it's very unfortunate that Joyce should have made this silly remark about seeing a murder.'

'Have you ever had a murder in Woodleigh Common?'

'Not that I can remember,' said Mrs Drake firmly.

'In this age of increased crime that we live in,' said Poirot, 'that really seems somewhat unusual, does it not?'

'Well, I think there was a lorry driver who killed a pal of his – something like that – and a little girl whom they found buried in a gravel pit about fifteen miles from here, but that was years ago. They were both rather sordid and uninteresting crimes. Mainly the result of drink, I think.'

'In fact, the kind of murder unlikely to have been witnessed by a girl of twelve or thirteen.'

'Most unlikely, I should say. And I can assure you, Monsieur Poirot, this statement that the girl made was solely in order to impress friends and perhaps interest a famous character.' She looked rather coldly across at Mrs Oliver.

'In fact,' said Mrs Oliver, 'it's all my fault for being at the party, I suppose.'

'Oh, of course not, my dear, of course I didn't mean it *that* way.'

Poirot sighed as he departed from the house with Mrs Oliver by his side.

'A very unsuitable place for a murder,' he said, as they walked down the path to the gate. 'No atmosphere, no haunting sense of tragedy, no character worth murdering, though I couldn't help thinking that just occasionally someone might feel like murdering Mrs Drake.'

'I know what you mean. She can be intensely irritating sometimes. So pleased with herself and so complacent.'

'What is her husband like?'

'Oh, she's a widow. Her husband died a year or two ago. He got polio and had been a cripple for years. He was a banker originally, I think. He was very keen on games and sport and hated having to give all that up and be an invalid.'

'Yes, indeed.' He reverted to the subject of the child Joyce. 'Just tell me this. Did anyone who was listening take this assertion of the child Joyce about murder seriously?'

'I don't know. I shouldn't have thought anyone did.'

'The other children, for instance?'

'Well, I was thinking really of them. No, I don't think they believed what Joyce was saying. They thought she was making up things.'

'Did you think that, too?'

'Well, I did really,' said Mrs Oliver. 'Of course,' she added, 'Mrs Drake would like to believe that the murder never really happened, but she can't very well go as far as that, can she?'

'I understand that this may be painful for her.'

'I suppose it is in a way,' said Mrs Oliver, 'but I think that by now, you know, she is actually getting quite pleased to talk about it. I don't think she likes to have to bottle it up all the time.'

'Do you like her?' asked Poirot. 'Do you think she's a nice woman?'

'You do ask the most difficult questions. Embarrassing ones,' said Mrs Oliver. 'It seems the only thing you are interested in is whether people are nice or not. Rowena Drake is the bossy type – likes running things and people. She runs this whole place more or less, I should think. But runs it very efficiently. It depends if you like bossy women. I don't much –'

'What about Joyce's mother whom we are on our way to see?'

'She's quite a nice woman. Rather stupid, I should think. I'm sorry for her. It's pretty awful to have your daughter murdered, isn't it? And everyone here thinks it was a sex crime which makes it worse.'

'But there was no evidence of sexual assault, or so I understand?'

'No, but people like to think these things happen. It makes it more exciting. You know what people are like.'

'One thinks one does – but sometimes – well – we do not really know at all.'

'Wouldn't it be better if my friend Judith Butler was to take you to see Mrs Reynolds? She knows her quite well, and I'm a stranger to her.'

'We will do as planned.'

'The Computer Programme will go on,' murmured Mrs Oliver rebelliously.

CHAPTER 7

Mrs Reynolds was a complete contrast to Mrs Drake. There was no air of poised competence about her, nor indeed was there ever likely to be.

She was wearing conventional black, had a moist handkerchief clasped in her hand and was clearly prepared to dissolve into tears at any moment.

'It's very kind of you, I'm sure,' she said to Mrs Oliver, 'to bring a friend of yours down here to help us.' She put a damp hand into Poirot's and looked at him doubtfully. 'And if he *can* help in any way I'm sure I'll be very grateful, though I don't see what anyone can do. Nothing will bring her back, poor child. It's awful to think of. How anyone could deliberately kill anyone of that age. If she had only cried out – though I suppose he rammed her head under water straight away and held it there. Oh, I can't bear to think of it. I really can't.'

'Indeed, Madame, I do not want to distress you. Please do not think of it. I only want to ask you a few questions that might help – help, that is, to find your daughter's murderer. You've no idea yourself, I suppose, who it can possibly be?'

'How could I have any idea? I shouldn't have thought there was anyone, anyone living here, I mean. This is such a nice place. And the people living here are such nice people. I suppose it was just someone – some awful man who came in through one of the windows. Perhaps he'd taken drugs or something. He saw the light and that it was a party, so he gate-crashed.'

'You are quite sure that the assailant was male?'

'Oh, it must have been.' Mrs Reynolds sounded shocked. 'I'm sure it was. It couldn't have been a *woman*, could it?'

'A woman might have been strong enough.'

'Well, I suppose in a way I know what you mean. You mean women are much more athletic nowadays and all that. But they wouldn't do a thing like this, I'm sure. Joyce was only a child – thirteen years old.'

'I don't want to distress you by staying here too long, Madame, or to ask you difficult questions. That already, I am sure, the police are doing elsewhere, and I don't want to upset you by dwelling on painful facts. It was just concerning a remark that your daughter made at the party. You were not there yourself, I think?'

'Well, no, I wasn't. I haven't been very well lately and children's parties can be very tiring. I drove them there, and then later I came back to fetch them. The three children went together, you know. Ann, that's the older one, she is sixteen, and Leopold who is nearly eleven. What was it Joyce said that you wanted to know about?'

'Mrs Oliver, who was there, will tell you what your daughter's words were exactly. She said, I believe, that she had once seen a murder committed.'

'Joyce? Oh, she couldn't have said a thing like that. What murder could she possibly have seen committed?'

'Well, everyone seems to think it was rather unlikely,' said Poirot. 'I just wondered if *you* thought it likely. Did she ever speak to you about such a thing?'

'Seeing a *murder*? Joyce?'

'You must remember,' said Poirot, 'that the term murder might have been used by someone of Joyce's age in a rather loose way. It might have been just a question of somebody being run over by a car, or of children fighting together perhaps and one pushing another into a stream or over a bridge. Something that was not meant seriously, but which had an unfortunate result.'

'Well, I can't think of anything like that happening here that Joyce could have seen, and she certainly never said anything about it to me. She must have been joking.'

'She was very positive,' said Mrs Oliver. 'She kept on saying that it was true and that she'd seen it.'

'Did anyone believe her?' asked Mrs Reynolds.

'I don't know,' said Poirot.

'I don't think they did,' said Mrs Oliver, 'or perhaps they didn't want to – er – well, encourage her by saying they believed it.'

'They were inclined to jeer at her and say she was making it all up,' said Poirot, less kind-hearted than Mrs Oliver.

'Well, that wasn't very nice of them,' said Mrs Reynolds. 'As though Joyce would tell a lot of lies about things like that.' She looked flushed and indignant.

'I know. It seems unlikely,' said Poirot. 'It was more possible, was it not, that she might have made a mistake, that she might have seen something she *did* think could have been described as a murder. Some accident, perhaps.'

'She'd have said something about it to me, if so, wouldn't she?' said Mrs Reynolds, still indignant.

'One would think so,' said Poirot. 'She did not say so at any time in the past? You might have forgotten. Especially if it wasn't really important.'

'When do you mean?'

'We don't know,' said Poirot. 'That is one of the difficulties. It might have been three weeks ago – or three years. She said she had been "quite young" at the time. What does a thirteen-year-old consider quite young? There was no sensational happening round here that you can recall?'

'Oh, I don't think so. I mean, you do hear of things. Or read about them in the papers. You know, I mean women being attacked, or a girl and her young man, or things like that. But nothing important that I can remember, nothing that Joyce took an interest in or anything of that kind.'

'But if Joyce said positively she saw a murder, would you think she really thought so?'

'She wouldn't say so unless she really did think so, would she?' said Mrs Reynolds. 'I think she must have got something mixed up really.'

'Yes, it seems possible. I wonder,' he asked, 'if I might speak to your two children who were also at the party?'

'Well, of course, though I don't know what you can expect them to tell you. Ann's doing her work for her "A" levels upstairs and Leopold's in the garden assembling a model aeroplane.'

Leopold was a solid, pudgy faced boy entirely absorbed, it seemed, in mechanical construction. It was some few moments before he could pay attention to the questions he was being asked.

'You were there, weren't you, Leopold? You heard what your sister said. What did she say?'

'Oh, you mean about the murder?' He sounded bored.

'Yes, that's what I mean,' said Poirot. 'She said she saw a murder once. Did she really see such a thing?'

'No, of course she didn't,' said Leopold. 'Who on earth would she see murdered? It was just like Joyce, that.'

'How do you mean, it was just like her?'

'Showing off,' said Leopold, winding round a piece of wire and breathing forcefully through his nose as he concentrated. 'She was an awfully stupid sort of girl,' he added. 'She'd say anything, you know, to make people sit up and take notice.'

'So you really think she invented the whole thing?'

Leopold shifted his gaze to Mrs Oliver.

'I expect she wanted to impress *you* a bit,' he said. 'You write detective stories, don't you? I think she was just putting it on so that you should take more notice of her than you did of the others.'

'That would also be rather like her, would it?' said Poirot.

'Oh, she'd say anything,' said Leopold. 'I bet nobody believed her though.'

'Were you listening? Do *you* think anyone believed it?'

'Well, I heard her say it, but I didn't really listen. Beatrice laughed at her and so did Cathie. They said "that's a tall story," or something.'

There seemed little more to be got out of Leopold. They went upstairs to where Ann, looking rather more than her sixteen years, was bending over a table with various study books spread round her.

'Yes, I was at the party,' she said.

'You heard your sister say something about having seen a murder?'

'Oh yes, I heard her. I didn't take any notice, though.'

'You didn't think it was true?'

'Of course it wasn't true. There haven't been any murders here for ages. I don't think there's been a proper murder for years.'

'Then why do you think she said so?'

'Oh, she likes showing off. I mean she used to like showing off. She had a wonderful story once about having travelled to India. My uncle had been on a voyage there and she pretended she went with him. Lots of girls at school actually *believed* her.'

'So you don't remember any what you call murders taking place here in the last three or four years?'

'No, only the usual kind,' said Ann. 'I mean, the ones you read every day in the newspaper. And they weren't actually *here* in Woodleigh Common. They were mostly in Medchester, I think.'

'Who do *you* think killed your sister, Ann? You must have known her friends, you would know any people who didn't like her.'

'I can't imagine who'd want to kill her. I suppose someone who was just batty. Nobody else would, would they?'

'There was no one who had – quarrelled with her or who did not get on with her?'

'You mean, did she have an enemy? I think that's silly. People don't have enemies really. There are just people you don't like.'

As they departed from the room, Ann said:

'I don't want to be nasty about Joyce, because she's dead, and it wouldn't be kind, but she really was the most awful liar, you know. I mean, I'm sorry to say things about my sister, but it's quite true.'

Are we making any progress?' said Mrs Oliver as they left the house.

'None whatever,' said Hercule Poirot. 'That is interesting,' he said thoughtfully.

Mrs Oliver looked as though she didn't agree with him.

CHAPTER 8

It was six o'clock at Pine Crest. Hercule Poirot put a piece of sausage into his mouth and followed it up with a sip of tea. The tea was strong and to Poirot singularly unpalatable. The sausage, on the other hand, was delicious. Cooked to perfection. He looked with appreciation across the table to where Mrs McKay presided over the large brown teapot.

Elspeth McKay was as unlike her brother, Superintendent Spence, as she could be in every way. Where he was broad, she was angular. Her sharp, thin face looked out on the world with shrewd appraisal. She was thin as a thread, yet there was a certain likeness between them. Mainly the eyes and the strongly marked line of the jaw. Either of them, Poirot thought, could be relied upon for judgement and good sense. They would express themselves differently, but that was all. Superintendent Spence would express himself slowly and carefully as the result of due thought and deliberation. Mrs McKay would pounce, quick and sharp, like a cat upon a mouse.

'A lot depends,' said Poirot, 'upon the character of this child. Joyce Reynolds. This is what puzzles me most.'

He looked inquiringly at Spence.

'You can't go by me,' said Spence, 'I've not lived here long enough. Better ask Elspeth.'

Poirot looked across the table, his eyebrows raised inquiringly. Mrs McKay was sharp as usual in response.

'I'd say she was a proper little liar,' she said.

'Not a girl whom you'd trust and believe what she said?'

Elspeth shook her head decidedly.

'No, indeed. Tell a tall tale, she would, and tell it well, mind you. But I'd never believe her.'

'Tell it with the object of showing off?'

'That's right. They told you the Indian story, didn't they? There's many as believed that, you know. Been away for the holidays, the family had. Gone abroad somewhere. I don't know if it was her father and mother or her uncle and aunt, but they went to India and she came back from those holidays with tall tales of how she'd been taken there with them. Made a good story of it, she did. A Maharajah and a tiger shoot and elephants – ah, it was fine hearing and a lot of those around her here believed it. But I said straight along, she's telling more than ever happened. Could be, I thought at first, she was just exaggerating. But the story got added to every time. There were more tigers, if you know what I mean. Far more tigers than could possibly happen. And elephants, too, for that matter. I'd known her before, too, telling tall stories.'

'Always to get attention?'

'Aye, you're right there. She was a great one for getting attention.'

'Because a child told a tall story about a travel trip she never took,' said Superintendent Spence, 'you can't say that every tall tale she told was a lie.'

'It might not be,' said Elspeth, 'but I'd say the likelihood was that it usually would be.'

'So you think that if Joyce Reynolds came out with a tale that she'd seen a murder committed, you'd say she was probably lying and you wouldn't believe the story was true?'

'That's what I'd think,' said Mrs McKay.

'You might be wrong,' said her brother.

'Yes,' said Mrs McKay. 'Anyone may be wrong. It's like the old story of the boy who cried "Wolf, wolf," and he cried it once too often, when it was a real wolf, and nobody believed him, and so the wolf got him.'

'So you'd sum it up –'

'I'd still say the probabilities are that she wasn't speaking the truth. But I'm a fair woman. She may have been. She *may* have seen something. Not quite so much as she said she saw, but *something*.'

'And so she got herself killed,' said Superintendent Spence. 'You've got to mind that, Elspeth. She got herself killed.'

'That's true enough,' said Mrs McKay. 'And that's why I'm saying maybe I've misjudged her. And if so, I'm sorry. But ask anyone who knew her and they'll tell you that lies came natural to her. It was a party she was at, remember, and she was excited. She'd want to make an effect.'

'Indeed, they didn't believe her,' said Poirot.

Elspeth McKay shook her head doubtfully.

'Who could she have seen murdered?' asked Poirot.

He looked from brother to sister.

'Nobody,' said Mrs McKay with decision.

'There must have been deaths here, say, over the last three years.'

'Oh that, naturally,' said Spence. 'Just the usual – old folks or invalids or what you'd expect – or maybe a hit-and-run motorist –'

'No unusual or unexpected deaths?'

'Well – ' Elspeth hesitated. 'I mean –'

Spence took over.

'I've jotted a few names down here.' He pushed the paper over to Poirot. 'Save you a bit of trouble, asking questions around.'

'Are these suggested victims?'

'Hardly as much as that. Say within the range of possibility.'

Poirot read aloud.

'Mrs Llewellyn-Smythe. Charlotte Benfield. Janet White. Lesley Ferrier –' He broke off, looked across the table and repeated the first name. Mrs Llewellyn-Smythe.

'Could be,' said Mrs McKay. 'Yes, you might have something there.' She added a word that sounded like 'opera.'

'Opera?' Poirot looked puzzled. He had heard of no opera.

'Went off one night, she did,' said Elspeth, 'was never heard of again.'

'Mrs Llewellyn-Smythe?'

'No, no. The opera girl. She could have put something in the medicine easily enough. And she came into all the money, didn't she – or so she thought at the time?'

Poirot looked at Spence for enlightenment.

'And never been heard of since,' said Mrs McKay. 'These foreign girls are all the same.'

The significance of the word 'opera' came to Poirot.

'An *au pair* girl,' he said.

'That's right. Lived with the old lady, and a week or two after the old lady died, the *au pair* girl just disappeared.'

'Went off with some man, I'd say,' said Spence.

'Well, nobody knew of him if so,' said Elspeth. 'And there's usually plenty to talk about here. Usually know just who's going with who.'

'Did anybody think there had been anything wrong about Mrs Llewellyn-Smythe's death?' asked Poirot.

'No. She'd got heart trouble. Doctor attended her regularly.'

'But you headed your list of possible victims with her, my friend?'

'Well, she was a rich woman, a very rich woman. Her death was not unexpected but it *was* sudden. I'd say offhand that Dr Ferguson was surprised, even if only slightly surprised. I think he expected her to live longer. But doctors do have these surprises. She wasn't one to do as the doctor ordered. She'd been told not to overdo things, but she did exactly as she liked. For one thing, she was a passionate gardener, and that doesn't do heart cases any good.'

Elspeth McKay took up the tale.

'She came here when her health failed. She was living abroad before. She came here to be near her nephew and niece, Mr and Mrs Drake, and she bought the Quarry House. A big Victorian house which included a disused quarry which attracted her as having possibilities. She spent thousands of pounds on turning that quarry into a sunk garden or whatever they call the thing. Had a landscape gardener down from Wisley or one of these places to design it. Oh, I can tell you, it's something to look at.'

'I shall go and look at it,' said Poirot. 'Who knows – it might give me ideas.'

'Yes, I would go if I were you. It's worth seeing.'

'And she was rich, you say?' said Poirot.

'Widow of a big shipbuilder. She had packets of money.'

'Her death was not unexpected because she had a heart condition, but it *was* sudden,' said Spence. 'No doubts arose that it was due to anything but natural causes. Cardiac failure, or whatever the longer name is that doctors use. Coronary something.'

'No question of an inquest ever arose?'

Spence shook his head.

'It has happened before,' said Poirot. 'An elderly woman told to be careful, not to run up and down stairs, not to do any intensive gardening, and so on and so on. But if you get an energetic woman who's been an enthusiastic gardener all her life and done as she liked in most ways, then she doesn't always treat these recommendations with due respect.'

'That's true enough. Mrs Llewellyn-Smythe made a wonderful thing of the quarry – or rather, the landscape artist did. Three of four years they worked at it, he and his employer. She'd seen some garden, in Ireland I think it was, when she went on a National Trust tour visiting gardens. With that in mind, they fairly transformed the place. Oh yes, it has to be seen to be believed.'

'Here is a natural death, then,' said Poirot, 'certified as such by the local doctor. Is that the same doctor who is here now? And whom I am shortly going to see?'

'Dr Ferguson – yes. He's a man of about sixty, good at his job and well liked here.'

'But you suspect that her death *might* have been murder? For any other reason than those that you've already given me?'

'The opera girl, for one thing,' said Elspeth.

'Why?'

'Well, she must have forged the Will. Who forged the Will if she didn't?'

'You must have more to tell me,' said Poirot. 'What is all this about a forged Will?'

'Well, there was a bit of fuss when it came to probating, or whatever you call it, the old lady's Will.'

'Was it a new Will?'

'It was what they call – something that sounded like fish – a codi – a codicil.'

Elspeth looked at Poirot, who nodded.

'She'd made Wills before,' said Spence. 'All much the same. Bequests to charities, legacies to old servants, but the bulk of her fortune always went to her nephew and his wife, who were her near relatives.'

'And this particular codicil?'

'Left everything to the opera girl,' said Elspeth, '*because of her devoted care and kindness*. Something like that.'

'Tell me, then, more about the *au pair* girl.'

'She came from some country in the middle of Europe. Some long name.'

'How long had she been with the old lady?'

'Just over a year.'

'You call her the old lady always. How old was she?'

'Well in the sixties. Sixty-five or six, say.'

'That is not so very old,' said Poirot feelingly.

'Made several Wills, she had, by all accounts,' said Elspeth. 'As Bert has told you, all of them much the same. Leaving money to one or two charities and then perhaps she'd change the charities and some different souvenirs to old servants and all that. But the bulk of the money always went to her nephew and his wife, and I think some other old cousin who was dead, though, by the time she died. She left the bungalow she'd built to the landscape man, for him to live in as long as he liked, and some kind of income for which he was to keep up the quarry garden and let it be walked in by the public. Something like that.'

'I suppose the family claimed that the balance of her mind had been disturbed, that there had been undue influence?'

'I think probably it might have come to that,' said Spence. 'But the lawyers, as I say, got on to the forgery sharply. It was not a very convincing forgery, apparently. They spotted it almost at once.'

'Things came to light to show that the opera girl could have done it quite easily,' said Elspeth. 'You see, she wrote a great many of Mrs Llewellyn-Smythe's letters for her and it seems Mrs Llewellyn-Smythe had a great dislike of typed letters being sent to friends or anything like that. If it wasn't a business letter, she'd always say "write it in handwriting and make it as much like mine as you can and sign it with my name." Mrs Minden, the cleaning woman, heard her say that one day, and I suppose the girl got used to doing it and copying her employer's handwriting and then it came to her suddenly that she could do this and get away with it. And that's how it all came about. But as I say, the lawyers were too sharp and spotted it.'

'Mrs Llewellyn-Smythe's own lawyers?'

'Yes. Fullerton, Harrison and Leadbetter. Very respectable firm in Medchester. They'd always done all her legal business for her. Anyway, they got experts on to it and questions were asked and the girl was asked questions and got the wind up. Just walked out one day leaving half her things behind her. They were preparing to take proceedings against her, but she didn't wait for that. She just got out. It's not so difficult, really, to get out of this country, if you do it in time. Why, you can go on day trips on the Continent without a passport, and if you've got a little arrangement with someone on the other side, things can be arranged long before there is any real hue and cry. She's probably gone back to her own country or changed her name or gone to friends.'

'But everyone thought that Mrs Llewellyn-Smythe died a natural death?' asked Poirot.

'Yes, I don't think there was ever any question of that. I

only say it's possible because, as I say, these things have happened before where the doctor has no suspicion. Supposing that girl Joyce had heard something, had heard the *au pair* girl giving medicines to Mrs Llewellyn-Smythe, and the old lady saying "this medicine tastes different to the usual one." Or "this has got a bitter taste" or "it's peculiar".'

'Anyone would think you'd been there listening to things yourself, Elspeth,' said Superintendent Spence. 'This is all your imagination.'

'When did she die?' said Poirot. 'Morning, evening, indoors, out of doors, at home or away from home?'

'Oh, at home. She'd come up from doing things in the garden one day, breathing rather heavily. She said she was very tired and she went to lie down on her bed. And to put it in one sentence, she never woke up. Which is all very natural, it seems, medically speaking.'

Poirot took out a little notebook. The page was already headed 'Victims.' Under, he wrote, 'No. 1. suggested, Mrs Llewellyn-Smythe.' On the next pages of his book he wrote down the other names that Spence had given him. He said, inquiringly:

'Charlotte Benfield?'

Spence replied promptly. 'Sixteen-year-old shop assistant. Multiple head injuries. Found on a footpath near the Quarry Wood. Two young men came under suspicion. Both had walked out with her from time to time. No evidence.'

'They assisted the police in their inquiries?' asked Poirot.

'As you say. It's the usual phrase. They didn't assist much. They were frightened. Told a few lies, contradicted themselves. They didn't carry conviction as likely murderers. But either of them *might* have been.'

'What were they like?'

'Peter Gordon, twenty-one. Unemployed. Had had one or two jobs but never kept them. Lazy. Quite good-looking. Had been on probation once or twice for minor pilferings, things of that kind. No record before of violence. Was in with a rather nasty lot of likely young criminals, but usually managed to keep out of serious trouble.'

'And the other one?'

'Thomas Hudd. Twenty. Stammered. Shy, Neurotic. Wanted to be a teacher, but couldn't make the grade. Mother a widow. The doting mother type. Didn't encourage girl friends. Kept him as close to her apron-strings as she could. He had a job in a stationer's. Nothing criminal known against him, but a possibility psychologically, so it seems. The girl played him up a good deal. Jealousy a possible motive, but no evidence that we could prosecute on. Both of them had alibis. Hudd's was his mother's. She would have sworn to kingdom come that he was indoors with her all that evening, and nobody can say he wasn't or had seen him elsewhere or in the neighbourhood of the murder. Young Gordon was given an alibi by some of his less reputable friends. Not worth much, but you couldn't disprove it.'

'This happened when?'

'Eighteen months ago.'

'And where?'

'In a footpath in a field not far from Woodleigh Common.'

'Three quarters of a mile,' said Elspeth.

'Near Joyce's house – the Reynold's house?'

'No, it was on the other side of the village.'

'It seems unlikely to have been the murder Joyce was talking about,' said Poirot thoughtfully. 'If you see a girl being bashed on the head by a young man you'd be likely to think of murder straight away. Not to wait for a year before you began to think it was murder.'

Poirot read another name.

'Lesley Ferrier.'

Spence spoke again. 'Lawyer's clerk, twenty-eight, employed by Messrs. Fullerton, Harrison and Leadbetter of Market Street, Medchester.'

'Those were Mrs Llewellyn-Smythe's solicitors, I think you said.'

'Yes. Same ones.'

'And what happened to Lesley Ferrier?'

'He was stabbed in the back. Not far from the Green Swan Pub. He was said to have been having an affair with the wife of the landlord, Harry Griffin. Handsome piece, she was, indeed still is. Getting perhaps a bit long in the tooth. Five or six years older than he was, but she liked them young.'

'The weapon?'

'The knife wasn't found. Les was said to have broken with her and taken up with some other girl, but what girl was never satisfactorily discovered.'

'Ah. And who was suspected in this case? The landlord or the wife?'

'Quite right,' said Spence. 'Might have been either. The wife seemed the more likely. She was half gypsy and a temperamental piece. But there were other possibilities. Our Lesley hadn't led a blameless life. Got into trouble in his early twenties, falsifying his accounts somewhere. With a spot of forgery. Was said to have come from a broken home and all the rest of it. Employers spoke up for him. He got a short sentence and was taken on by Fullerton, Harrison and Leadbetter when he came out of prison.'

'And after that he'd gone straight?'

'Well, nothing proved. He appeared to do so as far as his employers were concerned, but he *had* been mixed up in a few questionable transactions with his friends. He's what you might call a wrong 'un but a careful one.'

'So the alternative was?'

'That he might have been stabbed by one of his less reputable associates. When you're in with a nasty crowd you've got it coming to you with a knife if you let them down.'

'Anything else?'

'Well, he had a good lot of money in his bank account.

Paid in in cash, it had been. Nothing to show where it came from. That was suspicious in itself.'

'Possibly pinched from Fullerton, Harrison and Leadbetter?' suggested Poirot.

'They say not. They had a chartered account to work on it and look into things.'

'And the police had no idea where else it might have come from?'

'No.'

'Again,' said Poirot, 'not Joyce's murder, I should think.'

He read the last name, 'Janet White.'

'Found strangled on a footpath which was a short cut from the schoolhouse to her home. She shared a flat there with another teacher, Nora Ambrose. According to Nora Ambrose, Janet White had occasionally spoken of being nervous about some man with whom she'd broken off relations a year ago, but who had frequently sent her threatening letters. Nothing was ever found out about this man. Nora Ambrose didn't know his name, didn't know exactly where he lived.'

'Aha,' said Poirot, 'I like this better.'

He made a good, thick black tick against Janet White's name.

'For what reason?' asked Spence.

'It is a more likely murder for a girl of Joyce's age to have witnessed. She could have recognized the victim, a schoolteacher whom she knew and who perhaps taught her. Possibly she did not know the attacker. She might have seen a struggle, heard a quarrel between a girl whom she knew and a strange man. But thought no more of it than that at the time. When was Janet White killed?'

'Two and a half years ago.'

'That again,' said Poirot, 'is about the right time. Both for not realizing that the man she may have seen with his hands round Janet White's neck was not merely necking her, but might have been killing her. But then as she grew more mature, the proper explanation came to her.'

He looked at Elspeth. 'You agree with my reasoning?'

'I see what you mean,' said Elspeth. 'But aren't you going at all this the wrong way round? Looking for a victim of a past murder instead of looking for a man who killed a child here in Woodleigh Common not more than three days ago?'

'We go from the past to the future,' said Poirot. 'We arrive, shall we say, from two and a half years ago to three days ago. And, therefore, we have to consider – what you, no doubt, have already considered – who was there in Woodleigh Common amongst the people who were at the party who might have been connected with an older crime?'

'One can narrow it down a bit more than that now,' said Spence. 'That is if we are right in accepting your assumption that Joyce was killed because of what she claimed earlier in the day about seeing murder committed. She said those words during the time the preparations for the party were going on. Mind you, we may be wrong in believing that that was the motive for killing, but I don't think we are wrong. So let us say she claimed to have seen a murder, and someone who was present during the preparations for the party that afternoon could have heard her and acted as soon as possible.'

'Who *was* present?' said Poirot. 'You know, I presume.'

'Yes, I have the list for you here.'

'You have checked it carefully?'

'Yes, I've checked and re-checked, but it's been quite a job. Here are the eighteen names.'

List of people present during preparation for Hallowe'en
    Party
Mrs Drake (owner of house)
Mrs Butler
Mrs Oliver
Miss Whittaker (school-teacher)
Rev. Charles Cotterell (Vicar)
Simon Lampton (Curate)
Miss Lee (Dr Ferguson's dispenser)

Ann Reynolds
Joyce Reynolds
Leopold Reynolds
Nicholas Ransom
Desmond Holland
Beatrice Ardley
Cathie Grant
Diana Brent
Mrs Garlton (household help)
Mrs Minden (cleaning woman)
Mrs Goodbody (helper)

'You are sure these are all?'

'No,' said Spence. 'I'm not sure. I can't really be sure. Nobody can. You see, odd people brought things. Somebody brought some coloured light bulbs. Somebody else supplied some mirrors. There were some extra plates. Someone lent a plastic pail. People brought things, exchanged a word or two and went away again. They didn't remain to help. Therefore such a person *could* have been overlooked and not remembered as being present. But that somebody, even if they had only just deposited a bucket in the hall, could have overheard what Joyce was saying in the sitting-room. She was shouting, you know. We can't really limit it to this list, but it's the best we can do. Here you are. Take a look at it. I've made a brief descriptive note against the names.'

'I thank you. Just one question. You must have interrogated some of these people, those for instance who were also at the party. Did anyone, *anyone* at all, mention what Joyce had said about seeing a murder?'

'I think not. There is no record of it officially. The first I heard of it is what you told me.'

'Interesting,' said Poirot. 'One might also say remarkable.'

'Obviously no one took it seriously,' said Spence.

Poirot nodded thoughtfully.

'I must go now to keep my appointment with Dr Ferguson, after his surgery,' he said.

He folded up Spence's list and put it in his pocket.

CHAPTER 9

Dr Ferguson was a man of sixty, of Scottish extraction with a brusque manner. He looked Poirot up and down with shrewd eyes under bristling eyebrows, and said:

'Well, what's all this about? Sit down. Mind that chair leg. The castor's loose.'

'I should perhaps explain,' said Dr Ferguson. 'Everybody knows everything in a place like this. That authoress woman brought you down here as God's greatest detective to puzzle police officers. That's more or less right, isn't it?'

'In part,' said Poirot. 'I came here to visit an old friend ex-Superintendent Spence, who lives with his sister here.'

'Spence? Hm. Good type, Spence. Bull-dog breed. Good honest police officer of the old type. No graft. No violence. Not stupid either. Straight as a die.'

'You appraise him correctly.'

'Well,' said Ferguson, 'what did you tell him and what did he tell you?'

'Both he and Inspector Raglan have been exceedingly kind to me. I hope you will likewise.'

'I've nothing to be kind about,' said Ferguson. 'I don't know what happened. Child gets her head shoved in a bucket and is drowned in the middle of a party. Nasty business. Mind you, doing in a child isn't anything to be startled about nowadays. I've been called out to look at too many murdered children in the last seven to ten years – far too many. A lot of people who ought to be under mental restraint aren't under mental restraint. No room in the asylums. They go about, nicely spoken, nicely got up and looking like everybody else, looking for somebody they can do in. And enjoy themselves. Don't usually do it at a party, though. Too much chance of getting caught, I suppose, but novelty appeals even to a mentally disturbed killer.'

'Have you any idea who killed her?'

'Do you really suppose that's a question I can answer just like that? I'd have to have some evidence, wouldn't I? I'd have to be sure.'

'You could guess,' said Poirot.

'Anyone can guess. If I'm called in to a case I have to guess whether the chap's going to have measles or whether it's a case of an allergy to shell-fish or to feather pillows. I have to ask questions to find out what they've been eating, or drinking, or sleeping on, or what other children they've been meeting. Whether they've been in a crowded bus with Mrs Smith's or Mrs Robinson's children who've all got the measles, and a few other things. Then I advance a tentative opinion as to which it is of the various possibilities, and that, let me tell you, is what's called diagnosis. You don't do it in a hurry and you make sure.'

'Did you know this child?'

'Of course. She was one of my patients. There are two of us here. Myself and Worrall. I happen to be the Reynolds' doctor. She was quite a healthy child, Joyce. Had the usual small childish ailments. Nothing peculiar or out of the way. Ate too much, talked too much. Talking too much hadn't done her any harm. Eating too much gave her what used to be called in the old days a bilious attack from time to time. She'd had mumps and chicken pox. Nothing else.'

'But she had perhaps talked too much on one occasion, as you suggest she might be able to do?'

'So that's the tack you're on? I heard some rumour of that. On the lines of "what the butler saw" – only tragedy instead of comedy. Is that it?'

'It could form a motive, a reason.'

'Oh yes. Grant you that. But there *are* other reasons. Mentally disturbed seems the usual answer nowadays. At any rate, it does always in the Magistrates' courts. Nobody gained by her death, nobody hated her. But it seems to me with children nowadays you don't need to look for the reason. The reason's in another place. The reason's in the killer's mind. His disturbed mind or his evil mind or his kinky mind. Any kind of mind you like to call it. I'm not a psychiatrist. There are times when I get tired of hearing those words: "Remanded for a psychiatrist's report," after a lad has broken in somewhere, smashed the looking-glasses, pinched the bottles of whisky, stolen the silver, knocked an old woman on the head. Doesn't matter much what it is now. Remand them for the psychiatrist's report.'

'And who would you favour, in this case, to remand for a psychiatrist's report?'

'You mean of those there at the "do" the other night?'

'Yes.'

'The murderer would have had to be there, wouldn't he? Otherwise there wouldn't have been a murder. Right? He was among the guests, he was among the helpers or he walked in through the window with malice aforethought. Probably he knew the fastenings of that house. Might have been in there before, looking round. Take your man or boy. He wants to kill someone. Not at all unusual. Over in Medchester we had a case of that. Came to light after about six or seven years. Boy of thirteen. Wanted to kill someone, so he killed a child of nine, pinched a car, drove it seven or eight miles into a copse, burned her there, went away, and as far as we know led a blameless life until he was twenty-one or two. Mind you, we have only his word for that, he may have gone on doing it. Probably did. Found he liked killing people. Don't suppose he's killed too many, or some police force would have been on to him before now. But every now and then he felt the urge. Psychiatrist's report. Committed murder while mentally disturbed. I'm trying to say myself that that's what happened here. That sort of thing, anyway. I'm not a psychiatrist myself, thank goodness. I have a few psychiatrist friends. Some of them are sensible chaps. Some of them – well, I'll go as far as saying they ought to be remanded for a psychiatrist's report themselves. This chap who killed Joyce probably had nice parents, ordinary manners, good appearance. Nobody'd dream anything was wrong with him. Ever had a bite at a nice red juicy apple and there, down by the core, something rather nasty rears itself up and wags its head at you? Plenty of human beings about like that. More than there used to be, I'd say nowadays.'

'And you've no suspicion of your own?'

'I can't stick my neck out and diagnose a murderer without some evidence.'

'Still, you admit it must have been someone at the party. You cannot have a murder without a murderer.'

'You can easily in some detective stories that are written. Probably your pet authoress writes them like that. But in this case I agree. The murderer must have been there. A guest, a domestic help, someone who walked in through the window. Easily done if he'd studied the catch of the window beforehand. It might have struck some crazy brain that it would be a novel idea and a bit of fun to have a murder at a Hallowe'en party. That's all you've got to start off with, isn't it? Just someone who was at the party.'

Under bushy brows a pair of eyes twinkled at Poirot.

'I was there myself,' he said. 'Came in late, just to see what was doing.'

He nodded his head vigorously.

'Yes, that's the problem, isn't it? Like a social announcement in the papers:

"Amongst those present was – A Murderer".'

CHAPTER 10

Poirot looked up at The Elms and approved of it.

He was admitted and taken promptly by what he judged to be a secretary to the head-mistress's study. Miss Emlyn rose from her desk to greet him.

'I am delighted to meet you, Mr Poirot. I've heard about you.'

'You are too kind,' said Poirot.

'From a very old friend of mine, Miss Bulstrode. Former head-mistress of Meadowbank. You remember Miss Bulstrode, perhaps?'

'One would not be likely to forget her. A great personality.'

'Yes,' said Miss Emlyn. 'She made Meadowbank the school it is.' She sighed slightly and said, 'It has changed a little nowadays. Different aims, different methods, but it still holds its own as a school of distinction, of progress, and also of tradition. Ah well, we must not live too much in the past. You have come to see me, no doubt, about the death of Joyce Reynolds. I don't know if you have any particular interest in her case. It's out of your usual run of things, I imagine. You knew her personally, or her family perhaps?'

'No,' said Poirot. 'I came at the request of an old friend, Mrs Ariadne Oliver, who was staying down here and was present at the party.'

'She writes delightful books,' said Miss Emlyn. 'I have met her once or twice. Well, that makes the whole thing easier, I think, to discuss. So long as no personal feelings are involved, one can go straight ahead. It was a horrifying thing to happen. If I may say so, it was an unlikely thing to happen. The children involved seem neither old enough nor young enough for it to fall into any special class. A psychological crime is indicated. Do you agree?'

'No,' said Poirot. 'I think it was a murder, like most murders, committed for a motive, possibly a sordid one.'

'Indeed. And the reason?'

'The reason was a remark made by Joyce; not actually at the party, I understand, but earlier in the day when preparations were being made by some of the older children and other helpers. She announced that she had once seen a murder committed.'

'Was she believed?'

'On the whole, I think she was *not* believed.'

'That seems the most likely response. Joyce – I speak plainly to you, Monsieur Poirot, because we do not want unnecessary sentiment to cloud mental faculties – she was a rather mediocre child, neither stupid nor particularly intellectual. She was, quite frankly, a compulsive liar. And by that I do not mean that she was specially deceitful. She was not trying to avoid retribution or to avoid being found out in some peccadillo. She boasted. She boasted of things that had not happened, but that would impress her friends who were listening to her. As a result, of course, they inclined not to believe the tall stories she told.'

'You think that she boasted of having seen a murder committed in order to make herself important, to intrigue someone –?'

'Yes. And I would suggest that Ariadne Oliver was doubtless the person whom she wanted to impress . . .'

'So you don't think Joyce saw a murder committed at all?'

'I should doubt it very much.'

'You are of the opinion that she made the whole thing up?'

'I would not say that. She did witness, perhaps, a car accident, or someone perhaps who was hit with a ball on the golf links and injured – something that she could work up into an impressive happening that might, just conceivably, pass as an attempted murder.'

'So the only assumption we can make with any certainty

is that there was a murderer present at the Hallowe'en party.'

'Certainly,' said Miss Emlyn, without turning a grey hair. 'Certainly. That follows on logically, does it not?'

'Would you have any idea who that murderer might be?'

'That is certainly a sensible question,' said Miss Emlyn. 'After all, the majority of the children at the party were aged between nine and fifteen, and I suppose nearly all of them had been or were pupils at my school. I ought to know something about them. Something, too, about their families and their backgrounds.'

'I believe that one of your own teachers, a year or two ago, was strangled by an unknown killer.'

'You are referring to Janet White? About twenty-four years of age. An emotional girl. As far as is known, she was out walking alone. She may, of course, have arranged to meet some young man. She was a girl who was quite attractive to men in a modest sort of way. Her killer has not been discovered. The police questioned various young men or asked them to assist them in their inquiries, as the technique goes, but they were not able to find sufficient evidence to bring a case against anyone. An unsatisfactory business from their point of view. And, I may say, from mine.'

'You and I have a principle in common. We do not approve of murder.'

Miss Emlyn looked at him for a moment or two. Her expression did not change, but Poirot had an idea that he was being sized up with a great deal of care.

'I like the way you put it,' she said. 'From what you read and hear nowadays, it seems that murder under certain aspects is slowly but surely being made acceptable to a large section of the community.'

She was silent for a few minutes, and Poirot also did not speak. She was, he thought, considering a plan of action.

She rose and touched a bell.

'I think,' she said, 'that you had better talk to Miss Whittaker.'

Some five minutes passed after Miss Emlyn had left the

room and then the door opened and a woman of about forty entered. She had russet-coloured hair, cut short, and came in with a brisk step.

'Monsieur Poirot?' she said. 'Can I help you? Miss Emlyn seems to think that that might be so.'

'If Miss Emlyn thinks so, then it is almost a certainty that you can. I would take her word for it.'

'You know her?'

'I have only met her this afternoon.'

'But you have made up your mind quickly about her.'

'I hope you are going to tell me that I am right.'

Elizabeth Whittaker gave a short, quick sigh.

'Oh, yes, you're right. I presume that this is about the death of Joyce Reynolds. I don't know exactly how you come into it. Through the police?' She shook her head slightly in a dissatisfied manner.

'No, not through the police. Privately, through a friend.'

She took a chair, pushing it back a little so as to face him.

'Yes. What do you want to know?'

'I don't think there is any need to tell you. No need to waste time asking questions that may be of no importance. Something happened that evening at the party which perhaps it is well that I should know about. Is that it?'

'Yes.'

'You were at the party?'

'I was at the party.' She reflected a minute or two. 'It was a very good party. Well run. Well arranged. About thirty-odd people were there, that is, counting helpers of different kinds. Children – teenagers – grown-ups – and a few cleaning and domestic helpers in the background.'

'Did you take part in the arrangements which were made, I believe, earlier that afternoon or that morning?'

'There was nothing really to do. Mrs Drake was fully competent to deal with all the various preparations with a small number of people to help her. It was more domestic preparations that were needed.'

'I see. But you came to the party as one of the guests?'

'That is right.'

'And what happened?'

'The progress of the party, I have no doubt, you already know. You want to know if there is anything I can tell you that I specially noticed or that I thought might have a certain significance? I don't want to waste your time unduly, you understand.'

'I am sure you will not waste my time. Yes, Miss Whittaker, tell me quite simply.'

'The various events happened in the way already arranged for. The last event was what was really more a Christmas festivity or associated with Christmas, than it would be with Hallowe'en. The Snapdragon, a burning dish of raisins with brandy poured over them, and those round snatch at the raisins – there are squeals of laughter and excitement. It became very hot, though, in the room, with the burning dish, and I left it and came out in the hall. It was then, as I stood there, that I saw Mrs Drake coming out of the lavatory on the first floor landing. She was carrying a large vase of mixed autumn leaves and flowers. She stood at the angle of the staircase, pausing for a moment before coming downstairs. She was looking down over the well of the staircase. Not in my direction. She was looking towards the other end of the hall where there is a door leading into the library. It is set just across the hall from the door into the dining-room. As I say, she was looking that way and pausing for a moment before coming downstairs. She was shifting slightly the angle of the vase as it was a rather awkward thing to carry, and weighty if it was, as I presumed, full of water. She was shifting the position of it rather carefully so that she could hold it to her with one arm, and put out the other arm to the rail of the staircase as she came round the slightly shaped corner stairway. She stood there for a moment or two, still not looking at what she was carrying, but towards the hall below. And suddenly she made a sudden movement – a start I would describe it as – yes, definitely something had startled her. So much so that she relinquished her hold of the vase and it fell, re-versing itself as it did so so that the water streamed over her and the vase itself crashed down to the hall below, where it broke in smithereens on the hall floor.'

'I see,' said Poirot. He paused a minute or two, watching her. Her eyes, he noticed, were shrewd and knowledgeable. They were asking now his opinion of what she was telling him. 'What did you think had happened to startle her?'

'On reflection, afterwards, I thought she had seen some-thing.'

'You thought she had seen something,' repeated Poirot, thoughtfully. 'Such as?'

'The direction of her eyes, as I have told you, was towards the door of the library. It seems to me possible that she may have seen that door open or the handle turn, or indeed she might have seen something slightly more than that. She might have seen somebody who was opening that door and preparing to come out of it. She may have seen someone she did not expect to see.'

'Were you looking at the door yourself?'

'No. I was looking in the opposite direction up the stairs towards Mrs Drake.'

'And you think definitely that she saw something that startled her?'

'Yes. No more than that, perhaps. A door opening. A person, just possibly an unlikely person, emerging. Just sufficient to make her relinquish her grasp on the very heavy vase full of water and flowers, so that she dropped it.'

'Did you see anyone come out of that door?'

'No. I was not looking that way. I do not think anyone actually did come out into the hall. Presumably whoever it was drew back into the room.'

'What did Mrs Drake do next?'

'She made a sharp exclamation of vexation, came down the stairs and said to me, "Look what I've done now! What a mess!" She kicked some of the broken glass away. I helped her sweep it in a broken pile into a corner. It wasn't practicable to clear it all up at that moment. The children were beginning to come out of the Snapdragon room. I fetched a glass cloth and mopped her up a bit, and shortly after that the party came to an end.'

'Mrs Drake did not say anything about having been startled or make any reference as to what might have startled her?'

'No. Nothing of the kind.'

'But you think she *was* startled.'

'Possibly, Monsieur Poirot, you think that I am making a rather unnecessary fuss about something of no importance whatever?'

'No,' said Poirot, 'I do not think that at all. I have only met Mrs Drake once,' he added thoughtfully, 'when I went to her house with my friend, Mrs Oliver, to visit ¬ as one might say, if one wishes to be melodramatic – the scene of the crime. It did not strike me during the brief period I had for observation that Mrs Drake could be a woman who is easily startled. Do you agree with my view?'

'Certainly. That is why I, myself, since have wondered.'

'You asked no special questions at the time?'

'I had no earthly reason to do so. If your hostess has been unfortunate to drop one of her best glass vases, and it has smashed to smithereens, it is hardly the part of a guest to say "What on earth made you do that?"; thereby accusing her of a clumsiness which I can assure you is not one of Mrs Drake's characteristics.'

'And after that, as you have said, the party came to an end. The children and their mothers or friends left, and Joyce could not be found. We know now that Joyce was behind the library door and that Joyce was dead. So who could it have been who was about to come out of the library door, a little while earlier, shall we say, and then hearing voices in the hall shut the door again and made an exit later when there were people milling about in the hall making their farewells, putting on their coats and all the rest of it? It was not until after the body had been found, I presume,

Miss Whittaker, that you had time to reflect on what you had seen?'

'That is so.' Miss Whittaker rose to her feet. 'I'm afraid there's nothing else that I can tell you. Even this may be a very foolish little matter.'

'But noticeable. Everything noticeable is worth remembering. By the way, there is one question I should like to ask you. Two, as a matter of fact.'

Elizabeth Whittaker sat down again. 'Go on,' she said, 'ask anything you like.'

'Can you remember exactly the order in which the various events occured at the party?'

'I think so.' Elizabeth Whittaker reflected for a moment or two. 'It started with a broomstick competition. Decorated broomsticks. There were three or four different small prizes for that. Then there was a kind of contest with balloons, punching them and batting them about. A sort of mild horse-play to get the children warmed up. There was a looking-glass business where the girls went into a small room and held a mirror where a boy's or young man's face reflected in it.'

'How was that managed?'

'Oh, very simply. The transom of the door had been removed, and so different faces looked through and were reflected in the mirror a girl was holding.'

'Did the girls know who it was they saw reflected in the glass?'

'I presume some of them did and some of them didn't. A little make-up was employed on the male half of the arrangement. You know, a mask or a wig, sideburns, a beard, some greasepaint effects. Most of the boys were probably known to the girls already and one or two strangers might have been included. Anyway, there was a lot of quite happy giggling,' said Miss Whittaker, showing for a moment or two a kind of academic contempt for this kind of fun. 'After that there was an obstacle race and then there was flour packed into a glass tumbler and reversed, sixpence laid on top and everyone took a slice off. When the flour collapsed that person was out of the competition and the others remained until the last one claimed the sixpence. After that there was dancing, and then there was supper. After that, as a final climax, came the Snapdragon.'

'When did you yourself see the girl Joyce last?'

'I've no idea,' said Elizabeth Whittaker. 'I don't know her very well. She's not in my class. She wasn't a very interesting girl so I wouldn't have been watching her. I do remember I saw her cutting the flour because she was so clumsy that she capsized it almost at once. So she was alive then – but that was quite early on.'

'You did not see her go into the library with anyone?'

'Certainly not. I should have mentioned it before if I had. *That* at least might have been significant and important.'

'And now,' said Poirot, 'for my second question or questions. How long have you been at the school here?'

'Six years this next autumn.'

'And you teach –?'

'Mathematics and Latin.'

'Do you remember a girl who was teaching here two years ago – Janet White by name?'

Elizabeth Whittaker stiffened. She half rose from her chair, then sat down again.

'But that – that has nothing to do with all this, surely?'

'It could have,' said Poirot.

'But how? In what way?'

Scholastic circles were less well informed than village gossip, Poirot thought.

'Joyce claimed before witnesses to have seen a murder done some years ago. Could that possibly have been the murder of Janet White, do you think? How did Janet White die?'

'She was strangled, walking home from school one night.'

'Alone?'

'Probably not alone.'

'But not with Nora Ambrose?'

'What do you know about Nora Ambrose?'

'Nothing as yet,' said Poirot, 'but I should like to. What were they like, Janet White and Nora Ambrose?'

'Over-sexed,' said Elizabeth Whittaker, 'but in different ways. How could Joyce have seen anything of the kind or know anything about it? It took place in a lane near Quarry Wood. She wouldn't have been more than ten or eleven years old.'

'Which one had the boy friend?' asked Poirot. 'Nora or Janet?'

'All this is past history.'

'*Old sins have long shadows,*' quoted Poirot. 'As we advance through life, we learn the truth of that saying. Where is Nora Ambrose now?'

'She left the school and took another post in the North of England – she was, naturally, very upset. They were – great friends.'

'The police never solved the case?'

Miss Whittaker shook her head. She got up and looked at her watch.

'I must go now.'

'Thank you for what you have told me.'

CHAPTER 11

Hercule Poirot looked up at the façade of Quarry House. A solid, well-built example of mid-Victorian architecture. He had a vision of its interior – a heavy mahogany sideboard, a central rectangular table also of heavy mahogany, a billiard room, perhaps, a large kitchen with adjacent scullery, stone flags on the floor, a massive coal range now no doubt replaced by electricity or gas.

He noted that most of the upper windows were still curtained. He rang the front-door bell. It was answered by a thin, grey-haired woman who told him that Colonel and Mrs Weston were away in London and would not be back until next week.

He asked about the Quarry Woods and was told that they were open to the public without charge. The entrance was about five minutes' walk along the road. He would see a notice-board on an iron gate.

He found his way there easily enough, and passing through the gate began to descend a path that led downwards through trees and shrubs.

Presently he came to a halt and stood there lost in thought. His mind was not only on what he saw, on what lay around him. Instead he was conning over one or two sentences, and reflecting over one or two facts that had given him at the time, as he expressed it to himself, furiously to think. A forged Will, a forged Will and a girl. A girl who had disappeared, the girl in whose favour the Will had been forged. A young artist who had come here professionally to make out of an abandoned quarry of rough stone a garden, a sunk garden. Here again, Poirot looked round him and nodded his head with approval of the phrase. A Quarry Garden was an ugly term. It suggested the noise of blasting rock, the carrying away by lorries of vast masses of stone for road making. It had behind it industrial demand. But a Sunk Garden – that was different. It brought with it vague remembrances in his own mind. So Mrs Llewellyn-Smythe had gone on a National Trust tour of gardens in Ireland. He himself, he remembered, had been in Ireland five or six years ago. He had gone there to investigate a robbery of old family silver. There had been some interesting points about the case which had aroused his curiosity, and having (as usual) – Poirot added this bracket to his thoughts – solved his mission with full success, he had put in a few days travelling around and seeing the sights.

He could not remember now the particular garden he had been to see. Somewhere, he thought, not very far from Cork. Killarney? No, not Killarney. Somewhere not far from Bantry Bay. And he remembered it because it had been a garden quite different from the gardens which he had so far acclaimed as the great successes of this age, the gardens of the Châteaux in France, the formal beauty of Versailles. Here, he remembered, he had started with a little group of people in a boat. A boat difficult to get into if two strong and able boatmen had not practically lifted him in. They had rowed towards a small island, not a very interesting island, Poirot had thought, and began to wish that he had not come. His feet were wet and cold and the wind was blowing through the crevices of his mackintosh. What beauty, he had thought, what formality, what symmetrical arrangement of great beauty could there be on this rocky island with its sparse trees? A mistake – definitely a mistake.

They had landed at the little wharf. The fishermen had landed him with the same adroitness they had shown before. The remaining members of the party had gone on ahead, talking and laughing. Poirot, readjusting his mackintosh in position and tying up his shoes again, had followed them up the rather dull path with shrubs and bushes and a few sparse trees either side. A most uninteresting park, he thought.

And then, rather suddenly, they had come out from among the scrub on to a terrace with steps leading down from it. Below it he had looked down into what struck him at once as something entirely magical. Something as it might have been if elemental beings such as he believed were common in Irish poetry, had come out of their hollow hills and had created there, not so much by toil and hard labour as by waving a magic wand, a garden. You looked down into the garden. Its beauty, the flowers and bushes, the artificial water below in the fountain, the path round it, enchanted, beautiful and entirely unexpected. He wondered how it had been originally. It seemed too symmetrical to have been a quarry. A deep hollow here in the raised ground of the island, but beyond it you could see the waters of the Bay and the hills rising the other side, their misty tops an enchanting scene. He thought perhaps that it might have been that particular garden which had stirred Mrs Llewellyn-Smythe to possess such a garden of her own, to have the pleasure of taking an unkempt quarry set in this smug, tidy, elementary and essentially conventional countryside of that part of England.

And so she had looked about for the proper kind of well-paid slave to do her bidding. And she had found the professionally qualified young man called Michael Garfield and had brought him here and had paid him no doubt a large fee, and had in due course built a house for him. Michael Garfield, thought Poirot, had not failed her.

He went and sat down on a bench, a bench which had been strategically placed. He pictured to himself what the sunken quarry would look like in the spring. There were young beech trees and birches with their white shivering barks. Bushes of thorn and white rose, little juniper trees. But now it was autumn, and autumn had been catered for also. The gold and red of acers, a parrotia or two, a path that led along a winding way to fresh delights. There were flowering bushes of gorse or Spanish broom – Poirot was not famous for knowing the names of either flowers or shrubs – only roses and tulips could he approve and recognize.

But everything that grew here had the appearance of having grown by its own will. It had not been arranged or forced into submission. And yet, thought Poirot, that is not really so. All has been arranged, all has been planned to this tiny little plant that grows here and to that large towering bush that rises up so fiercely with its golden and red leaves. Oh yes. All has been planned here and arranged. What is more, I would say that it had obeyed.

He wondered then whom it had obeyed. Mrs Llewellyn-Smythe or Michael Garfield? It makes a difference, said Poirot to himself, yes, it makes a difference. Mrs Llewellyn-Smythe was knowledgeable, he felt sure. She had gardened for many years, she was no doubt a Fellow of the Royal Horticultural Society, she went to shows, she consulted catalogues, she visited gardens. She took journeys abroad, no doubt, for botanical reasons. She would know what she wanted, she would say what she wanted. Was that enough? Poirot thought it was not quite enough. She could have given orders to gardeners and made sure her orders were carried out. But did she know – really know – see in her mind's eye exactly what her orders would look like when they had been carried out? Not in the first year of their planting, not even the second, but things that she would see two years later, three years later, perhaps, even six or seven years later. Michael Garfield, thought Poirot, Michael Garfield knows what she wants because she has told him what she wants, and he knows how to make this bare quarry of stone and rock blossom as a desert can blossom. He planned and he brought it about; he had no doubt the intense pleasure that comes to an artist who is commissioned by a client with plenty of money. Here was his conception of a fairy-land tucked away in a conventional and rather dull hillside, and here it would grow up. Expensive shrubs for which large cheques would have to be written, and rare plants that perhaps would only be obtainable through the goodwill of a friend, and here, too, the humble things that were needed and which cost next to nothing at all. In spring on the bank just to his left there would be primroses, their modest green leaves all bunched together up the side of it told him that.

'In England,' said Poirot, 'people show you their herbaceous borders and they take you to see their roses and they talk at inordinate length about their iris gardens, and to show they appreciate one of the great beauties of England, they take you on a day when the sun shines and the beech trees are in leaf, and underneath them are all the bluebells. Yes, it is a very beautiful sight, but I have been shown it, I think, once too often. I prefer –' the thought broke off in his mind as he thought back to what he had preferred. A drive through Devon lanes. A winding road with great banks up each side of it, and on those banks a great carpet and showing of primroses. So pale, so subtly and timidly yellow, and coming from them that sweet, faint, elusive smell that the primrose has in large quantities, which is the smell of spring almost more than any other smell. And so it would not be all rare shrubs here. There would be spring and autumn, there would be little wild cyclamen and there would be autumn crocus here too. It was a beautiful place.

He wondered about the people who lived in Quarry House now. He had their names, a retired elderly Colonel and his wife, but surely, he thought, Spence might have told him more about them. He had the feeling that whoever owned this now had not got the love of it that dead Mrs Llewellyn-Smythe had had. He got up and walked along the path a little way. It was an easy path, carefully levelled, designed, he thought, to be easy for an elderly person to walk where she would at will, without undue amount of steep steps, and at a convenient angle and convenient intervals a seat that looked rustic but was much less rustic than it looked. In fact, the angle for the back and for one's feet was remarkably comfortable. Poirot thought to himself, I'd like to see this Michael Garfield. He made a good thing of this. He knew his job, he was a good planner and he got experienced people to carry his plans out, and he managed, I think, to get his patron's plans so arranged that she would think that the whole planning had been hers. But I don't think it was only hers. It was mostly his. Yes, I'd like to see him. If he's still in the cottage – or the bungalow – that was built for him, I suppose – his thought broke off.

He stared. Stared across a hollow that lay at his feet where the path ran round the other side of it. Stared at one particular golden red branching shrub which framed something that Poirot did not know for a moment was really there or was a mere effect of shadow and sunshine and leaves.

What am I seeing? thought Poirot. Is this the result of enchantment? It could be. In this place here, it could be. Is it a human being I see, or is it – what could it be? His mind reverted to some adventures of his many years ago which he had christened 'The Labours of Hercules'. Somehow, he thought, this was not an English garden in which he was sitting. There was an atmosphere here. He tried to pin it down. It had qualities of magic, of enchantment, certainly of beauty, bashful beauty, yet wild. Here, if you were staging a scene in the theatre, you would have your nymphs, your fauns, you would have Greek beauty, you would have fear too. Yes, he thought, in this sunk garden there is fear. What did Spence's sister say? Something about a murder that took place in the original quarry years ago? Blood had stained the rock there, and afterwards, death had been forgotten, all had been covered over, Michael Garfield had come, had planned and had created a garden of great beauty, and an elderly woman who had not many more years to live had paid out money for it.

He saw now it was a young man who stood on the other side of the hollow, framed by golden red leaves, and a young man, so Poirot now recognized, of an unusual beauty. One didn't think of young men that way nowadays. You said of a young man that he was sexy or madly attractive, and these evidences of praise are often quite justly made. A man with a craggy face, a man with wild greasy hair and whose features were far from regular. You didn't say a young man was beautiful. If you did say it, you said it apologetically as though you were praising some quality that had been long dead. The sexy girls didn't want Orpheus with his lute, they wanted a pop singer with a raucous voice, expressive eyes and large masses of unruly hair.

Poirot got up and walked round the path. As he got to the other side of the steep descent, the young man came out from the trees to meet him. His youth seemed the most characteristic thing about him, yet, as Poirot saw, he was not really young. He was past thirty, perhaps nearer forty. The smile on his face was very, very faint. It was not quite a welcoming smile, it was just a smile of quiet recognition. He was tall, slender, with features of great perfection such as a classical sculptor might have producd. His eyes were dark, his hair was black and fitted him as a woven chain mail helmet or cap might have done. For a moment Poirot wondered whether he and this young man might not be meeting in the course of some pageant that was being rehearsed. If so, thought Poirot, looking down at his galoshes, I, alas, shall have to go to the wardrobe mistress to get myself better equipped. He said:

'I am perhaps trespassing here. If so, I must apologize. I am a stranger in this part of the world. I only arrived yesterday.'

'I don't think one could call it trespassing.' The voice was very quiet; it was polite yet in a curious way uninterested, as if this man's thoughts were really somewhere quite far away. 'It's not exactly open to the public, but people do walk round here. Old Colonel Weston and his wife don't mind. They would mind if there was any damage done, but that's not really very likely.'

'No vandalism,' said Poirot, looking round him. 'No

litter that is noticeable. Not even a little basket. That is very unusual, is it not? And it seems deserted – strange. Here you would think,' he went on, 'there would be lovers walking.'

'Lovers don't come here,' said the young man. 'It's supposed to be unlucky for some reason.'

'Are you, I wonder, the architect? But perhaps I'm guessing wrong.'

'My name is Michael Garfield,' said the young man.

'I thought it might be,' said Poirot. He gesticulated with a hand around him. 'You made this?'

'Yes,' said Michael Garfield.

'It is beautiful,' said Poirot. 'Somehow one feels it is always rather unusual when something beautiful is made in – well, frankly, what is a dull part of the English landscape.

'I congratulate you,' he said. 'You must be satisfied with what you have done here.'

'Is one ever satisfied? I wonder.'

'You made it, I think, for a Mrs Llewellyn-Smythe. No longer alive, I believe. There is a Colonel and Mrs Weston, I believe? Do they own it now?'

'Yes. They got it cheap. It's a big, ungainly house – not easy to run – not what most people want. She left it in her Will to me.'

'And you sold it.'

'I sold the house.'

'And not the Quarry Garden?'

'Oh yes. The Quarry Garden went with it, practically thrown in, as one might say.'

'Now why?' said Poirot. 'It is interesting, that. You do not mind if I am perhaps a little curious?'

'Your questions are not quite the usual ones,' said Michael Garfield.

'I ask not so much for facts as for reasons. Why did A do so and so? Why did B do something else? Why was C's behaviour quite different from that of A and B?'

'You should be talking to a scientist,' said Michael. 'It is a

95

matter – or so we are told nowadays – of genes or chromosomes. The arrangement, the pattern, and so on.'

'You said just now you were not entirely satisfied because no-one ever was. Was your employer, your patron, whatever you like to call her – was she satisfied? With this thing of beauty?'

'Up to a point,' said Michael. 'I saw to that. She was easy to satisfy.'

'That seems most unlikely,' said Hercule Poirot. 'She was, I have learned, over sixty. Sixty-five at least. Are people of that age often satisfied?'

'She was assured by me that what I had carried out was the exact carrying out of her instructions and imagination and ideas.'

'And was it?'

'Do you ask me that seriously?'

'No,' said Poirot. 'No. Frankly I do not.'

'For success in life,' said Michael Garfield, 'one has to pursue the career one wants, one has to satisfy such artistic leanings as one has got, but one has as well to be a tradesman. You have to sell your wares. Otherwise you are tied to carrying out other people's ideas in a way which will not accord with one's own. I carried out mainly my own ideas and I sold them, marketed them perhaps is a better word, to the client who employed me, as a direct carrying out of her plans and schemes. It is not a very difficult art to learn. There is no more to it than selling a child brown eggs rather than white ones. The customer has to be assured they are the best ones, the right ones. The essence of the countryside. Shall we say, the hen's own preference? Brown, farm, *country* eggs. One does not sell them if one says "they are just eggs. There is only one difference in eggs. They are new laid or they are not".'

'You are an unusual young man,' said Poirot. 'Arrogant,' he said thoughtfully.'

'Perhaps.'

'You have made here something very beautiful. You have

added vision and planning to the rough material of stone hollowed out in the pursuit of industry, with no thought of beauty in that hacking out. You have added imagination, a result seen in the mind's eye, that you have managed to raise the money to fulfil. I congratulate you. I pay my tribute. The tribute of an old man who is approaching a time when the end of his own work is come.'

'But at the moment you are still carrying it on?'

'You know who I am, then?'

Poirot was pleased indubitably. He liked people to know who he was. Nowadays, he feared, most people did not.

'You follow the trail of blood . . . It is already known here. It is a small community, news travels. Another public success brought you here.'

'Ah, you mean Mrs Oliver.'

'Ariadne Oliver. A best seller. People wish to interview her, to know what she thinks about such subjects as student unrest, socialism, girls' clothing, should sex be permissive, and many other things that are no concern of hers.'

'Yes, yes,' said Poirot, 'deplorable, I think. They do not learn very much, I have noticed, from Mrs Oliver. They learn only that she is fond of apples. That has now been known for twenty years at least, I should think, but she still repeats it with a pleasant smile. Although now, I fear, she no longer likes apples.'

'It was apples that brought you here, was it not?'

'Apples at a Hallowe'en party,' said Poirot. 'You were at that party?'

'No.'

'You were fortunate.'

'Fortunate?' Michael Garfield repeated the word, something that sounded faintly like surprise in his voice.

'To have been one of the guests at a party where murder is committed is not a pleasant experience. Perhaps you have not experienced it, but I tell you, you are fortunate because – ' Poirot became a little more foreign ' – *il y a des ennuis, vous comprenez?* People ask you times, dates, impertinent questions.' He went on, 'You knew the child?'

'Oh yes. The Reynolds are well known here. I know most of the people living round here. We all know each other in Woodleigh Common, though in varying degrees. There is some intimacy, some friendships, some people remain the merest acquaintances, and so on.'

'What was she like, the child Joyce?'

'She was – how can I put it? – not important. She had rather an ugly voice. Shrill. Really, that's about all I remember about her. I'm not particularly fond of children. Mostly they bore me. Joyce bored me. When she talked, she talked about herself.'

'She was not interesting?'

Michael Garfield looked slightly surprised.

'I shouldn't think so,' he said. 'Does she have to be?'

'It is my view that people devoid of interest are unlikely to be murdered. People are murdered for gain, for fear or for love. One takes one's choice, but one has to have a starting point –'

He broke off and glanced at his watch.

'I must proceed. I have an engagement to fulfil. Once more, my felicitations.'

He went on down, following the path and picking his way carefully. He was glad that for once he was not wearing his tight patent leather shoes.

Michael Garfield was not the only person he was to meet in the sunk garden that day. As he reached the bottom he noted that three paths led from here in slightly different directions. At the entrance of the middle path, sitting on a fallen trunk of a tree, a child was awaiting him. She made this clear at once.

'I expect you are Mr Hercule Poirot, aren't you?' she said.

Her voice was clear, almost bell-like in tone. She was a fragile creature. Something about her matched the sunk garden. A dryad or some elf-like being.

'That is my name,' said Poirot.

'I came to meet you,' said the child. 'You are coming to tea with us, aren't you?'

'With Mrs Butler and Mrs Oliver? Yes.'

'That's right. That's Mummy and Aunt Ariadne.' She added with a note of censure: 'You're rather late.'

'I am sorry. I stopped to speak to someone.'

'Yes, I saw you. You were talking to Michael, weren't you?'

'You know him?'

'Of course. We've lived here quite a long time. I know everybody.'

Poirot wondered how old she was. He asked her. She said,

'I'm twelve years old. I'm going to boarding-school next year.'

'Will you be sorry or glad?'

'I don't really know till I get there. I don't think I like this place very much, not as much as I did.' She added, 'I think you'd better come with me now, please.'

'But certainly. But certainly. I apologize for being late.'

'Oh, it doesn't really matter.'

'What's your name?'

'Miranda.'

'I think it suits you,' said Poirot.

'Are you thinking of Shakespeare?'

'Yes. Do you have it in lessons?'

'Yes. Miss Emlyn read us some of it. I asked Mummy to read some more. I liked it. It has a wonderful sound. *A brave new world*. There isn't anything really like that, is there?'

'You don't believe in it?'

'Do you?'

'There is always a brave new world,' said Poirot, 'but only, you know, for very special people. The lucky ones. The ones who carry the making of that world within themselves.'

'Oh, I see,' said Miranda, with an air of apparently seeing with the utmost ease, though what she saw Poirot rather wondered.

She turned, started along the path and said,

'We go this way. It's not very far. You can go through the hedge of our garden.'

Then she looked back over her shoulder and pointed, saying:

'In the middle there, that's where the fountain was.'

'A fountain?'

'Oh, years ago. I suppose it's still there, underneath the shrubs and the azaleas and the other things. It was all broken up, you see. People took bits of it away but nobody has put a new one there.'

'It seems a pity.'

'I don't know. I'm not sure. Do you like fountains very much?'

'*Ça dépend*,' said Poirot.

'I know some French,' said Miranda. 'That's it depends, isn't it?'

'You are quite right. You seem very well educated.'

'Everyone says Miss Emlyn is a very fine teacher. She's our head-mistress. She's awfully strict and a bit stern, but she's terribly interesting sometimes in the things she tells us.'

'Then she is certainly a good teacher,' said Hercule Poirot. 'You know this place very well – you seem to know all the paths. Do you come here often?'

'Oh yes, it's one of my favourite walks. Nobody knows where I am, you see, when I come here. I sit in trees – on the branches, and watch things. I like that. Watching things happen.'

'What sort of things?'

'Mostly birds and squirrels. Birds are very quarrelsome, aren't they? Not like in the bit of poetry that says "birds in their little nests agree." They don't really, do they? And I watch squirrels.'

'And you watch people?'

'Sometimes. But there aren't many people who come here.'

'Why not, I wonder?'

'I suppose they are afraid.'

'Why should they be afraid?'

'Because someone was killed here long ago. Before it was a garden, I mean. It was a quarry once and then there was a gravel pile or a sand pile and that's where they found her. In that. Do you think the old saying is true – about you're born to be hanged or born to be drowned?'

'Nobody is born to be hanged nowadays. You do not hang people any longer in this country.'

'But they hang them in some other countries. They hang them in the streets. I've read it in the papers.'

'Ah. Do you think that is a good thing or a bad thing?'

Miranda's response was not strictly in answer to the question, but Poirot felt that it was perhaps meant to be.

'Joyce was drowned,' she said. 'Mummy didn't want to tell me, but that was rather silly, I think, don't you? I mean, I'm twelve years old.'

'Was Joyce a friend of yours?'

'Yes. She was a great friend in a way. She told me very interesting things sometimes. All about elephants and rajahs. She'd been to India once. I wish I'd been to India. Joyce and I used to tell each other all our secrets. I haven't so much to tell as Mummy. Mummy's been to Greece, you know. That's where she met Aunt Ariadne, but she didn't take me.'

'Who told you about Joyce?'

'Mrs Perring. That's our cook. She was talking to Mrs Minden who comes and cleans. Someone held her head down in a bucket of water.'

'Have you any idea who that someone was?'

'I shouldn't think so. They didn't seem to know, but then they're both rather stupid really.'

'Do *you* know, Miranda?'

'I wasn't there. I had a sore throat and a temperature so Mummy wouldn't take me to the party. But I think I could know. Because she was drowned. That's why I asked if you thought people were born to be drowned. We go through the hedge here. Be careful of your clothes.'

Poirot followed her lead. The entrance through the hedge from the Quarry Garden was more suited to the build of his childish guide with her elfin slimness – it was practically a highway to her. She was solicitous for Poirot, however, warning him of adjacent thorn bushes and holding back the more prickly components of the hedge. They emerged at a spot in the garden adjacent to a compost heap and turned a corner by a derelict cucumber frame to where two dustbins stood. From there on a small neat garden mostly planted with roses gave easy access to the small bungalow house. Miranda led the way through an open french window, announcing with the modest pride of a collector who has just secured a sample of a rare beetle:

'I've got him all right.

'Miranda, you didn't bring him through the hedge, did you? You ought to have gone round by the path at the side gate.'

'This is a better way,' said Miranda. 'Quicker and shorter.'

'And much more painful, I suspect.'

'I forget,' said Mrs Oliver – 'I did introduce you, didn't I, to my friend Mrs Butler?'

'Of course. In the post office.'

The introduction in question had been a matter of a few moments while there had been a queue in front of the counter. Poirot was better able now to study Mrs Oliver's friend at close quarters. Before it had been a matter of a slim woman in a disguising head-scarf and a mackintosh. Judith Butler was a woman of about thirty-five, and whilst her daughter resembled a dryad or a wood-nymph, Judith had more the attributes of a water-spirit. She could have been a Rhine maiden. Her long blonde hair hung limply on her shoulders, she was delicately made with a rather long face and faintly hollow cheeks, whilst above them were big sea-green eyes fringed with long eyelashes.

'I'm very glad to thank you properly Monsieur Poirot,' said Mrs Butler. 'It was very good of you to come down here when Ariadne asked you.'

'When my friend, Mrs Oliver, asks me to do anything I always have to do it,' said Poirot.

'What nonsense,' said Mrs Oliver.

'She was sure, quite sure, that you would be able to find out all about this beastly thing. Miranda, dear, will you go into the kitchen? You'll find the scones on the wire tray above the oven.'

Miranda disappeared. She gave, as she went, a knowledgeable smile directed at her mother that said as plainly as a smile could say, 'She's getting me out of the way for a short time.'

'I tried not to let her know,' said Miranda's mother, 'about this – this horrible thing that happened. But I suppose that was a forlorn chance from the start.'

'Yes indeed,' said Poirot. 'There's nothing that goes round any residential centre with the same rapidity as news of a disaster, and particularly an unpleasant disaster. And anyway,' he added, 'one cannot go long through life without knowing what goes on around one. And children seem particularly apt at that sort of thing.'

'I don't know if it was Burns or Sir Walter Scott who said "There's a chiel among you taking notes",' said Mrs Oliver, 'but he certainly knew what he was talking about.'

'Joyce Reynolds certainly seems to have noticed such a thing as a murder,' said Mrs Butler. 'One can hardly believe it.'

'Believe that Joyce noticed it?'

'I meant believe that if she saw such a thing she never spoke about it earlier. That seems very unlike Joyce.'

'The first thing that everybody seems to tell me here,' said Poirot, in a mild voice, 'is that this girl, Joyce Reynolds, was a liar.'

'I suppose it's possible,' said Judith Butler, 'that a child might make up a thing and then it might turn out to be true?'

'That is certainly the focal point from which we start,' said Poirot. 'Joyce Reynolds was unquestionably murdered.'

'And you *have* started. Probably you know already all about it,' said Mrs Oliver.

'Madame, do not ask impossibilities of me. You are always in such a hurry.'

'Why not?' said Mrs Oliver. 'Nobody would ever get anything done nowadays if they weren't in a hurry.'

Miranda returned at this moment with a plateful of scones.

'Shall I put them down here?' she asked. 'I expect you've finished talking by now, haven't you? Or is there anything else you would like me to get from the kitchen?'

There was a gentle malice in her voice. Mrs Butler lowered the Georgian silver teapot to the fender, switched on an electric kettle which had been turned off just before it came to the boil, duly filled the teapot and served the tea. Miranda handed hot scones and cucumber sandwiches with a serious elegance of manner.

'Ariadne and I met in Greece,' said Judith.

'I fell into the sea,' said Mrs Oliver, 'when we were coming back from one of the islands. It had got rather rough and the sailors always say "jump" and, of course, they always say jump just when the thing's at its furthest point which makes it come right for you, but you don't think that can possibly happen and so you dither and you lose your nerve and you jump when it looks close and, of course, that's the moment when it goes far away.' She paused for breath. 'Judith helped fish me out and it made a kind of bond between us, didn't it?'

'Yes, indeed,' said Mrs Butler. 'Besides, I liked your Christian name,' she added. 'It seemed very appropriate, somehow.'

'Yes, I suppose it is a Greek name,' said Mrs Oliver. 'It's

my own, you know. I didn't just make it up for literary purposes. But nothing Ariadne-like has ever happened to me. I've never been deserted on a Greek island by my own true love or anything like that.'

Poirot raised a hand to his moustache in order to hide the slight smile that he could not help coming to his lips as he envisaged Mrs Oliver in the rôle of a deserted Greek maiden.

'We can't all live up to our names,' said Mrs Butler.

'No, indeed. I can't see you in the rôle of cutting off your lover's head. That is the way it happened, isn't it, Judith and Holofernes, I mean?'

'It was her patriotic duty,' said Mrs Butler, 'for which, if I remember rightly, she was highly commended and rewarded.'

'I'm not really very well up in Judith and Holofernes. It's the Apochrypha, isn't it? Still, if one comes to think of it, people do give other people – their children, I mean – some very queer names, don't they? Who was the one who hammered some nails in someone's head? Jael or Sisera. I never remember which is the man or which is the woman there. Jael, I think. I don't think I remember any child having been christened Jael.'

'She laid butter before him in a lordly dish,' said Miranda unexpectedly, pausing as she was about to remove the tea-tray.

'Don't look at me,' said Judith Butler to her friend, 'it wasn't I who introduced Miranda to the Apochrypha. 'That's her school training.'

'Rather unusual for schools nowadays, isn't it?' said Mrs Oliver. 'They give them ethical ideas instead, don't they?'

'Not Miss Emlyn,' said Miranda. 'She says that if we go to church nowadays we only get the modern version of the Bible read to us in the lessons and things, and that it has no literary merit whatsoever. We should at least know the fine prose and blank verse sometimes of the Authorized Version. I enjoyed the story of Jael and Sisera very much,' she added.

'It's not a thing,' she said meditatively, 'that I should ever have thought of doing myself. Hammering nails, I mean, into someone's head when they were asleep.'

'I hope not indeed,' said her mother.

'And how *would* you dispose of your enemies, Miranda?' asked Poirot.

'I should be very kind,' said Miranda in a gently contemplative tone. 'It would be more difficult, but I'd rather have it that way because I don't like hurting things. I'd use a sort of drug that gives people euthanasia. They would go to sleep and have beautiful dreams and they just wouldn't wake up.' She lifted some tea cups and the bread and butter plate. 'I'll wash up, Mummy,' she said, 'if you like to take Monsieur Poirot to look at the garden. There are still some Queen Elizabeth roses at the back of the border.'

She went out of the room carefully carrying the tea-tray.

'She's an astonishing child, Miranda,' said Mrs Oliver.

'You have a very beautiful daughter, Madame,' said Poirot.

'Yes, I think she is beautiful *now*. One doesn't know what they will look like by the time they grow up. They acquire puppy fat and look like well-fattened pigs sometimes. But now – now she is like a wood-nymph.'

'One does not wonder that she is fond of the Quarry Garden which adjoins your house.'

'I wish she wasn't so fond of it sometimes. One gets nervous about people wandering about in isolated places, even if they are quite near people or a village. One's – oh, one's very frightened all the time nowadays. That's why – why you've got to find out why this awful thing happened to Joyce, Monsieur Poirot. Because until we know who that was, we shan't feel safe for a minute – about *our* children, I mean. Take Monsieur Poirot out in the garden, will you, Ariadne? I'll join you in a minute or two.'

She took the remaining two cups and a plate and went into the kitchen. Poirot and Mrs Oliver went out through the french window. The small garden was like most autumn gardens. It retained a few candles of golden rod and michaelmas daisies in a border, and some Queen Elizabeth roses held their pink statuesque heads up high. Mrs Oliver walked rapidly down to where there was a stone bench, sat down, and motioned Poirot to sit down beside her.

'You said you thought Miranda was like a wood-nymph,' she said. 'What do you think of Judith?'

'I think Judith's name ought to be Undine,' said Poirot.

'A water-spirit, yes. Yes, she does look as though she'd just come out of the Rhine or the sea or a forest pool or something. Her hair looks as though it had been dipped in water. Yet there's nothing untidy or scatty about her, is there?'

'She, too, is a very lovely woman,' said Poirot.

'What do you think about her?'

'I have not had time to think as yet. I just think that she is beautiful and attractive and that something is giving her great concern.'

'Well, of course, wouldn't it?'

'What I would like, Madame, is for you to tell me what *you* know or think about her.'

'Well, I got to know her very well on the cruise. You know, One does make quite intimate friends. Just one or two people. The rest of them, I mean, they like each other and all that, but you don't really go to any trouble to see them again. But one or two you do. Well, Judith was one of the ones I *did* want to see again.'

'You did not know her before the cruise?'

'No.'

'But you know something about her?'

'Well, just ordinary things. She's a widow,' said Mrs Oliver. 'Her husband died a good many years ago – he was an air pilot. He was killed in a car accident. One of those pile-up things, I think it was, coming off the M what-is-it that runs near here on to the ordinary road one evening, or something of that kind. He left her rather badly off, I imagine. She was very broken up about it, I think. She doesn't like talking about him.'

'Is Miranda her only child?'

'Yes. Judith does some part-time secretarial work in the neighbourhood, but she hasn't got a fixed job.'

'Did she know the people who lived at the Quarry House?'

'You mean old Colonel and Mrs Weston?'

'I mean the former owner, Mrs Llewellyn-Smythe, wasn't it?'

'I think so. I think I've heard that name mentioned. But she died two or three years ago, so of course one doesn't hear about her much. Aren't the people who are alive enough for you?' demanded Mrs Oliver with some irritation.

'Certainly not,' said Poirot. 'I have also to inquire into those who have died or disappeared from the scene.'

'Who's disappeared?'

'An *au pair* girl,' said Poirot.

'Oh well,' said Mrs Oliver, 'they're always disappearing, aren't they?' I mean, they come over here and get their fare paid and then they go straight into hospital because they're pregnant and have a baby, and call it Auguste, or Hans or Boris, or some name like that. Or they've come over to marry someone, or to follow up some young man they're in love with. You wouldn't believe the things friends tell me! The thing about *au pair* girls seems to be either they're Heaven's gift to over-worked mothers and you never want to part with them, or they pinch your stockings – or get themselves murdered –' She stopped. 'Oh!' she said.

'Calm yourself, Madame,' said Poirot. 'There seems no reason to believe that an *au pair* girl has been murdered – quite the contrary.'

'What do you mean by quite the contrary? It doesn't make sense.'

'Probably not. All the same –'

He took out his notebook and made an entry in it.

'What are you writing down there?'

'Certain things that have occurred in the past.'

'You seem to be very perturbed by the past altogether.'

'The past is the father of the present,' said Poirot sententiously.

He offered her the notebook.

'Do you wish to see what I have written?'

'Of course I do. I daresay it won't mean anything to me. The things *you* think important to write down, I never do.'

He held out the small black notebook.'

'Deaths: e.g. Mrs Llewellyn-Smythe (Wealthy). Janet White (School-teacher). Lawyer's clerk – Knifed, Former prosecution for forgery.'

Below it was written 'Opera girl disappears.'

'What opera girl?'

'It is the word my friend, Spence's sister, uses for what you and I call an *au pair* girl.'

'Why should she disappear?'

'Because she was possibly about to get into some form of legal trouble.'

Poirot's finger went down to the next entry. The word was simply 'Forgery,' with two question marks after it.

'Forgery?' said Mrs Oliver. 'Why forgery?'

'That is what *I* asked. *Why* forgery?'

'What kind of forgery?'

'A Will was forged, or rather a codicil to a Will. A codicil in the *au pair* girl's favour.'

'Undue influence?' suggested Mrs Oliver.

'Forgery is something rather more serious than undue influence,' said Poirot.

'I don't see what that's got to do with the murder of poor Joyce.'

'Nor do I,' said Poirot. 'But, therefore, it is interesting.'

'What is the next word? I can't read it.'

'Elephants.'

'I don't see what that's got to do with anything.'

'It might have,' said Poirot, 'believe me, it might have.'

He rose.

'I must leave you now,' he said. 'Apologize, please, to my

hostess for my not saying goodbye to her. I much enjoyed meeting her and her lovely and unusual daughter. Tell her to take care of that child.'

"'*My mother said I never should, play with the children in the wood*",' quoted Mrs Oliver. 'Well, goodbye. If you like to be mysterious, I suppose you will go on being mysterious. You don't even say what you're going to do next.'

'I have made an appointment for tomorrow morning with Messrs Fullerton, Harrison and Leadbetter in Medchester.'

'Why?'

'To talk about forgery and other matters.'

'And after that?'

'I want to talk to certain people who were also present.'

'At the party?'

'No – at the preparation for the party.'

CHAPTER 12

The premises of Fullerton, Harrison and Leadbetter were typical of an old-fashioned firm of the utmost respectability. The hand of time had made itself felt. There were no more Harrisons and no more Leadbetters. There was a Mr Atkinson and a young Mr Cole, and there was still Mr Jeremy Fullerton, senior partner.

A lean, elderly man, Mr Fullerton, with an impassive face, a dry, legal voice, and eyes that were unexpectedly shrewd. Beneath his hand rested a sheet of notepaper, the few words on which he had just read. He read them once again, assessing their meaning very exactly. Then he looked at the man whom the note introduced to him.

'Monsieur Hercule Poirot?' He made his own assessment of the visitor. An elderly man, a foreigner, very dapper in his dress, unsuitably attired as to the feet in patent leather shoes which were, so Mr Fullerton guessed shrewdly, too tight for him. Faint lines of pain were already etching themselves round the corners of his eyes. A dandy, a fop, a foreigner and recommended to him by, of all people, Inspector Henry Raglan, C.I.D., and also vouched for by Superintendent Spence (retired), formerly of Scotland Yard.

'Superintendent Spence, eh?' said Mr Fullerton.

Fullerton knew Spence. A man who had done good work in his time, had been highly thought of by his superiors. Faint memories flashed across his mind. Rather a celebrated case, more celebrated actually than it had showed any signs of being, a case that had seemed cut and dried. Of course! It came to him that his nephew Robert had been connected with it, had been Junior Counsel. A psychopathic killer, it had seemed, a man who had hardly bothered to try and defend himself, a man whom you might have thought really wanted to be hanged (because it had meant hanging at that time). No fifteen years, or indefinite number of years in prison. No. You paid the full penalty – and more's the pity they've given it up, so Mr Fullerton thought in his dry mind. The young thugs nowadays thought they didn't risk much by prolonging assault to the point where it became mortal. Once your man was dead, there'd be no witness to identify you.

Spence had been in charge of the case, a quiet, dogged man who had insisted all along that they'd got the wrong man. And they *had* got the wrong man, and the person who found the evidence that they'd got the wrong man was some sort of an amateurish foreigner. Some retired detective chap from the Belgian police force. A good age then. And now – senile, probably, thought Mr Fullerton, but all the same he himself would take the prudent course. Information, that's what was wanted from him. Information which, after all, could not be a mistake to give, since he could not see that he was likely to have any information that could be useful in this particular matter. A case of child homicide.

Mr Fullerton might think he had a fairly shrewd idea of who had committed that homicide, but he was not so sure as he would like to be, because there were at least three claimants in the matter. Any one of three young ne'er-do-wells might have done it. Words floated through his head. Mentally retarded. Psychiatrist's report. That's how the whole matter would end, no doubt. All the same, to drown a child during a party – that was rather a different cup of tea from one of the innumerable school children who did not arrive home and who had accepted a lift in a car after having been repeatedly warned not to do so, and who had been found in a nearby copse or gravel pit. A gravel pit now. When was that? Many, many years ago now.

All this took about four minutes time and Mr Fullerton then cleared his throat in a slightly asthmatic fashion, and spoke.

'Monsieur Hercule Poirot,' he said again. 'What can I do for you? I suppose it's the business of this young girl, Joyce Reynolds. Nasty business, very nasty business. I can't see actually where I can assist you. I know very little about it all.'

'But you are, I believe, the legal adviser to the Drake family?'

'Oh yes, yes. Hugo Drake, poor chap. Very nice fellow. I've known them for years, ever since they bought Apple Trees and came here to live. Sad thing, polio – he contracted it when they were holidaying abroad one year. Mentally, of course, his health was quite unimpaired. It's sad when it happens to a man who has been a good athlete all his life, a sportsman, good at games and all the rest of it. Yes. Sad business to know you're a cripple for life.'

'You were also, I believe, in charge of the legal affairs of Mrs Llewellyn-Smythe?'

'The aunt, yes. Remarkable woman really. She came here to live after her health broke down, so as to be near her nephew and his wife. Bought that white elephant of a place, Quarry House. Paid far more than it was worth – but money was no object to her. She was very well off. She could have found a more attractive house, but it was the quarry itself that fascinated her. Got a landscape gardener on to it, fellow quite high up in his profession, I believe. One of those handsome, long-haired chaps, but he had ability all right. He did well for himself in this quarry garden work. Got himself quite a reputation over it, illustrated in *Homes and Gardens* and all the rest of it. Yes, Mrs Llewellyn-Smythe knew how to pick people. It wasn't just a question of a handsome young man as a protégé. Some elderly women are foolish that way, but this chap had brains and was at the top of his profession. But I'm wandering on a bit. Mrs Llewellyn-Smythe died nearly two years ago.'

'Quite suddenly.'

Fullerton looked at Poirot sharply.

'Well, no, I wouldn't say that. She had a heart condition

and doctors tried to keep her from doing too much, but she was the sort of woman that you couldn't dictate to. She wasn't a hypochondriac type.' He coughed and said, 'But I expect we are getting away from the subject about which you came to talk to me.'

'Not really,' said Poirot, 'although I would like, if I may, to ask you a few questions on a completely different matter. Some information about one of your employees, by name Lesley Ferrier.'

Mr Fullerton looked somewhat surprised. 'Lesley Ferrier?' he said. 'Lesley Ferrier. Let me see. Really you know, I'd nearly forgotten his name. Yes, yes, of course. Got himself knifed, didn't he?'

'That is the man I mean.'

'Well, I don't really know that I can tell you much about him. It took place some years ago. Knifed near the Green Swan one night. No arrest was ever made. I daresay the police had some idea who was responsible, but it was mainly, I think, a matter of getting evidence.'

'The motive was emotional?' inquired Poirot.

'Oh yes, I should think certainly so. Jealousy, you know. He'd been going steady with a married woman. Her husband had a pub. The Green Swan at Woodleigh Common. Unpretentious place. Then it seems young Lesley started playing around with another young woman – or more than one, it was said. Quite a one for the girls, he was. There was a bit of trouble once or twice.'

'You were satisfied with him as an employee?'

'I would rather describe it as not dissatisfied. He had his points. He handled clients well and was studying for his articles, and if only he'd paid more attention to his position and keeping up a good standard of behaviour, it would have been better instead of mixing himself up with one girl after another, most of whom I am apt in my old-fashioned way to consider as considerably beneath him in station. There was a row one night at the Green Swan, and Lesley Ferrier was knifed on his way home.'

114

'Was one of the girls responsible, or would it be Mrs Green Swan, do you think?'

'Really, it is not a case of knowing anything *definite*. I believe the police considered it was a case of jealousy – but –' He shrugged his shoulders.

'But you are not sure?'

'Oh, it happens,' said Mr Fullerton. '"*Hell hath no fury like a woman scorned.*" That is always being quoted in Court. Sometimes it's true.'

'But I think I discern that you yourself are not at all sure that that was the case here.'

'Well, I should have preferred rather more evidence, shall we say. The police would have preferred rather more evidence, too. Public prosecutor threw it out, I believe.'

'It *could* have been something quite different?'

'Oh yes. One could propound several theories. Not a very stable character, young Ferrier. Well brought up. Nice mother – a widow. Father not so satisfactory. Got himself out of several scrapes by the skin of his teeth. Hard luck on his wife. Our young man in some ways resembled his father. He was associated once or twice with rather a doubtful crowd. I gave him the benefit of the doubt. He was still young. But I warned him that he was getting himself mixed up with the wrong lot. Too closely connected with fiddling transactions outside the law. Frankly, but for his mother, I wouldn't have kept him. He was young, and he had ability; I gave him a warning or two which I hoped might do the trick. But there's a lot of corruption about these days. It's been on the increase for the last ten years.'

'Someone might have had it in for him, you think?'

'Quite possible. These associations – gangs is a rather melodramatic word – but you run a certain danger when you get tangled up with them. Any idea that you may split on them, and a knife between your shoulder blades isn't an uncommon thing to happen.'

'Nobody saw it happen?'

'No. Nobody saw it happen. They wouldn't, of course.

Whoever took the job on would have all the arrangments nicely made. Alibi at the proper place and time, and so on and so on.'

'Yet *somebody* might have seen it happen. Somebody quite unlikely. A child, for instance.'

'Late at night? In the neighbourhood of the Green Swan? Hardly a very credible idea, Monsieur Poirot.'

'A child,' persisted Poirot, 'who might remember. A child coming home from a friend's house. At some short distance, perhaps, from her own home. She might have been coming by a footpath or seen something from behind a hedge.'

'Really, Monsieur Poirot, what an imagination you have got. What you are saying seems to me *most* unlikely.'

'It does not seem so unlikely to me,' said Poirot. 'Children *do* see things. They are so often, you see, not expected to be where they are.'

'But surely when they go home and relate what they have seen?'

'They might not,' said Poirot. 'They might not, you see, be sure of what they *had* seen. Especially if what they had seen had been faintly frightening to them. Children do not always go home and report a street accident they have seen, or some unexpected violence. Children keep their secrets very well. Keep them and think about them. Sometimes they like to feel that they know a secret, a secret which they are keeping to themselves.'

'They'd tell their mothers,' said Mr Fullerton.

'I am not so sure of that,' said Poirot. 'In my experience the the things that children do *not* tell their mothers are quite numerous.'

'What interests you so much, may I know, about this case of Lesley Ferrier? The regrettable death of a young man by a violence which is so lamentably often amongst us nowadays?'

'I know nothing about him. But I wanted to know something about him because his is a violent death that occurred not many years ago. That might be important to me.'

'You know, Mr Poirot,' said Mr Fullerton, with some

slight acerbity. 'I really cannot quite make out why you have come to me, and in what you are really interested. You cannot surely suspect any tie-up between the death of Joyce Reynolds and the death of a young man of promise but slightly criminal activities who has been dead for some years?'

'One can suspect anything,' said Poirot. 'One has to find out more.'

'Excuse me, what one has to have in all matters dealing with crime, is evidence.'

'You have perhaps heard that the dead girl Joyce was heard by several witnesses to say that she had with her own eyes witnessed a murder.'

'In a place like this,' said Mr Fullerton, 'one usually hears any rumour that may be going round. One usually hears it, too, if I may add these words, in a singularly exaggerated form not usually worthy of credence.'

'That also,' said Poirot, 'is quite true. Joyce was, I gather, just thirteen years of age. A child of nine could remember something she had seen – a hit-and-run accident, a fight or a struggle with knives on a dark evening, or a school teacher who was strangled, say – all these things might leave a very strong impression on a child's mind about which she would not speak, being uncertain, perhaps, of the actual facts she had seen, and mulling them over in her own mind. Forgetting about them even, possibly, until something happened to remind her. You agree that that is a possible happening?'

'Oh yes, yes, but I hardly – I think it is an extremely far-fetched supposition.'

'You had, also, I believe, a disappearance here of a foreign girl. Her name, I believe, was Olga or Sonia – I am not sure of the surname.'

'Olga Seminoff. Yes, indeed.'

'Not, I fear, a very reliable character?'

'No.'

'She was companion or nurse attendant to Mrs Llewellyn-

Smythe, was she not, whom you described to me just now? Mrs Drake's aunt –'

'Yes. She had had several girls in that position – two other foreign girls, I think, one of them with whom she quarrelled almost immediately, and another one who was nice but painfully stupid. Mrs Llewellyn-Smythe was not one to suffer fools gladly. Olga, her last venture, seems to have suited her very well. She was not, if I remember rightly, a particularly attractive girl,' said Mr Fullerton. 'She was short, rather stocky, had rather a dour manner, and people in the neighbourhood did not like her very much.'

'But Mrs Llewellyn-Smythe *did* like her,' suggested Poirot.

'She became very much attached to her – unwisely so, it seemed at one moment.'

'Ah, indeed.'

'I have no doubt,' said Mr Fullerton, 'that I am not telling you anything that you have not heard already. These things, as I say, go round the place like wildfire.'

'I understand that Mrs Llewellyn-Smythe left a large sum of money to the girl.'

'A most surprising thing to happen,' said Mr Fullerton. 'Mrs Llewellyn-Smythe had not changed her fundamental testamentary disposition for many years, except for adding new charities or altering legacies left void by death. Perhaps I am telling you what you know already, if you are interested in this matter. Her money had always been left jointly to her nephew, Hugo Drake, and his wife, who was also his first cousin, and so also niece to Mrs Llewellyn-Smythe. If either of them predeceased her the money went to the survivor. A good many bequests were left to charities and to old servants. But what was alleged to be her final disposal of her property was made about three weeks before her death, and not, as heretofore, drawn up by our firm. It was a codicil written in her own handwriting. It included one or two charities – not so many as before – the old servants had no legacies at all, and the whole residue of her considerable fortune was left to Olga Seminoff in gratitude for the devoted service and affection she had shown her. A most astonishing disposition, one that seemed totally unlike anything Mrs Llewellyn-Smythe had ever done before.'

'And then?' said Poirot.

'You have presumably heard more or less the developments. From the evidence of handwriting experts, it became clear that the codicil was a complete forgery. It bore only a faint resemblance to Mrs Llewellyn-Smythe's handwriting, no more than that. Mrs Smythe had disliked the typewriter and had frequently got Olga to write letters of a personal nature, as far as possible copying her employer's handwriting – sometimes, even, signing the letter with her employer's signature. She had had plenty of practice in doing this. It seems that when Mrs Llewellyn-Smythe died the girl went one step further and thought that she was proficient enough to make the handwriting acceptable as that of her employer. But that sort of thing won't do with experts. No, indeed it won't.'

'Proceedings were about to be taken to contest the document?'

'Quite so. There was, of course, the usual legal delay before the proceedings actually came to court. During that period the young lady lost her nerve and well, as you said yourself just now, she – disappeared.'

CHAPTER 13

When Hercule Poirot had taken his leave and departed, Jeremy Fullerton sat before his desk drumming gently with his fingertips. His eyes, however, were far away – lost in thought.

He picked up a document in front of him and dropped his eyes down to it, but without focusing his glance. The discreet buzz of the house telephone caused him to pick up the receiver on his desk.

'Yes, Miss Miles?'

'Mr Holden is here, sir.'

'Yes. Yes, his appointment, I believe was for nearly three quarters of an hour ago. Did he give any reason for having been so late? . . . Yes, yes. I quite see. Rather the same excuse he gave last time. Will you tell him I've seen another client, and I am now too short of time. Make an appointment with him for next week, will you? We can't have this sort of thing going on.'

'Yes, Mr Fullerton.'

He replaced the receiver and sat looking thoughtfully down at the document in front of him. He was still not reading it. His mind was going over events of the past. Two years – close on two years ago – and that strange little man this morning with his patent leather shoes and his big moustaches, had brought it back to him, asking all those questions.

Now he was going over in his own mind a conversation of nearly two years ago.

He saw again, sitting in the chair opposite him, a girl, a short, stocky figure – the olive brown skin, the dark red generous mouth, the heavy cheekbones and the fierceness of the blue eyes that looked into his beneath the heavy, beetling brows. A passionate face, a face full of vitality, a face that had known suffering – would probably always know suffering – but would never learn to accept suffering. The kind of woman who would fight and protest until the end. Where was she now, he wondered? Somehow or other she had managed – what had she managed exactly? Who had helped her? Had anyone helped her? Somebody must have done so.

She was back again, he supposed, in some trouble-stricken spot in Central Europe where she had come from, where she belonged, where she had had to go back to because there was no other course for her to take unless she was content to lose her liberty.

Jeremy Fullerton was an upholder of the law. He believed in the law, he was contemptuous of many of the magistrates of today with their weak sentences, their acceptance of scholastic needs. The students who stole books, the young married women who denuded the supermarkets, the girls who filched money from their employers, the boys who wrecked telephone boxes, none of them in real need, none of them desperate, most of them had known nothing but over-indulgence in bringing-up and a fervent belief that anything they could not afford to buy was theirs to take. Yet along with his intrinsic belief in the administration of the law justly, Mr Fullerton was a man who had compassion. He could be sorry for people. He could be sorry, and was sorry, for Olga Seminoff though he was quite unaffected by the passionate arguments she advanced for herself.

'I came to you for help. I thought you would help me. You were kind last year. You helped me with forms so that I could remain another year in England. So they say to me: "You need not answer any questions you do not wish to. You can be represented by a lawyer." So I come to you.'

'The circumstances you have instanced –' and Mr Fullerton remembered how drily and coldly he had said that, all the more drily and coldly because of the pity that lay behind the dryness of the statement ' – do not apply. In this case I am not at liberty to act for you legally. I am representing already the Drake family. As you know, I was Mrs Llewellyn-Smythe's solicitor.'

'But she is dead. She does not want a solicitor when she is dead.'

'She was fond of you,' said Mr Fullerton.

'Yes, she was fond of me. That is what I am telling you. That is why she wanted to give me the money.'

'All her money?'

'Why not? Why not? She did not like her relations.'

'You are wrong. She was very fond of her niece and nephew.'

'Well, then, she may have liked Mr Drake but she did not like Mrs Drake. She found her very tiresome. Mrs Drake interfered. She would not let Mrs Llewellyn-Smythe do always what she liked. She would not let her eat the food she liked.'

'She is a very conscientious woman, and she tried to get her aunt to obey the doctor's orders as to diet and not too much exercise and many other things.'

'People do not always want to obey a doctor's orders. They do not want to be interfered with by relations. They like living their own lives and doing what they want and having what they want. She had plenty of money. She could have what she wanted! She could have as much as she liked of everything. She was rich – rich – rich, and she could do what she liked with her money. They have already quite enough money, Mr and Mrs Drake. They have a fine house and clothes and two cars. They are very well-to-do. Why should they have any more?'

'They were her only living relations.'

'She wanted *me* to have the money. She was sorry for me. She knew what I had been through. She knew about my father, arrested by the police and taken away. We never saw him again, my mother and I. And then my mother and how she died. All my family died. It is terrible, what I have endured. You do not know what it is like to live in a police state, as I have lived in it. No, no. You are on the side of the police. You are not on *my* side.'

'No,' Mr Fullerton said, 'I am not on your side. I am very sorry for what has happened to you, but you've brought this trouble about yourself.'

'That is not true! It is not true that I have done anything I should not do. What have I done? I was kind to her, I was nice to her. I brought her in lots of things that she was not supposed to eat. Chocolates and butter. All the time nothing but vegetable fats. She did not like vegetable fats. She wanted butter. She wanted lots of butter.'

'It's not just a question of butter,' said Mr Fullerton.

'I looked after her, I was nice to her! And so she was grateful. And then when she died and I find that in her kindness and her affection she has left a signed paper leaving all her money to me, then those Drakes come along and say I shall not have it. They say all sorts of things. They say I had a bad influence. And then they say worse things than that. Much worse. They say *I* wrote the Will myself. That is nonsense. *She* wrote it. *She* wrote it. And then she sent me out of the room. She got the cleaning woman and Jim the gardener. She said they had to sign the paper, not me. Because I was going to get the money. Why should not I have the money? Why should I not have some good luck in my life, some happiness? It seemed so wonderful. All the things I planned to do when I knew about it.'

'I have no doubt, yes, I have no doubt.'

'Why shouldn't I have plans? Why should not I rejoice? I am going to be happy and rich and have all the things I want. What did I do wrong? Nothing. *Nothing*, I tell you. *Nothing*.'

'I have tried to explain to you,' said Mr Fullerton.

'That is all lies. You say I tell lies. You say I wrote the paper myself. I did not write it myself. *She* wrote it. Nobody can say anything different.'

'Certain people say a good many things,' said Mr Fullerton. 'Now listen. Stop protesting and listen to me. It is true, is it not, that Mrs Llewellyn-Smythe in the letters you wrote for her, often asked you to copy her handwriting as nearly as you could? That was because she had an old-fashioned idea that to write typewritten letters to people who are friends or with whom you have a personal acquaintance, is an act of rudeness. That is a survival from Victorian days. Nowadays nobody cares whether they receive hand-written letters or typewritten ones. But to Mrs Llewellyn-Smythe that was discourtesy. You understand what I am saying?'

'Yes, I understand. And so she asks me. She says, "Now, Olga," she says. "These four letters you will answer as I have told you and that you have taken down in shorthand. But you will write them in handwriting and you will make the handwriting as close to mine as possible." And she told me to practise writing her hand-writing, to notice how she made her a's, and her b's and her l's and all the different letters. "So long as it is reasonably like my handwriting," she said, "that will do, and then you can sign my name. But I do not want people to think that I am no longer able to write my own letters. Although, as you know, the rheumatism in my wrist is getting worse and I find it more difficult, but I don't want my personal letters typewritten".'

'You could have written them in your ordinary hand-writing,' said Mr Fullerton, 'and put a note at the end saying "per secretary" or per initials if you liked.'

'She did not want me to do that. She wanted it to be thought that *she* wrote the letters herself.'

And that, Mr Fullerton thought, could be true enough. It was very like Louise Llewellyn-Smythe. She was always passionately resentful of the fact that she could no longer do the things she used to do, that she could no longer walk far or go up hills quickly or perform certain actions with her hands, her right hand especially. She wanted to be able to say 'I'm perfectly well, perfectly all right and there's nothing I can't do if I set my mind to it.' Yes, what Olga was telling him now was perfectly true, and because it was true it was one of the reasons why the codicil appended to the last Will properly drawn out and signed by Louise Llewellyn-Smythe had been accepted at first without suspicion. It was in his own office, Mr Fullerton reflected, that suspicions had arisen because both he and his younger partner knew Mrs Llewellyn-Smythe's handwriting very well. It was young Cole who had first said,

'You know, I really can't believe that Louise Llewellyn-Smythe wrote that codicil. I know she had arthritis lately but look at these specimens of her own writing that I've brought along from amongst her papers to show you. There's something wrong about that codicil.

Mr Fullerton had agreed that there was something wrong about it. He had said they would take expert opinion on this handwriting question. The answer had been quite definite. Separate opinions had not varied. The handwriting of the codicil was definitely not that of Louise Llewellyn-Smythe. If Olga had been less greedy, Mr Fullerton thought, if she had been content to write a codicil beginning as this one had done – 'Because of her great care and attention to me and the affection and kindness she has shown me, I leave –' That was how it had begun, that was how it could have begun, and if it gone on to specify a good round sum of money left to the devoted *au pair girl*, the relations might have considered it over-done, but they would have accepted it without questioning. But to cut out the relations altogether, the nephew who had been his aunt's residuary legatee in the last four wills she had made during a period of nearly twenty years, to leave everything to the stranger Olga Seminoff – that was not in Louise Llewellyn-Smythe's character. In fact, a plea of undue influence could upset such a document anyway. No. She had been greedy, this hot, passionate child. Possibly Mrs Llewellyn-Smythe had told her that some money would be left to her because of her kindness, because of her attention, because of a fondness the old lady was beginning to feel for this girl who fulfilled all her whims, who did whatever she asked her. And that had opened up a vista for Olga. She would have everything. The old lady should leave everything to her, and she would have *all* the money. All the money and the house and the clothes and the jewels. Everything. A greedy girl. And now retribution had caught up with her.

And Mr Fullerton, against his will, against his legal instincts and against a good deal more, felt sorry for her. Very sorry for her. She had known suffering since she was a child, had known the rigours of a police state, had lost her parents, lost a brother and a sister and known injustice and fear, and it had developed in her a trait that she had no doubt been born with but which she had never been able so far to indulge. It had developed a childish passionate greed.

'Everyone is against me,' said Olga. 'Everyone. You are all against me. You are not fair because I am a foreigner, because I do not belong to this country, because I do not know what to say, what to do. What *can* I do? Why do you not tell me what I can do?'

'Because I do not really think there is anything much you can do.' said Mr Fullerton. 'Your best chance is to make a clean breast of things.'

'If I say what you want me to say, it will be all lies and not true. She made that Will. She wrote it down there. She told me to go out of the room while the others signed it.'

'There is evidence against you, you know. There are people who will say that Mrs Llewellyn-Smythe often did not know what she was signing. She had several documents of different kinds, and she did not always re-read what was put before her.'

'Well, then she did not know what she was saying.'

'My dear child,' said Mr Fullerton, 'your best hope is the fact that you are a first offender, that you are a foreigner, that you understand the English language only in a rather rudimentary form. In that case you may get off with a minor sentence – or you may, indeed, get put on probation.'

'Oh, words. Nothing but words. I shall be put in prison and never let out again.'

'Now you are talking nonsense,' Mr Fullerton said.

'It would be better if I ran away, if I ran away and hid myself so that nobody could find me.'

'Once there is a warrant out for your arrest, you would be found.'

'Not if I did it quickly. Not if I went at once. Not if someone helped me. I could get away. Get away from England. In a boat or a plane. I could find someone who forges passports or visas, or whatever you have to have. Someone who will do something for me. I have friends. I have people who are fond of me. Somebody could help me to disappear. That is what I needed. I could put on a wig. I could walk about on crutches.'

'Listen,' Mr Fullerton had said, and he had spoken then with authority, 'I am sorry for you. I will recommend you to a lawyer who will do his best for you. You can't hope to disappear. You are talking like a child.'

'I have got enough money. I have saved money.' And then she had said, 'You have tried to be kind. Yes, I believe that. But you will not do anything because it is all the law – the law. But someone will help me. Someone will. And I shall get away where nobody will ever find me.'

Nobody, Mr Fullerton thought, had found her. He wondered – yes; he wondered very much – where she was or could be now.

CHAPTER 14

Admitted to Apple Trees, Hercule Poirot was shown into the drawing-room and told that Mrs Drake would not be long.

In passing through the hall he heard the hum of female voices behind what he took to be the dining-room door.

Poirot crossed to the drawing-room window and surveyed the neat and pleasant garden. Well laid out, kept studiously in control. Rampant autumn michaelmas daisies still survived, tied up severely to sticks; chrysanthemums had not yet relinquished life. There were still a persistent rose or two scorning the approach of winter.

Poirot could discern no sign as yet of the preliminary activities of a landscape gardener. All was care and convention. He wondered if Mrs Drake had been one too many for Michael Garfield. He had spread his lures in vain. It showed every sign of remaining a splendidly kept suburban garden.

The door opened.

'I am sorry to have kept you waiting, Monsieur Poirot,' said Mrs Drake.

Outside in the hall there was a diminishing hum of voices as various people took their leave and departed.

'It's our church Christmas fête,' explained Mrs Drake. 'A Committee Meeting for arrangements for it and all the rest of it. These things always go on much longer than they ought to, of course. Somebody always objects to something, or has a good idea – the good idea usually being a perfectly impossible one.'

There was a slight acerbity in her tone. Poirot could well imagine that Rowena Drake would put things down as quite absurd, firmly and definitely. He could understand well enough from remarks he had heard from Spence's sister, from hints of what other people had said and from various other sources, that Rowena Drake was that dominant type of personality whom everyone expects to run the show, and whom nobody has much affection for while she is doing it. He could imagine, too, that her conscientiousness had not been the kind to be appreciated by an elderly relative who was herself of the same type. Mrs Llewellyn-Smythe, he gathered, had come here to live so as to be near to her nephew and his wife, and that the wife had readily undertaken the supervision and care of her husband's aunt as far as she could do so without actually living in the house. Mrs Llewellyn-Smythe had probably acknowledged in her own mind that she owed a great deal to Rowena, and had at the same time resented what she had no doubt thought of as her bossy ways.

'Well, they've all gone now,' said Rowena Drake, hearing the final shutting of the hall door. 'Now what can I do for you? Something more about that dreadful party? I wish I'd never had it here. But no other house really seemed suitable. Is Mrs Oliver still staying with Judith Butler?'

'Yes. She is, I believe, returning to London in a day or two. You had not met her before?'

'No. I love her books.'

'She is, I believe, considered a very good writer,' said Poirot.

'Oh well, she *is* a good writer. No doubt of that. She's a very amusing person too. Has she any ideas herself – I mean about who might have done this dreadful thing?'

'I think not. And you, Madame?'

'I've told you already. I've no idea whatever.'

'You would perhaps say so, and yet – you might, might you not, have, perhaps, what amounts to a very good idea, but only an idea. A half-formed idea. A *possible* idea.'

'Why should you think that?'

She looked at him curiously.

'You might have seen something – something quite small

129

and unimportant but which on reflection might seem more significant to you, perhaps, than it had done at first.'

'You must have something in your mind, Monsieur Poirot, some definite incident.'

'Well, I admit it. It is because of what someone said to me.'

'Indeed! And who was that?'

'A Miss Whittaker. A school-teacher.'

'Oh yes, of course. Elizabeth Whittaker. She's the mathematics mistress, isn't she, at The Elms? She *was* at the party, I remember. Did she see something?'

'It was not so much that she saw something as she had the idea that *you* might have seen something.'

Mrs Drake looked surprised and shook her head.

'I can't think of anything I can possibly have seen,' said Rowena Drake, 'but one never knows.'

'It had to do with a vase,' said Poirot. 'A vase of flowers.'

'A vase of flowers?' Rowena Drake looked puzzled. Then her brow cleared. 'Oh, of course, I know. Yes, there was a big vase of autumn leaves and chrysanthemums on the table in the angle of the stairs. A very nice glass vase. One of my wedding presents. The leaves seemed to be drooping and so did one or two of the flowers. I remember noticing it as I passed through the hall – it was near the end of the party, I think, by then, but I'm not sure – I wondered why it looked like that, and I went up and dipped my fingers into it and found that some idiot must have forgotten to put any water into it after arranging it. It made me very angry. So I took it into the bathroom and filled it up. But what could I have seen in that bathroom? There was nobody in it. I am quite sure of that. I think one or two of the older girls and boys had done a little harmless, what the Americans call "necking", there during the course of the party, but there was certainly nobody when I went into it with the vase.'

'No, no, I do not mean that,' said Poirot. 'But I understood that there was an accident. That the vase slipped out of your hand and it fell to the hall below and was shattered to pieces.'

'Oh yes,' said Rowena. 'Broken to smithereens. I *was*

130

rather upset about it because as I've said, it had been one of our wedding presents, and it was really a perfect flower vase, heavy enough to hold big autumn bouquets and things like that. It was very stupid of me. My fingers just slipped. It went out of my hand and crashed on the hall floor below. Elizabeth Whittaker was standing there. She helped me to pick up the pieces and sweep some of the broken glass out of the way in case someone stepped on it. We just swept it into a corner by the Grandfather clock to be cleared up later.'

She looked inquiringly at Poirot.

'Is that the incident you mean?' she asked.

'Yes,' said Poirot. 'Miss Whittaker wondered, I think, how you had come to drop the vase. She thought that something perhaps had startled you.'

'Startled me?' Rowena Drake looked at him, then frowned as she tried to think again. 'No, I don't think I was startled, anyway. It was just one of those ways things do slip out of your hands. Sometimes when you're washing up. I think, really, it's a result of being tired. I was pretty tired by that time, what with the preparations for the party and running the party and all the rest of it. It went very well, I must say. I think it was – oh, just one of those clumsy actions that you can't help when you're tired.'

'There was nothing – you are sure – that startled you? Something unexpected that you saw?'

'Saw? Where? In the hall below? I didn't see anything in the hall below. It was empty at the moment because every-one was in at the Snapdragon excepting, of course, for Miss Whittaker. And I don't think I even noticed her until she came forward to help when I ran down.'

'Did you see someone, perhaps, leaving the library door?'

'The library door . . . I see what you mean. Yes, I *could* have seen that.' She paused for quite a long time, then she looked at Poirot with a very straight, firm glance. 'I didn't see *anyone* leave the library,' she said. 'Nobody at all . . .'

He wondered. The way in which she said it was what aroused the belief in his mind that she was not speaking the truth, that instead she *had* seen someone or something, perhaps the door just opening a little, a mere glance perhaps of a figure inside. But she was quite firm in her denial. Why, he wondered, had she been so firm? Because the person she had seen was a person she did not want to believe for one moment had had anything to do with the crime committed on the other side of the door? Someone she cared about, or someone – which seemed more likely, he thought – someone whom she wished to protect. Someone, perhaps, who had not long passed beyond childhood, someone whom she might feel was not truly conscious of the awful thing they had just done.

He thought her a hard creature but a person of integrity. He thought that she was, like many women of the same type, women who were often magistrates, or who ran councils or charities, or interested themselves in what used to be called 'good works.' Women who had an inordinate belief in extenuating circumstances, who were ready, strangely enough, to make excuses for the young criminal. An adolescent boy, a mentally retarded girl. Someone perhaps who had already been – what is the phrase – 'in care.' If that had been the type of person she had seen coming out of the library, then he thought it possible that Rowena Drake's protective instinct might have come into play. It was not unknown in the present age for children to commit crimes, quite young children. Children of seven, of nine and so on, and it was often difficult to know how to dispose of these natural, it seemed, young criminals who came before the juvenile courts. Excuses had to be brought for them. Broken homes. Negligent and unsuitable parents. But the people who spoke the most vehemently for them, the people who sought to bring forth every excuse for them, were usually the type of Rowena Drake. A stern and censorious woman, except in such cases.

For himself, Poirot did not agree. He was a man who thought first always of justice. He was suspicious, had always been suspicious, of mercy – too much mercy, that is to say. Too much mercy, as he knew from former experience both in Belgium and this country, often resulted in further crimes which were fatal to innocent victims who need not have been victims if justice had been put first and mercy second.

'I see,' said Poirot. 'I see.'

'You don't think it's possible that Miss Whittaker might have seen someone go into the library?' suggested Mrs Drake.

Poirot was interested.

'Ah, you think that that might have been so?'

'It seemed to me merely a possibility. She might have caught sight of someone going in through the library, say, perhaps five minutes or so earlier, and then, when I dropped the vase it might have suggested to her that I could have caught a glimpse of the same person. That I might have seen who it was. Perhaps she doesn't like to say anything that might suggest, unfairly perhaps, some person whom she had perhaps only half glimpsed – not enough to be sure of. Some back view perhaps of a child, or a young boy.'

'You think, do you not, Madame, that it was – shall we say, a child – a boy or girl, a mere child, or a young adolescent? You think it was not any definite one of these but, shall we say, you think that that is the most likely type to have committed the crime we are discussing?'

She considered the point thoughtfully, turning it over in her mind.

'Yes,' she said at last, 'I suppose I do. I haven't thought it out. It seems to me that crimes are so often associated nowadays with the young. People who don't really know quite what they are doing, who want silly revenges, who have an instinct for destruction. Even the people who wreck telephone boxes, or who slash the tyres of cars, do all sorts of things just to hurt people, just because they hate – not anyone in particular, but the whole world. It's a sort of symptom of this age. So I suppose when one comes across something like a child drowned at a party for no reason really, one does assume that it's someone who is not yet fully responsible for their actions. Don't you agree with me that – that – well, that that is certainly the most likely possibility here?'

'The police, I think, share your point of view – or did share it.'

'Well, they should know. We have a very good class of policeman in this district. They've done well in several crimes. They are painstaking and they never give up. I think probably they will solve this murder, though I don't think it will happen very quickly. These things seem to take a long time. A long time of patient gathering of evidence.'

'The evidence in this case will not be very easy to gather, Madame.'

'No, I suppose it won't. When my husband was killed – He was a cripple, you know. He was crossing the road and a car ran over him and knocked him down. They never found the person who was responsible. As you know, my husband – or perhaps you don't know – my husband was a polio victim. He was partially paralyzed as a result of polio, six years ago. His condition had improved, but he was still crippled, and it would be difficult for him to get out of the way if a car bore down upon him quickly. I almost felt that I had been to blame, though he always insisted on going out without me or without anyone with him, because he would have resented very much being in the care of a nurse, or a wife who took the part of a nurse, and he was always careful before crossing a road. Still, one does blame oneself when accidents happen.'

'That came on top of the death of your aunt?'

'No. She died not long afterwards. Everything seems to come at once, doesn't it?'

'That is very true,' said Hercule Poirot. He went on: 'The police were not able to trace the car that ran down your husband?'

'It was a Grasshopper Mark 7, I believe. Every third car

you notice on the road is a Grasshopper Mark 7 – or was then. It's the most popular car on the market, they tell me. They believe it was pinched from the Market Place in Medchester. A car park there. It belonged to a Mr Waterhouse, an elderly seed merchant in Medchester. Mr Waterhouse was a slow and careful driver. It was certainly not he who caused the accident. It was clearly one of those cases where irresponsible young men help themselves to cars. Such careless, or should I say such callous young men, should be treated, one sometimes feels, more severely than they are now.'

'A long gaol sentence, perhaps. Merely to be fined, and the fine paid by indulgent relatives, makes little impression.'

'One has to remember,' said Rowena Drake, 'that there are young people at an age when it is vital that they should continue with their studies if they are to have the chance of doing well in life.'

'The sacred cow of education,' said Hercule Poirot. 'That is a phrase I have heard uttered,' he added quickly, 'by people – well, should I say people who ought to know. People who themselves hold academic posts of some seniority.'

'They do not perhaps make enough allowances for youth, for a bad bringing up. Broken homes.'

'So you think they need something other than gaol sentences?'

'Proper remedial treatment,' said Rowena Drake firmly.

'And that will make – (another old-fashioned proverb) – a silk purse out of a sow's ear? You do not believe in the maxim "the fate of every man have we bound about his neck"?'

Mrs Drake looked extremely doubtful and slightly displeased.

"An Islamic saying. I believe," said Poirot. Mrs Drake looked unimpressed.

'I hope,' she said, 'we do not take our ideas – or perhaps I should say our ideals – from the Middle East.'

'One must accept facts,' said Poirot, 'and a fact that is expressed by modern biologists – Western biologists –' he hastened to add, ' – seems to suggest very strongly that the root of a person's actions lies in his genetic make-up. That a murderer of twenty-four was a murderer in potential at two or three or four years old. Or of course a mathematician or a musical genius.'

'We are not discussing murderers,' said Mrs Drake. 'My husband died as a result of an accident. An accident caused by a careless and badly adjusted personality. Whoever the boy or young man was, there is always the hope of eventual adjustment to a belief and acceptance that it is a duty to consider others, to be taught to feel an abhorrence if you have taken life unawares, simply out of what may be described as criminal carelessness that was not really criminal in intent?'

'You are quite sure, therefore, that it was not criminal in intent?'

'I should doubt it very much.' Mrs Drake looked slightly surprised. 'I do not think that the police ever seriously considered that possibility. I certainly did not. It was an accident. A very tragic accident which altered the pattern of many lives, including my own.'

'You say we are not discussing murderers,' said Poirot. 'But in the case of Joyce that is just what we are discussing. There was no accident about that. Deliberate hands pushed that child's head down into water, holding her there till death occurred. Deliberate intent.'

'I know. I know. It's terrible. I don't like to think of it, to be reminded of it.'

She got up, moving about restlessly. Poirot pushed on relentlessly.

'We are still presented with a choice there. We still have to find the motive involved.'

'It seems to me that such a crime must have been quite motiveless.'

'You mean committed by someone mentally disturbed to the extent of enjoying killing someone? Presumably killing someone young and immature.'

'One does hear of such cases. What is the original cause of

them is difficult to find out. Even psychiatrists do not agree.'

'You refuse to accept a simpler explanation?'

She looked puzzled. 'Simpler?'

'Someone *not* mentally disturbed, *not* a possible case for psychiatrists to disagree over. Somebody perhaps who just wanted to be safe.'

'Safe? Oh, you mean –'

'The girl had boasted that same day, some hours previously, that she had seen someone commit a murder.'

'Joyce,' said Mrs Drake, with calm certainty, 'was really a very silly little girl. Not, I am afraid, always very truthful.'

'So everyone has told me,' said Hercule Poirot. 'I am beginning to believe, you know, that what everybody has told me must be right,' he added with a sigh. 'It usually is.'

He rose to his feet, adopting a different manner.

'I must apologize, Madame. I have talked of painful things to you, things that do not truly concern me here. But it seemed from what Miss Whittaker told me –'

'Why don't you find out more from her?'

'You mean –?'

'She is a teacher. She knows, much better than I can, what potentialities (as you have called them) exist amongst the children she teaches.'

She paused and then said:

'Miss Emlyn, too.'

'The head-mistress?' Poirot looked surprised.

'Yes. She knows things. I mean, she is a natural psychologist. You said I might have ideas – half-formed ones – as to who killed Joyce. I haven't – but I think Miss Emlyn might.'

'This is interesting . . .'

'I don't mean has *evidence*. I mean she just *knows*. *She* could tell you – but I don't think she will.'

'I begin to see,' said Poirot, 'that I have still a long way to go. People know things – but they will not tell them to me.' He looked thoughtfully at Rowena Drake.

'Your aunt, Mrs Llewellyn-Smythe, had an *au pair* girl who looked after her, a foreign girl.'

'You seem to have got hold of all the local gossip.' Rowena spoke dryly. 'Yes, that is so. She left here rather suddenly soon after my aunt's death.'

'For good reasons, it would seem.'

'I don't know whether it's libel or slander to say so – but there seems no doubt that she forged a codicil to my aunt's Will – or that someone helped her to do so.'

'Someone?'

'She was friendly with a young man who worked in a solicitor's office in Medchester. He had been mixed up in a forgery case before. The case never came to court because the girl disappeared. She realized the Will would not be admitted to probate, and that there was going to be a court case. She left the neighbourhood and has never been heard of since.'

'She too came, I have heard, from a broken home,' said Poirot.

Rowena Drake looked at him sharply but he was smiling amiably.

'Thank you for all you have told me, Madame,' he said.

When Poirot had left the house, he went for a short walk along a turning off the main road which was labelled 'Helpsly Cemetery Road.' The cemetery in question did not take him long to reach. It was at most ten minutes' walk. It was obviously a cemetery that had been made in the last ten years, presumably to cope with the rising importance of Woodleigh as a residential entity. The church, a church of reasonable size dating from some two or three centuries back, had had a very small enclosure round it already well filled. So the new cemetery had come into being with a foot-path connecting it across two fields. It was, Poirot thought, a business-like, modern cemetery with appropriate sentiments on marble or granite slabs; it had urns, chippings, small plantations of bushes or flowers. No interesting old epitaphs or inscriptions. Nothing much for an antiquarian. Cleaned, neat, tidy and with suitable sentiments expressed.

He came to a halt to read a tablet erected on a grave contemporary with several others near it, all dating within two or three years back. It bore a simple inscription, 'Sacred to the Memory of Hugo Edmund Drake, beloved husband of Rowena Arabella Drake, who departed this life March the 20th 19–'

He giveth his beloved sleep

It occurred to Poirot, fresh from the impact of the dynamic Rowena Drake, that perhaps sleep might have come in welcome guise to the late Mr Drake.

An alabaster urn had been fixed in position there and contained the remains of flowers. An elderly gardener, obviously employed to tend the graves of good citizens departed this life, approached Poirot in the pleasurable hopes of a few minutes' conversation while he laid his hoe and his broom aside.

'Stranger in these parts, I think,' he said, 'aren't you, sir?'

'It is very true,' said Poirot. 'I am a stranger with you as were my fathers before me.'

'Ah, aye. We've got that text somewhere or summat very like it. Over down the other corner, it is.' He went on, 'He was a nice gentleman, he were, Mr Drake. A cripple, you know. He had that infant paralysis, as they call it, though as often as not it isn't infants as suffer from it. It's grown-ups. Men and women too. My wife, she had an aunt, who caught it in Spain, she did. Went there with a tour, she did, and bathed somewhere in some river. And they said afterwards as it was the water infection, but I don't think they know much. Doctors don't, if you ask me. Still, it's made a lot of difference nowadays. All this inoculation they give the children, and that. Not nearly as many cases as there were.

'Yes, he were a nice gentleman and didn't complain, though he took it hard, being a cripple, I mean. He'd been a good sportsman, he had, in his time. Used to bat for us here in the village team. Many a six he's hit to the boundary. Yes, he were a nice gentleman.'

'He died of an accident, did he not?'

'That's right. Crossing the road, towards twilight this was. One of these cars come along, a couple of these young thugs in it with beards growing up to their ears. That's what they say. Didn't stop either. Went on. Never looked to see. Abandoned the car somewhere in a car park twenty miles away. Wasn't their own car either. Pinched from a car park somewhere. Ah, it's terrible, a lot of those accidents nowadays. And the police often can't do anything about them. Very devoted to him, his wife was. Took it very hard, she did. She comes here, nearly every week, brings flowers and puts them here. Yes, they were a very devoted couple. If you ask me, she won't stay here much longer.'

'Really? But she has a very nice house here.'

'Yes, oh yes. And she does a lot in the village, you know. All these things – women's institutes and teas and various societies and all the rest of it. Runs a lot of things, she does. Runs a bit too many for some people. Bossy, you know. Bossy and interfering, some people say. But the vicar relies on her. She starts things. Women's activities and all the rest of it. Gets up tours and outings. Ah yes. Often thought myself, though I wouldn't like to say it to my wife, that all these good works as ladies does, doesn't make you any fonder of the ladies themselves. Always know best, they do. Always telling you what you should do and what you shouldn't do. No freedom. Not much freedom anywhere nowadays.'

'Yet you think Mrs Drake may leave here?'

'I shouldn't wonder if she didn't go away and live somewhere abroad. They liked being abroad, used to go there for holidays.'

'Why do you think she wants to leave here?'

A sudden rather roguish smile appeared on the old man's face.

'Well, I'd say, you know, that she's done all she can do here. To put it scriptural, she needs another vineyard to work in. She needs more good works. Aren't no more good works to be done round here. She's done all there is, and even more than there need be, so some think. Yes.'

'She needs a new field in which to labour?' suggested Poirot.

'You've hit it. Better settle somewhere else where she can put a lot of things right and bully a lot of other people. She'd got us where she wants us here and there's not much more for her to do.'

'It may be,' said Poirot.

'Hasn't even got her husband to look after. She looked after him a good few years. That gave her a kind of object in life, as you might say. What with that and a lot of outside activities, she could be busy all the time. She's the type likes being busy all the time. And she's no children, more's the pity. So it's my view as she'll start all over again somewhere else.'

'You may have something there. Where would she go?'

'I couldn't say as to that. One of these Riviery places, maybe – or there's them as goes to Spain or Portugal. Or Greece – I've heard her speak of Greece – Islands. Mrs Butler, she's been to Greece on one of them tours. Hellenic, they call them, which sounds more like fire and brimstone to me.'

Poirot smiled.

'The isles of Greece,' he murmured. Then he asked: 'Do you like her?'

'Mrs Drake? I wouldn't say I exactly *like* her. She's a good woman. Does her duty to her neighbour and all that – but she'll always need a power of neighbours to do her duty to – and if you ask me, nobody really likes people who are always doing their duty. Tells me how to prune my roses which I know well enough myself. Always at me to grow some new-fangled kind of vegetable. Cabbage is good enough for me, and I'm sticking to cabbage.'

Poirot smiled. He said, 'I must be on my way. Can you tell me where Nicholas Ransom and Desmond Holland live?'

'Past the church, third house on the left. They board with Mrs Brand, go into Medchester Technical every day to study. They'll be home by now.'

He gave Poirot an interested glance.

'So that's the way your mind is working, is it? There's some already as thinks the same.'

'No, I think nothing as yet. But they were among those present – that is all.'

As he took leave and walked away, he mused, 'Among those present – I have come nearly to the end of my list.'

CHAPTER 15

Two pairs of eyes looked at Poirot uneasily.

'I don't see what else we can tell you. We've both been interviewed by the police, M. Poirot.'

Poirot looked from one boy to the other. They would not have described themselves as boys; their manner was carefully adult. So much so that if one shut one's eyes, their conversation could have passed as that of elderly clubmen. Nicholas was eighteen. Desmond was sixteen.

'To oblige a friend, I make my inquiries of those present on a certain occasion. Not the Hallowe'en party itself – the preparations for that party. You were both active in these.'

'Yes, we were.'

'So far,' Poirot said, 'I have interviewed cleaning women, I have had the benefit of police views, of talks to a doctor – the doctor who examined the body first – have talked to a school-teacher who was present, to the headmistress of the school, to distraught relatives, have heard much of the village gossip – By the way, I understand you have a local witch here?'

The two young men confronting him both laughed.

'You mean Mother Goodbody. Yes, she came to the party and played the part of the witch.'

'I have come now,' said Poirot, 'to the younger generation, to those of acute eyesight and acute hearing and who have up-to-date scientific knowledge and shrewd philosphy. I am eager – very eager – to hear your views on this matter.'

Eighteen and sixteen, he thought to himself, looking at the two boys confronting him. Youths to the police, boys to him, adolescents to newspaper reporters. Call them what you will. Products of today. Neither of them, he judged, at all stupid, even if they were not quite of the high mentality that he had just suggested to them by way of a flattering sop to start the conversation. They had been at the party. They had also been there earlier in the day to do helpful offices for Mrs Drake.

They had climbed up step-ladders, they had placed yellow pumpkins in strategic positions, they had done a little electrical work on fairy lights, one or other of them had produced some clever effects in a nice batch of phoney photographs of possible husbands as imagined hopefully by teenage girls. They were also, incidentally, of the right age to be in the forefront of suspects in the mind of Inspector Raglan and, it seemed, in the view of an elderly gardener. The percentage of murders committed by this group had been increasing in the last few years. Not that Poirot inclined to that particular suspicion himself, but anything was possible. It was even possible that the killing which had occurred two or three years ago might have been committed by a boy, youth, or adolescent of fourteen or twelve years of age. Such cases had occurred in recent newspaper reports.

Keeping all these possibilities in mind he pushed them, as it were, behind a curtain for the moment, and concentrated instead on his own appraisement of these two, their looks, their clothes, their manner, their voices and so on and so forth, in the Hercule Poirot manner, masked behind a foreign shield of flattering words and much increased foreign mannerisms, so that they themselves should feel agreeably contemptuous of him, though hiding that under politeness and good manners. For both of them had excellent manners. Nicholas, the eighteen-year-old, was good-looking, wearing side-burns, hair that grew fairly far down his neck, and a rather funereal outfit of black. Not as a mourning for the recent tragedy, but what was obviously his personal taste in modern clothes. The younger one was wearing a rose-coloured velvet coat, mauve trousers and a kind of frilled shirting. They both obviously spent a good deal of money on their clothes which were certainly not purchased locally and were probably paid for by themselves and not by their parents or guardians.

Desmond's hair was ginger coloured and there was a good deal of fluffy profusion about it.

'You were there in the morning or afternoon of the party, I understand, helping with the preparations for it?'

'Early afternoon,' corrected Nicholas.

'What sort of preparations were you helping with? I have heard of preparation from several people, but I am not quite clear. They don't all agree.'

'A good deal of the lighting, for one thing.'

'Getting up on steps for things that had to be put high up.'

'I understand there were some very good photographic results too.'

Desmond immediately dipped into his pocket and took out a folder from which he proudly brought certain cards.

'We faked up these beforehand,' he said. 'Husbands for the girls,' he explained. 'They're all alike, birds are. They all want something up-to-date. Not a bad assortment, are they?'

He handed a few specimens to Poirot who looked with interest at a rather fuzzy reproduction of a ginger-bearded young man and another young man with an aureole of hair, a third one whose hair came to his knees almost, and there were a few assorted whiskers, and other facial adornments.

'Made 'em pretty well all different. It wasn't bad, was it?'

'You had models, I suppose?'

'Oh, they're all ourselves. Just make-up, you know. Nick and I got 'em done. Some Nick took of me and some I took of him. Just varied what you might call the hair *motif*.'

'Very clever,' said Poirot.

'We kept 'em a bit out of focus, you know, so that they'd look more like spirit pictures, as you might say.'

The other boy said.

'Mrs Drake was very pleased with them. She congratulated us. They made her laugh too. It was mostly electrical work we did at the house. You know, fitting up a light or two so that when the girls sat with the mirror one or other of us could take up a position, you'd only to bob up over a screen and the girl would see a face in the mirror with, mind you, the right kind of hair. Beard or whiskers or something or other.'

'Did they know it was you and your friend?'

'Oh, I don't think so for a moment. Not at the party, they didn't. They knew we had been helping at the house with some things, but I don't think they recognized us in the mirrors. Weren't smart enough, I should say. Besides, we'd got sort of an instant make-up to change the image. First me, then Nicholas. The girls squeaked and shrieked. Damned funny.'

'And the people who were there in the afternoon? I do not ask you to remember who was at the party.'

'At the party, there must have been about thirty, I suppose, knocking about. In the afternoon there was Mrs Drake, of course, and Mrs Butler. One of the schoolteachers, Whittaker I think her name is. Mrs Flatterbut or some name like that. She's the organist's sister or wife. Dr Ferguson's dispenser, Miss Lee; it's her afternoon off and she came along and helped too and some of the kids came to make themselves useful if they could. Not that I think they were very useful. The girls just hung about and giggled.'

'Ah yes. Do you remember what girls there were there?'

'Well, the Reynolds were there. Poor old Joyce, of course. The one who got done in and her elder sister Ann. Frightful girl. Puts no end of side on. Thinks she's terribly clever. Quite sure she's going to pass all her "A" levels. And the small kid, Leopold, he's awful,' said Desmond. 'He's a sneak. He eavesdrops. Tells tales. Real nasty bit of goods. And there was Beatrice Ardley and Cathie Grant, who is dim as they make and a couple of useful women, of course. Cleaning women, I mean. And the authoress woman – the one who brought you down here.'

'Any men?'

'Oh, the vicar looked in if you count him. Nice old boy, rather dim. And the new curate. He stammers when he's nervous. Hasn't been here long. That's all I can think of now.'

'And then I understand you heard this girl – Joyce Reynolds – saying something about having seen a murder committed.'

'I never heard that,' said Desmond. 'Did she?'

'Oh, they're saying so,' said Nicholas. 'I didn't hear her, I suppose I wasn't in the room when she said it. Where was she – when she said that, I mean?'

'In the drawing-room.'

'Yes, well, most of the people were in there unless they were doing something special. Of course Nick and I,' said Desmond, 'were mostly in the room where the girls were going to look for their true loves in mirrors. Fixing up wires and various things like that. Or else we were out on the stairs fixing fairy lights. We were in the drawing-room once or twice putting the pumpkins up and hanging up one or two that had been hollowed out to hold lights in them. But I didn't hear anything of that kind when we were there. What about you, Nick?'

'I didn't,' said Nick. He added with some interest, 'Did Joyce really say that she'd seen a murder committed? Jolly interesting, you know, if she did, isn't it?'

'Why is it so interesting?' asked Desmond.

'Well, it's E.S.P., isn't it? I mean there you are. She saw a murder committed and within an hour or two she herself was murdered. I suppose she had a sort of vision of it. Makes you think a bit. You know these last experiments they've been having seems as though there is something you can do to help it by getting an electrode, or something of that kind, fixed up to your jugular vein. I've read about it somewhere.'

'They've never got very far with this E.S.P. stuff,' said Nicholas, scornfully. 'People sit in different rooms looking at

147

cards in a pack or words with squares and geometrical figures on them. But they never see the right things, or hardly ever.'

'Well, you've got to be pretty young to do it. Adolescents are much better than older people.'

Hercule Poirot, who had no wish to listen to this high-level scientific discussion, broke in.

'As far as you can remember, nothing occurred during your presence in the house which seemed to you sinister or significant in any way. Something which probably nobody else would have noticed, but which might have come to *your* attention.'

Nicholas and Desmond frowned hard, obviously racking their brains to produce some incident of importance.

'No, it was just a lot of clacking and arranging and doing things.'

'Have you any theories yourself?'

Poirot addressed himself to Nicholas.

'What, theories as to who did Joyce in?'

'Yes. I mean something that you might have noticed that could lead you to a suspicion on perhaps purely psychological grounds.'

'Yes, I can see what you mean. There might be something in that.'

'Whittaker for my money,' said Desmond, breaking into Nicholas's absorption in thought.'

'The school-mistress?' asked Poirot.

'Yes. Real old spinster, you know. Sex starved. And all that teaching, bottled up among a lot of women. You remember, one of the teachers got strangled a year or two ago. She was a bit queer, they say.'

'Lesbian?' asked Nicholas, in a man of the world voice.

'I shouldn't wonder. D'you remember Nora Ambrose, the girl she lived with? She wasn't a bad looker. She had a boy friend or two, so they said, and the girl she lived with got mad with her about it. Someone said she was an unmarried mother. She was away for two terms with some illness and then came back. They'd say anything in this nest of gossip.'

'Well, anyway, Whittaker was in the drawing-room most of the morning. She probably heard what Joyce said. Might have put it into her head, mightn't it?'

'Look here,' said Nicholas, 'supposing Whittaker – what age is she, do you think? Forty odd? Getting on for fifty – Women do go a bit queer at that age.'

They both looked at Poirot with the air of contented dogs who have retrieved something useful which master has asked for.

'I bet Miss Emlyn knows if it is so. There's not much she doesn't know, about what goes on in her school.'

'Wouldn't she say?'

'Perhaps she feels she has to be loyal and shield her.'

'Oh, I don't think she'd do that. If she thought Elizabeth Whittaker was going off her head, well then, I mean, a lot of the pupils at the school might get done in.'

'What about the curate?' said Desmond hopefully. '*He* might be a bit off his nut. You know, original sin perhaps, and all that, and the water and the apples and the things and then – look here, I've got a good idea now. Suppose *he* is a bit barmy. Not been here very long. Nobody knows much about him. Supposing it's the Snapdragon put it into his head. Hell fire! All those flames going up! Then, you see, he took hold of Joyce and he said "come along with me and I'll show you something," and he took her to the apple room and he said "kneel down." He said "This is baptism," and pushed her head in. See? It would all fit. Adam and Eve and the apple and hell fire and the Snapdragon and being baptised again to cure you of sin.'

'Perhaps he exposed himself to her first,' said Nicholas hopefully. 'I mean, there's always got to be a sex background to all these things.'

They both looked with satisfied faces to Poirot.

'Well,' said Poirot, 'you've certainly given me something to think about.'

CHAPTER 16

Hercule Poirot looked with interest at Mrs Goodbody's face. It was indeed perfect as a model for a witch. The fact that it almost undoubtedly went with extreme amiability of character did not dispel the illusion. She talked with relish and pleasure.

'Yes, I was up there right enough, I was. I always does the witches round here. Vicar he complimented me last year and he said as I'd done such a good job in the pageant as he'd give me a new steeple hat. A witch's hat wears out just like anything else does. Yes, I was right up there that day. I does the rhymes, you know. I mean the rhymes for the girls, using their own Christian name. One for Beatrice, one for Ann and all the rest of it. And I gives them to whoever is doing the spirit voice and they recite it out to the girl in the mirror, and the boys, Master Nicholas and young Desmond, they send the phoney photographs floating down. Make me die of laughing, some of it does. See those boys sticking hair all over their faces and photographing each other. And what they dress up in! I saw Master Desmond the other day, and what he was wearing you'd hardly believe. Rose-coloured coat and fawn breeches. Beat the girls hollow, they do. All the girls can think of is to push their skirts higher and higher, and that's not much good to them because they've got to put on more underneath. I mean what with the things they call body stockings and tights, which used to be for chorus girls in my day and none other – they spend all their money on that. But the boys – my word, they look like kingfishers and peacocks or birds of paradise. Well, I like to see a bit of colour and I always think it must have been fun in those old historical days as you see on the pictures. You know, everybody with lace and curls and cavalier hats and all the rest of it. Gave the girls something to look at, they did. And doublet and hose. All the girls could think of in historical times, as far as I can see, was to put great balloon skirts on, crinolines they called them later, and great ruffles round their necks! My grandmother, she used to tell me that her young ladies – she was in service, you know, in a good Victorian family – and her young ladies (before the time of Victoria I think it was) – it was the time the King what had a head like a pear was on the throne – Silly Billy, wasn't it, William IVth – well then, her young ladies, I mean my grandmother's young ladies, they used to have muslin gowns very long down to their ankles, very prim but they used to damp their muslins with water so they stuck to them. You know, stuck to them so it showed everything there was to show. Went about looking ever so modest, but it tickled up the gentlemen, all right, it did.

'I lent Mrs Drake my witch ball for the party. Bought that witch ball at a jumble sale somewhere. There it is hanging up there now by the chimney, you see? Nice bright dark blue. I keep it over my door.'

'Do you tell fortunes?'

'Mustn't say I do, must I?' she chuckled. 'The police don't like that. Not that they mind the kind of fortunes *I* tell. Nothing to it, as you might say. Place like this you always know who's going with who, and so that makes it easy.'

'Can you look in your witch ball, look in there, see who killed that little girl, Joyce?'

'You got mixed up, you have,' said Mrs Goodbody. 'It's a crystal ball you look in to see things, not a witch ball. If I told you who I thought it was did it, you wouldn't like it. Say it was against nature, you would. But lots of things go on that are against nature.'

'You may have something there.'

'This is a good place to live, on the whole. I mean, people are decent, most of them, but wherever you go, the devil's always got some of his own. Born and bred to it.'

'You mean – black magic?'

'No, I don't mean that.' Mrs Goodbody was scornful. 'That's nonsense, that is. That's for people who like to dress up and do a lot of tomfoolery. Sex and all that. No, I mean those that the devil has touched with his hand. They're born that way. The sons of Lucifer. They're born so that killing don't mean nothing to them, not if they profit by it. When they want a thing, they want it. And they're ruthless to get it. Beautiful as angels, they can look like. Knew a little girl once. Seven years old. Killed her little brother and sister. Twins they were. Five or six months old, no more. Stifled them in their prams.'

'That took place here in Woodleigh Common?'

'No, no, it wasn't in Woodleigh Common. I came across that up in Yorkshire, far as I remember. Nasty case. Beautiful little creature she was, too. You could have fastened a pair of wings on her, let her go on a platform and sing Christmas hymns, and she'd have looked right for the part. But she wasn't. She was rotten inside. You'll know what I mean. You're not a young man. You know what wickedness there is about in the world.'

'Alas!' said Poirot. 'You are right. I do know only too well. If Joyce really saw a murder committed –'

'Who says she did?' said Mrs Goodbody.

'She said so herself.'

'That's no reason for believing. She's always been a little liar.' She gave him a sharp glance. 'You won't believe that, I suppose?'

'Yes,' said Poirot, 'I do believe it. Too many people have told me so, for me to continue disbelieving it.'

'Odd things crop up in families,' said Mrs Goodbody. 'You take the Reynolds, for example. There's Mr Reynolds. In the estate business he is. Never cut much ice at it and never will. Never got on much, as you'd say. And Mrs Reynolds, always getting worried and upset about things. None of their three children take after their parents. There's Ann, now, she's got brains. She's going to do well with her schooling, she is. She'll go to college, I shouldn't wonder, maybe get herself trained as a teacher. Mind you, she's pleased with herself. She's so pleased with herself that nobody can stick her. None of the boys look at her twice. And then there was Joyce. She wasn't clever like Ann, nor as clever as her little brother Leopold, either, but she wanted to be. She wanted always to know more than other people and to have done better than other people and she'd say anything to make people sit up and take notice. But don't you believe any single word she ever said was true. Because nine times out of ten it wasn't.'

'And the boy?'

'Leopold? Well, he's only nine or ten, I think, but he's clever all right. Clever with his fingers and other ways, too. He wants to study things like physics. He's good at mathematics, too. Quite surprised about it they were, in school. Yes, he's clever. He'll be one of these scientists, I expect. If you ask me, the things he does when he's a scientist and the things he'll think of – they'll be nasty, like atom bombs! He's one of the kind that studies and are ever so clever and think up something that'll destroy half the globe, and all us poor folk with it. You beware of Leopold. He plays tricks on people, you know, and eavesdops. Finds out all their secrets. Where he gets all his pocket money from I'd like to know. It isn't from his mother or his father. They can't afford to give him much. He's got lots of money always. Keeps it in a drawer under his socks. He buys things. Quite a lot of expensive gadgets. Where does he get the money from? That's what I'd like to know. Find's people's secrets out, I'd say, and makes them pay him for holding his tongue.'

She paused for breath.

'Well, I can't help you, I'm afraid, in any way.'

'You have helped me a great deal,' said Poirot. 'What happened to the foreign girl who is said to have run away?'

'Didn't go far, in my opinion. "*Ding dong dell, pussy's in the well*." That's what I've always thought, anyway.'

CHAPTER 17

'Excuse me, Ma'am, I wonder if I might speak to you a minute.'

Mrs Oliver, who was standing on the verandah of her friend's house looking out to see if there were any signs of Hercule Poirot approaching – he had notified her by telephone that he would be coming round to see her about now – looked round.

A neatly attired woman of middle age was standing, twisting her hands nervously in their neat cotton gloves.

'Yes?' said Mrs Oliver, adding an interrogation point by her intonation.

'I'm sorry to trouble you, I'm sure, Madam, but I thought – well, I thought . . .'

Mrs Oliver listened but did not attempt to prompt her. She wondered what was worrying the woman so much.

'I take it rightly as you're the lady who writes stories, don't I? Stories about crimes and murders and things of that kind.'

'Yes,' said Mrs Oliver, 'I'm the one.'

Her curiosity was now aroused. Was this a preface for a demand for an autograph or even a signed photograph? One never knew. The most unlikely things happened.

'I thought as you'd be the right one to tell me,' said the woman.

'You'd better sit down,' said Mrs Oliver.

She foresaw that Mrs Whoever-it-was – she was wearing a wedding ring so she was a Mrs – was the type who takes some time in getting to the point. The woman sat down and went on twisting her hands in their gloves.

'Something you're worried about?' said Mrs Oliver, doing her best to start the flow.

'Well, I'd like advice, and it's true. It's about something that happened a good while ago and I wasn't really worried at the time. But you know how it is. You think things over and you wish you knew someone you could go and ask about it.'

'I see,' said Mrs Oliver, hoping to inspire confidence by this entirely meretricious statement.

'Seeing the things what have happened lately, you never do know, do you?'

'You mean –?'

'I mean what happened at the Hallowe'en party, or whatever they called it. I mean it shows you there's people who aren't dependable here, doesn't it? And it shows you things before that weren't as you thought they were. I mean, they mightn't have been what you thought they were, if you understand what I mean.'

'Yes?' said Mrs Oliver, adding an even greater tinge of interrogation to the monosyllable. 'I don't think I know your name,' she added.

'Leaman. Mrs Leaman. I go out and do cleaning to oblige ladies here. Ever since my husband died, and that was five years ago. I used to work for Mrs Llewellyn-Smythe, the lady who lived up at the Quarry House, before Colonel and Mrs Weston came. I don't know if you ever knew her.'

'No,' said Mrs Oliver, 'I never knew her. This is the first time I have been down to Woodleigh Common.'

'I see. Well, you wouldn't know much about what was going on perhaps at that time, and what was said at that time.'

'I've heard a certain amount about it since I've been down here this time,' said Mrs Oliver.

'You see, I don't know anything about the law, and I'm worried always when it's a question of law. Lawyers, I mean. They might tangle it up and I wouldn't like to go to the police. It wouldn't be anything to do with the police, being a legal matter, would it?'

'Perhaps not,' said Mrs Oliver, cautiously.

155

'You know perhaps what they said at the time about the codi – I don't know, some word like codi. Like the fish I mean.'

'A codicil to the Will?' suggested Mrs Oliver.

'Yes, that's right. That's what I'm meaning. Mrs Llewellyn-Smythe, you see, made one of these cod – codicils and she left all her money to the foreign girl what looked after her. And it was a surprise, that, because she'd got relations living here, and she'd come here anyway to live near them. She was very devoted to them, Mr Drake, in particular. And it struck people as pretty queer, really. And then the lawyers, you see, they began saying things. They said as Mrs Llewellyn-Smythe hadn't written the codicil at all. That the foreign pair girl had done it, seeing as she got all the money left to her. And they said as they were going to law about it. That Mrs Drake was going to counterset the Will – if that is the right word.'

'The lawyers were going to contest the Will. Yes, I believe I did hear something about that,' said Mrs Oliver encouragingly. 'And you know something about it, perhaps?'

'I didn't mean no harm,' said Mrs Leaman. A slight whine came into her voice, a whine with which Mrs Oliver had been acquainted several times in the past.

Mrs Leaman, she thought, was presumably an unreliable woman in some ways, a snooper perhaps, a listener at doors.

'I didn't say nothing at the time,' said Mrs Leaman, 'because you see I didn't rightly know. But you see I thought it was queer and I'll admit to a lady like you, who knows what these things are, that I did want to know the truth about it. I'd worked for Mrs Llewellyn-Smythe for some time, I had, and one wants to know how things happened.'

'Quite,' said Mrs Oliver.

'If I thought I'd done what I oughtn't to have done, well, of course, I'd have owned up to it. But I didn't think as I'd done anything really wrong, you see. Not at the time, if you understand,' she added.

'Oh yes,' said Mrs Oliver, 'I'm sure I shall understand. Go on. It was about this codicil.'

'Yes, you see one day Mrs Llewellyn-Smythe – she hadn't

felt too good that day and so she asked us to come in. Me that was, and young Jim who helps down in the garden and brings the sticks in and the coals, and things like that. So we went into her room, where she was, and she'd got papers before her there on the desk. And she turns to this foreign girl – Miss Olga we all called her – and said "You go out of the room now, dear, because you mustn't be mixed up in this part of it," or something like that. So Miss Olga, she goes out of the room and Mrs Llewellyn-Smythe, she tells us to come close and she says "This is my Will, this is." She got a bit of blotting paper over the top part of it but the bottom of it's quite clear. She said "I'm writing something here on this piece of paper and I want you to be a witness of what I've written and of my signature at the end of it." So she starts writing along the page. Scratchy pen she always used, she wouldn't use Biros or anything like that. And she writes two or three lines of writing and then she signed her name, and then she says to me, "Now, Mrs Leaman, you write your name there. Your name and your address" and then she says to Jim "And now you write your name underneath there, and your address too. There. That'll do. Now you've seen me write that and you've seen my signature and you've written your names, both of you, to say that's that." And then she says "That's all. Thank you very much." So we goes out of the room. Well, I didn't think nothing more of it at the time, but I wondered a bit. And it happened as I turns my head just as I was going out of the room. You see the door doesn't always latch properly. You have to give it a pull, to make it click. And so I was doing that – I wasn't really looking, if you know what I mean –'

'I know what you mean,' said Mrs Oliver, in a non-committal voice.

'And so I sees Mrs Llewellyn-Smythe pull herself up from the chair – she'd got arthritis and had pain moving about sometimes – and go over to the bookcase and she pulled out a book and she puts that piece of paper she'd just signed – in an envelope it was – in one of the books. A big tall book it was in the bottom shelf. And she sticks it back in the bookcase. Well, I never thought of it again, as you might say. No, really I didn't. But when all this fuss came up, well, of course I felt – at least, I –' She came to a stop.

Mrs Oliver had one of her useful intuitions.

'But surely,' she said, 'you didn't wait as long as all that –'

'Well, I'll tell you the truth, I will. I'll admit I was curious. After all, I mean, you want to know when you've signed anything, *what* you've signed, don't you? I mean, it's only human nature.'

'Yes,' said Mrs Oliver, 'it's only human nature.'

Curiosity, she thought, was a highly component part in Mrs Leaman's human nature.

'So I will admit that next day, when Mrs Llewellyn-Smythe had driven into Medchester and I was doing her bedroom as usual – a bedsitting room she had because she had to rest a lot. And I thinks, "Well, one ought really to know when you've signed a thing, what it is you've signed." I mean they always say with these hire purchase things, you should read the small print.'

'Or in this case, the handwriting,' suggested Mrs Oliver.

'So I thought, well, there's no harm – it's not as though I was taking anything. I mean to say I'd had to sign my name there, and I thought I really ought to know what I'd signed. So I had a look along the bookshelves. They needed dusting anyway. And I found the one. It was on the bottom shelf. It was an old book, a sort of Queen Victoria's kind of book. And I found this envelope with a folded paper in it and the title of the book said *Enquire Within upon Everything*. And it seemed then as though it was, sort of meant, if you know what I mean?'

'Yes,' said Mrs Oliver. 'It was clearly meant. And so you took out the paper and looked at it.'

'That's right, Madam. And whether I did wrong or not I don't know. But anyway, there it was. It was a legal document all right. On the last page there was the writing what she'd made the morning before. New writing with a new scratchy pen she was using. It was clear enough to read, though, although she had a rather spiky handwriting.'

'And what did it say,' said Mrs Oliver, her curiosity now having joined itself to that previously felt by Mrs Leaman.

'Well, it said something like, as far as I remember – the exact words I'm not quite sure of – something about a codicil and that after the legacies mentioned in her Will, she bequeathed her entire fortune to Olga – I'm not sure of the surname, it began with an S. Seminoff, or something like that – in consideration of her great kindness and attention to her during her illness. And there it was written down and she'd signed it and I'd signed it, and Jim had signed it. So I put it back where it was because I shouldn't like Mrs Llewellyn-Smythe to know that I'd been poking about in her things.

'But well, I said to myself, well, this *is* a surprise. And I thought, fancy that foreign girl getting all that money because we all know as Mrs Llewellyn-Smythe was very rich. Her husband had been in shipbuilding and he'd left her a big fortune, and I thought, well, some people have all the luck. Mind you, I wasn't particularly fond of Miss Olga myself. She had a sharp way with her sometimes and she had quite a bad temper. But I will say as she was always very attentive and polite and all that, to the old lady. Looking out for herself, all right, she was, *and* she got away with it. And I thought, well, leaving all that money away from her own family. Then I thought, well, perhaps she's had a tiff with them and likely as not that will blow over, so maybe she'll tear this up and make another Will or codicil after all. But anyway, that was that, and I put it back and I forgot about it, I suppose.

'But when all the fuss came up about the Will, and there was talk of how it had been forged and Mrs Llewellyn-Smythe could never have written that codicil herself – for that's what they were saying, mind you, as it wasn't the old lady who had written that at all, it was somebody else –'

'I see,' said Mrs Oliver. 'And so, what did you do?'

'I didn't do anything. And that's what's worrying me. . . . I didn't get the hang of things at once. And when I'd thought things over a bit I didn't know rightly *what* I ought to do and I thought, well, it was all talk because the lawyers were against the foreigner, like people always are. I'm not very fond of foreigners myself, I'll admit. At any rate, there it was, and the young lady herself was swanking about, giving herself airs, looking as pleased as Punch and I thought, well, maybe it's all a legal thing of some kind and they'll say she's no right to the money because she wasn't related to the old lady. So everything will be all right. And it was in a way because, you see, they gave up the idea of bringing the case. It didn't come to court at all and as far as anyone knew, Miss Olga ran away. Went off back to the Continent somewhere, where she came from. So it looks as though there must have been some hocus-pocus of some kind on her part. Maybe she threatened the old lady and made her do it. You never know, do you? One of my nephews who's going to be a doctor, says you can do wonderful things with hypnotism. I thought perhaps she hypnotised the old lady.'

'This was how long ago?'

'Mrs Llewellyn-Smythe's been dead for – let me see, nearly two years.'

'And it didn't worry you?'

'No, It didn't worry me. Not at the time. Because you see, I didn't rightly see that it mattered. Everything was all right, there wasn't any question of that Miss Olga getting away with the money, so I didn't see as it was any call for me –'

'But now you feel differently?'

'It's that nasty death – the child that was pushed into a bucket of apples. Saying things about a murder, saying she'd seen something or known something about a murder. And I thought maybe as Miss Olga had murdered the old lady because she knew all this money was coming to her and then she got the wind up when there was a fuss and lawyers and the police, maybe, and so she ran away. So then I thought well, perhaps I ought to – well, I ought to tell someone, and I thought you'd be a lady as has got friends in legal departments. Friends in the police perhaps, and you'd explain to them that I was only dusting a bookshelf, and this paper was there in a book and I put it back where it belonged. I didn't take it away or anything.'

'But that's what happened, was it, on that occasion? You saw Mrs Llewellyn-Smythe write a codicil to her Will. You saw her write her name and you yourself and this Jim someone were both there and you both wrote your own names yourselves. That's it, isn't it?'

'That's right.'

'So if you both saw Mrs Llewellyn-Smythe write her name, then that signature couldn't have been a forgery, could it? Not if you saw her write it herself.'

'I saw her write it herself and that's the absolute truth I'm speaking. And Jim'd say so too only he's gone to Australia, he has. Went over a year ago and I don't know his address or anything. He didn't come from these parts, anyway.'

'And what do you want me to do?

'Well, I want you to tell me if there's anything I ought to say, or do – now. Nobody's asked me, mind you. Nobody ever asked me if I knew anything about a Will.'

'Your name is Leaman. What Christian name?'

'Harriet.'

'Harriet Leaman. And Jim, what was his last name?'

'Well, now, what was it? Jenkins. That's right. James Jenkins. I'd be much obliged if you could help me because it worries me, you see. All this trouble coming along and if that Miss Olga did it, murdered Mrs Llewellyn-Smythe, I mean, and young Joyce saw her do it . . . She was ever so cock-a-hoop about it all, Miss Olga was, I mean about hearing from the lawyers as she'd come into a lot of money. But it was different when the police came round asking questions, and she went off very sudden, she did.

Nobody asked me anything, they didn't. But now I can't help wondering if I ought to have said something at the time.'

'I think,' said Mrs Oliver, 'that you will probably have to tell this story of yours to whoever represented Mrs Llewellyn-Smythe as a lawyer. I'm sure a good lawyer will quite understand your feelings and your motive.'

'Well, I'm sure if you'd say a word for me and tell them, being a lady as knows what's what, how it came about, and how I never meant to – well, not to do anything dishonest in any way. I mean, all I did –'

'All you did was to say nothing,' said Mrs Oliver. 'It seems quite a reasonable explanation.'

'And if it could come from you – saying a word for me first, you know, to explain, I'd be ever so grateful.'

'I'll do what I can,' said Mrs Oliver.

Her eyes strayed to the garden path where she saw a neat figure approaching.

'Well, thanks ever so much. They said as you were a very nice lady, and I'm sure I'm much obliged to you.'

She rose to her feet, replaced the cotton gloves which she had twisted entirely off in her anguish, made a kind of half nod or bob, and trotted off. Mrs Oliver waited until Poirot approached.

'Come here,' she said, 'and sit down. What's the matter with you? You look upset.'

'My feet are extremely painful,' said Hercule Poirot.

'It's those awful tight patent leather shoes of yours,' said Mrs Oliver. 'Sit down. Tell me what you came to tell me, and then *I'll* tell *you* something that you may be surprised to hear!'

CHAPTER 18

Poirot sat down, stretched out his legs and said: 'Ah! that is better.'

'Take your shoes off,' said Mrs Oliver, 'and rest your feet.'

'No, no, I could not do that.' Poirot sounded shocked at the possibility.

'Well, we're old friends together,' said Mrs Oliver, 'and Judith wouldn't mind if she came out of the house. You know, if you'll excuse me saying so, you oughtn't to wear patent leather shoes in the country. Why don't you get yourself a nice pair of suède shoes? Or the things all the hippy-looking boys wear nowadays? You know, the sort of shoes that slip on, and you never have to clean them – apparently they clean themselves by some extraordinary process or other. One of these labour-saving gimmicks.'

'I would not care for that at all,' said Poirot severely. 'No, indeed!'

'The trouble with you is,' said Mrs Oliver, beginning to unwrap a package on the table which she had obviously recently purchased, 'the trouble with you is that you insist on being *smart*. You mind more about your clothes and your moustaches and how you look and what you wear than *comfort*. Now comfort is really the great thing. Once you've passed, say, fifty, comfort is the only thing that matters.'

'Madame, chère Madame, I do not know that I agree with you.'

'Well, you'd better,' said Mrs Oliver. 'If not, you will suffer a great deal, and it will be worse year after year.'

Mrs Oliver fished a gaily covered box from its paper bag. Removing the lid of this, she picked up a small portion of its contents and transferred it to her mouth. She then licked her fingers, wiped them on a handkerchief, and murmured, rather indistinctly:

'Sticky.'

'Do you no longer eat apples? I have always seen you with a bag of apples in your hand, or eating them, or on occasions the bag breaks and they tumble out on the road.'

'I told you,' said Mrs Oliver, 'I told you that I never want to see an apple again. No. I hate apples. I suppose I shall get over it some day and eat them again, but – well, I don't like the associations of apples.'

'And what is it that you eat now?' Poirot picked up the gaily coloured lid decorated with a picture of a palm tree. 'Tunis dates,' he read. 'Ah, dates now.'

'That's right,' said Mrs Oliver. 'Dates.'

She took another date and put it in her mouth, removed a stone which she threw into a bush and continued to munch.

'Dates,' said Poirot. 'It is extraordinary.'

'What is extraordinary about eating dates? People do.'

'No, no, I did not mean that. Not eating them. It is extraordinary that you should say to me like that – *dates*.'

'Why?' asked Mrs Oliver.

'Because,' said Poirot, 'again and again you indicate to me the path, the how do you say, the *chemin* that I should take or that I should have already taken. You show me the way that I should go. Dates. Till this moment I did not realize how important dates were.'

'I can't see that dates have anything to do with what's happened here. I mean, there's no real *time* involved. The whole thing took place what – only five days ago.'

'That event took place four days ago. Yes, that is very true. But to everything that happens there has to be a past. A past which is by now incorporated in today, but which existed yesterday or last month or last year. The present is nearly always rooted in the past. A year, two years, perhaps even three years ago, a murder was committed. A child saw that murder. Because that child saw that murder on a certain date now long gone by, that child died four days ago. Is not that so?'

'Yes. That's so. At least, I suppose it is. It mightn't have been at all. It might be just some mentally disturbed nut who liked killing people and whose idea of playing with water is to push somebody's head under it and hold it there. It might have been described as a mental delinquent's bit of fun at a party.'

'It was not that belief that brought you to me, Madame.'

'No,' said Mrs Oliver, 'no, it wasn't. I didn't like the feel of things. I still don't like the feel of things.'

'And I agree with you. I think you are quite right. If one does not like the feel of things, one must learn why. I am trying very hard, though you may not think so, to learn why.'

'By going around and talking to people, finding out if they are nice or not and then asking them questions?'

'Exactly.'

'And what have you learnt?'

'Facts,' said Poirot. 'Facts which will have in due course to be anchored in their place by dates, shall we say.'

'Is that all? What else have you learnt?'

'That nobody believes in the veracity of Joyce Reynolds.'

'When she said she saw someone killed? But I heard her.'

'Yes, she *said* it. But nobody believes it is true. The probability is, therefore, that it was not true. That she saw no such thing.'

'It seems to me,' said Mrs Oliver, 'as though your facts were leading you backwards instead of remaining on the spot or going forward.'

'Things have to be made to accord. Take forgery, for instance. The fact of forgery. Everybody says that a foreign girl, the *au pair* girl, so endeared herself to an elderly and very rich widow that that rich widow left a Will, or a codicil to a Will, leaving all her money to this girl. Did the girl forge that Will or did somebody else forge it?'

'Who else could have forged it?'

'There was another forger in this village. Someone, that is, who had once been accused of forgery but had got off lightly as a first offender and with extenuating circumstances.'

'Is this a new character? One I know?'

'No, you do not know him. He is dead.'

'Oh? When did he die?'

'About two years ago. The exact date I do not as yet know. But I shall have to know. He is someone who had practised forgery and who lived in this place. And because of a little what you might call girl trouble arousing jealousy and various emotions, he was knifed one night and died. I have the idea, you see, that a lot of separated incidents might tie up more closely than anyone has thought. Not any of them. Probably not all of them, but several of them.'

'It sounds interesting,' said Mrs Oliver, 'but I can't see –'

'Nor can I as yet,' said Poirot. 'But I think dates might help. Dates of certain happenings, where people were, what happened to them, what they were doing. Everybody thinks that the foreign girl forged the Will and probably,' said Poirot, 'everybody was right. She was the one to gain by it, was she not? Wait – wait –'

'Wait for what?' said Mrs Oliver.

'An idea that passed through my head,' said Poirot.

Mrs Oliver sighed and took another date.

'You return to London, Madame? Or are you making a long stay here?'

'Day after tomorrow,' said Mrs Oliver. 'I can't stay any longer. I've got a good many things cropping up.'

'Tell me, now – in your flat, your house, I cannot remember which it is now, you have moved so many times lately, there is room there to have guests?'

'I never admit that there is,' said Mrs Oliver. 'If you ever admit that you've got a free guest room in London, you've asked for it. All your friends, and not only your friends, your acquaintances or indeed your acquaintances' third cousins sometimes, write you letters and say would you mind just putting them up for a night. Well, I do mind. What with sheets and laundry, pillow cases and wanting early morning tea and very often expecting meals served to them, people come. So I don't let on that I have got an available spare room. My *friends* come and stay with me. The people I *really* want to see, but the others – no, I'm not helpful. I don't like just being made use of.'

'Who does?' said Hercule Poirot. 'You are very wise.'

'And anyway, what's all this about?'

'You could put up one or two guests, if need arose?'

'I *could*,' said Mrs Oliver. 'Who do you want me to put up? Not you yourself. You've got a splendid flat of your own. Ultra modern, very abstract, all squares and cubes.'

'It is just that there might be a wise precaution to take.'

'For whom? Somebody else going to be killed?'

'I trust and pray not, but it might be within the bound of possibility.'

'But who? Who? I can't understand.'

'How well do you know your friend?'

'Know her? Not well. I mean, we liked each other on a cruise and got in the habit of pairing off together. There was something – what shall I say? – exciting about her. Different.'

'Did you think you might put her in a book some day?'

'I do hate that phrase being used. People are always saying it to me and it's not true. Not really. I don't put people in books. People I meet, people I know.'

'Is it perhaps not true to say, Madame, that you do put people in books sometimes? People that you meet, but *not*, I agree, people that you *know*. There would be no fun in that.'

'You're quite right,' said Mrs Oliver. 'You're really rather good at guessing things sometimes. It does happen that way. I mean, you see a fat woman sitting in a bus eating a currant bun and her lips are moving as well as eating, and you can see she's either saying something to someone or thinking up a telephone call that she's going to make, or perhaps a letter she's going to write. And you look at her and you study her shoes and the skirt she's got on and her hat and guess her age and whether she's got a wedding ring on and a few other things. And then you get out of the bus. You don't want ever to see her again, but you've got a story in your mind about somebody called Mrs Carnaby who is going home in a bus, having had a very strange interview somewhere where she saw someone in a pastry cook's and was reminded of someone she'd only met once and who she had heard was dead and apparently isn't dead. Dear me,' said Mrs Oliver, pausing for breath. 'You know, it's quite true. I did sit across from someone in a bus just before I left London, and here it is all working out beautifully inside my head. I shall have the whole story soon. The whole sequence, what she's going back to say, whether it'll run her into danger or somebody else into danger. I think I even know her name. Her name's Constance. Constance Carnaby. There's only one thing would ruin it.'

'And what is that?'

'Well, I mean, if I met her again in another bus, or spoke to her or she talked to me or I began to know something about her. That would ruin everything, of course.'

'Yes, yes. The story must be yours, the character is yours. She is your child. You have made her, you begin to understand her, you know how she feels, you know where she lives and you know what she does. But that all started with a real, live human being and if you found out what the real live human being was like – well then, there would be no story, would there?'

'Right again,' said Mrs Oliver. 'As to what you were saying about Judith, I think that is true. I mean, we were together a lot on the cruise, and we went to see the places but I didn't really get to know her particularly well. She's a widow, and her husband died and she was left badly off with one child, Miranda, whom you've seen. And it's true that I've got rather a funny feeling about them. A feeling as though they mattered, as though they're mixed up in some interesting drama. I don't want to know what the drama is. I don't want them to tell me. I want to think of the sort of drama I would like them to be in.'

'Yes. Yes, I can see that they are – well, candidates for inclusion for another best seller by Ariadne Oliver.'

'You really are a beast sometimes,' said Mrs Oliver. 'You make it all sound so vulgar.' She paused thoughtfully. 'Perhaps it is.'

'No, no, it is not vulgar. It is just human.'

'And you want me to invite Judith and Miranda to my flat or house in London?'

'Not yet,' said Poirot. 'Not yet until I am sure that one of my little ideas might be right.'

'You and your litle ideas! Now I've got a piece of news for you.'

'Madame, you delight me.'

'Don't be too sure. It will probably upset your ideas. Supposing I tell you that the forgery you have been so busy talking about wasn't a forgery at all.'

'What is that you say?'

'Mrs Ap Jones Smythe, or whatever her name is, *did* make a codicil to her Will leaving all her money to the *au pair* girl *and* two witnesses saw her sign it, and signed it also in the presence of each other. Put that in your moustache and smoke it.'

CHAPTER 19

'Mrs – Leaman –' said Poirot, writing down the name.

'That's right. Harriet Leaman. And the other witness seems to have been a James Jenkins. Last heard of going to Australia. And Miss Olga Seminoff seems to have been last heard of returning to Czechoslovakia, or wherever she came from. Everybody seems to have gone somewhere else.'

'How reliable do you think this Mrs Leaman is?'

'I don't think she made it all up, if that's what you mean. I think she signed something, that she was curious about it, and that she took the first opportunity she had of finding out what she'd signed.'

'She can read and write?'

'I suppose so. But I agree that people aren't very good sometimes, at reading old ladies' handwriting, which is very spiky and very hard to read. If there were any rumours flying about later, about this Will or codicil, she might have thought that that was what she'd read in this rather undecipherable handwriting.'

'A genuine document,' said Poirot. 'But there *was* also a forged codicil.'

'Who says so?'

'Lawyers.'

'Perhaps it wasn't forged at all.'

'Lawyers are very particular about these matters. They were prepared to come into court with expert witnesses.'

'Oh well,' said Mrs Oliver, 'then it's easy to see what must have happened, isn't it?'

'What is easy? What happened?'

'Well, of course, the next day or a few days later, or even as much as a week later, Mrs Llewellyn-Smythe either had a bit of a tiff with her devoted *au pair* attendant, or she had a delicious reconciliation with her nephew, Hugo, or her niece Rowena, and she tore up the Will or scratched out the codicil or something like that, or burnt the whole thing.'

'And after that?'

'Well, after that, I suppose, Mrs Llewellyn-Smythe dies, and the girl seizes her chance and writes a new codicil in roughly the same terms in as near to Mrs Llewellyn-Smythe's handwriting as she can, and the two witnessing signatures as near as she can. She probably knows Mrs Leaman's writing quite well. It would be on national health cards or something like that, and she produces it, thinking that someone will agree to having witnessed the Will and that all would be well. But her forgery isn't good enough and so trouble starts.'

'Will you permit me, chère Madame, to use your telephone?'

'I will permit you to use Judith Butler's telephone, yes.'

'Where is your friend?'

'Oh, she's gone to get her hair done. And Miranda has gone for a walk. Go on, it's in the room through the window there.'

Poirot went in and returned about ten minutes later.

'Well? What have you been doing?'

'I rang up Mr Fullerton, the solicitor. I will now tell you something. The codicil, the forged codicil that was produced for probate was not witnessed by Harriet Leaman. It was witnessed by a Mary Doherty, deceased, who had been in service with Mrs Llewellyn-Smythe but had recently died. The other witness was the James Jenkins, who, as your friend Mrs Leaman has told you, departed for Australia.'

'So there was a forged codicil,' said Mrs Oliver. 'And there seems to have been a real codicil as well. Look here, Poirot, isn't this all getting a little too complicated?'

'It is getting incredibly complicated,' said Hercule Poirot. 'There is, if I may mention it, too much forgery about.'

'Perhaps the real one is still in the library at Quarry House, within the pages of *Enquire Within upon Everything*.'

'I understand all the effects of the house were sold up at Mrs Llewellyn-Smythe's death, except for a few pieces of family furniture and some family pictures.'

'What we need,' said Mrs Oliver, 'is something like *Enquire Within* here now. It's a lovely title, isn't it? I remember my grandmother had one. You could, you know, inquire within about everything, too. Legal information and cooking recipes and how to take ink stains out of linen. How to make home-made face powder that would not damage the complexion. Oh – and lots more. Yes, wouldn't you like to have a book like that now?'

'Doubtless,' said Hercule Poirot, 'it would give the recipe for treatment of tired feet.'

'Plenty of them, I should think. But why don't you wear proper country shoes?'

'Madame, I like to look *soigné* in my appearance.'

'Well, then you'll have to go on wearing things that are painful, and grin and bear it,' said Mrs Oliver. 'All the same, I don't understand anything now. Was that Leaman woman telling me a pack of lies just now?'

'It is always possible.'

'Did someone *tell* her to tell a pack of lies?'

'That too is possible.'

'Did someone *pay* her to tell me a pack of lies?'

'Continue,' said Poirot, 'continue. You are doing very nicely.'

'I suppose,' said Mrs Oliver thoughtfully, 'that Mrs Llewellyn-Smythe, like many another rich woman, enjoyed making Wills. I expect she made a good many during her life. You know; benefiting one person and then another. Changing about. The Drakes were well off, anyway. I expect she always left them at least a handsome legacy, but I wonder if she ever left anyone else as much as she appears, according to Mrs Leaman and according to the forged Will as well, to that girl Olga. I'd like to know a bit more about that girl, I must say. She certainly seems a very successful disappearess.'

'I hope to know more about her shortly,' said Hercule Poirot.

'How?'

'Information that I shall receive shortly.'

'I know you've been asking for information down here.'

'Not here only. I have an agent in London who obtains information for me both abroad and in this country. I should have some news possibly soon from Herzogovinia.'

'Will you find out if she ever arrived back there?'

'That might be one thing I should learn, but it seems more likely that I may get information of a different kind – letters perhaps written during her sojourn in this country, mentioning friends she may have made here, and become intimate with.'

'What about the school-teacher?' said Mrs Oliver.

'Which one do you mean?'

'I mean the one who was strangled – the one Elizabeth Whittaker told you about?' She added, 'I don't like Elizabeth Whittaker much. Tiresome sort of woman, but clever, I should think.' She added dreamily, 'I wouldn't put it past her to have thought up a murder.'

'Strangle another teacher, do you mean?'

'One has to exhaust all the possibilities.'

'I shall rely, as so often, on your intuition, Madame.'

Mrs Oliver ate another date thoughtfully.

CHAPTER 20

When he left Mrs Butler's house, Poirot took the same way as had been shown him by Miranda. The aperture in the hedge, it seemed to him, had been slightly enlarged since last time. Somebody, perhaps, with slightly more bulk than Miranda, had used it also. He ascended the path in the quarry, noticing once more the beauty of the scene. A lovely spot, and yet in some way, Poirot felt as he had felt before, that it could be a haunted spot. There was a king of pagan ruthlessness about it. It could be along these winding paths that the fairies hunted their victims down or a cold goddess decreed that sacrifices would have to be offered.

He could understand why it had not become a picnic spot. One would not want for some reason to bring your hard-boiled eggs and your lettuce and your oranges and sit down here and crack jokes and have a jollification. It was different, quite different. It would have been better, perhaps, he thought suddenly, if Mrs Llewellyn-Smythe had not wanted this fairy-like transformation. Quite a modest sunk garden could have been made out of a quarry without the atmosphere, but she had been an ambitious woman, ambitious and a very rich woman. He thought for a moment or two about Wills, the kind of Wills made by rich women, the kind of lies told about Wills made by rich women, the places in which the Wills of rich widows were sometimes hidden, and he tried to put himself back into the mind of a forger. Undoubtably the Will offered for probate had been a forgery. Mr Fullerton was a careful and competent lawyer. He was sure of that. The kind of lawyer, too, who would never advise a client to bring a case or to take legal proceedings unless there was very good evidence and justification for so doing.

He turned a corner of the pathway feeling for the moment that his feet were much more important than his speculations. Was he taking a short cut to Superintendent Spence's dwelling or was he not? As the crow flies, perhaps, but the main road might have been more good to his feet. This path was not a grassy or mossy one, it had the quarry hardness of stone. Then he paused.

In front of him were two figures. Sitting on an outcrop of rock was Michael Garfield. He had a sketching block on his knees and he was drawing, his attention fully on what he was doing. A little way away from him, standing close beside a minute but musical stream that flowed down from above, Miranda Butler was standing. Hercule Poirot forgot his feet, forgot the pains and ills of the human body, and concentrated again on the beauty that human beings could attain. There was no doubt that Michael Garfield was a very beautiful young man. He found it difficult to know whether he himself liked Michael Garfield or not. It is always difficult to know if you like anyone beautiful. You like beauty to look at, at the same time you dislike beauty almost on principle. Women could be beautiful, but Hercule Poirot was not at all sure that he liked beauty in men. He would not have liked to be a beautiful young man himself, not that there had ever been the least chance of that. There was only one thing about his own appearance which really pleased Hercule Poirot, and that was the profusion of his moustaches, and the way they responded to grooming and treatment and trimming. They were magnificent. He knew of nobody else who had any moustache half as good. He had never been handsome or good-looking. Certainly never beautiful.

And Miranda? He thought again, as he had thought before, that it was her gravity that was so attractive. He wondered what passed through her mind. It was the sort of thing one would never know. She would not say what she was thinking easily. He doubted if she would tell you what she was thinking, if you asked her. She had an original mind, he thought, a reflective mind. He thought too she was vulnerable. Very vulnerable. There were other things about her that he knew, or thought he knew. It was only thinking so far, but yet he was almost sure.

Michael Garfield looked up and said,

'Ha! Señor Moustachios. A very good afternoon to you, sir.'

'Can I look at what you are doing or would it incommode you? I do not want to be intrusive.'

'You can look,' said Michael Garfield, 'it makes no difference to me.' He added gently, 'I'm enjoying myself very much.'

Poirot came to stand behind his shoulder. He nodded. It was a very delicate pencil drawing, the lines almost invisible. The man could draw, Poirot thought. Not only design gardens. He said, almost under his breath:

'Exquisite!'

'I think so too,' said Michael Garfield.

He let it be left doubtful whether he referred to the drawing he was making, or to the sitter.

'Why?' asked Poirot.

'Why am I doing it? Do you think I have a reason?'

'You might have.'

'You're quite right. If I go away from here, there are one or two things I want to remember. Miranda is one of them.'

'Would you forget her easily?'

'Very easily. I am like that. But to have forgotten something or someone, to be unable to bring a face, a turn of a shoulder, a gesture, a tree, a flower, a contour of landscape, to know what it was like to see it but not to be able to bring that image in front of one's eyes, that sometimes causes – what shall I say – almost agony. You see, you record – and it all passes away.'

'Not the Quarry Garden or park. That has not passed away.'

'Don't you think so? It soon will. It soon will if no one is here. Nature takes over, you know. It needs love and attention and care and skill. If a Council takes it over – and that's what happens very often nowadays – then it will be what they call "kept up". The latest sort of shrubs may be put in, extra paths will be made, seats will be put at certain distances. Litter bins even may be erected. Oh, they are so careful, so kind at preserving. You can't preserve this. It's wild. To keep something wild is far more difficult than to preserve it.'

'Monsieur Poirot.' Miranda's voice came across the stream.

Poirot moved forward, so that he came within earshot of her.

'So I find you here. So you came to sit for your portrait, did you?'

She shook her head.

'I didn't come for that. That just happened.'

'Yes,' said Michael Garfield, 'yes, it just happened. A piece of luck sometimes comes one's way.'

'You were just walking in your favourite garden?'

'I was looking for the well, really,' said Miranda.

'A well?'

'There was a wishing well once in this wood.'

'In a former quarry? I didn't know they kept wells in quarries.'

'There was always a wood round the quarry. Well, there were always trees here. Michael knows where the well is but he won't tell me.'

'It will be much more fun for you,' said Michael Garfield, 'to go on looking for it. Especially when you're not at all sure it really exists.'

'Old Mrs Goodbody knows all about it.'

And added:

'She's a witch.'

'Quite right,' said Michael. 'She's the local witch, Monsieur Poirot. There's always a local witch, you know, in most places. They don't always call themselves witches, but everyone knows. They tell a fortune or put a spell on your

177

begonias or shrivel up your peonies or stop a farmer's cow from giving milk and probably give love potions as well.'

'It was a wishing well,' said Miranda. 'People used to come here and wish. They had to go round it three times backwards and it was on the side of the hill, so it wasn't always very easy to do.' She looked past Poirot at Michael Garfield. 'I shall find it one day,' she said, 'even if you won't tell me. It's here somewhere, but it was sealed up, Mrs Goodbody said. Oh! years ago. Sealed up because it was said to be dangerous. A child fell into it years ago – Kitty Somebody. Someone else might have fallen into it.'

'Well, go on thinking so,' said Michael Garfield. 'It's a good local story, but there *is* a wishing well over at Little Belling.'

'Of course,' said Miranda. 'I know all about that one. It's a very common one,' she said. 'Everybody knows about it, and it's very silly. People throw pennies into it and there's not any water in it any more so there's not even a splash.'

'Well, I'm sorry.'

'I'll tell you when I find it,' said Miranda.

'You mustn't always believe everything a witch says. I don't believe any child ever fell into it. I expect a cat fell into it once and got drowned.'

'Ding dong dell, pussy's in the well,' said Miranda. She got up. 'I must go now,' she said. 'Mummy will be expecting me.'

She moved carefully from the knob of rock, smiled at both the men and went off down an even more intransigent path that ran the other side of the water.

'"Ding dong dell",' said Poirot, thoughtfully. 'One believes what one wants to believe, Michael Garfield. Was she right or was she not right?'

Michael Garfield looked at him thoughtfully, then he smiled.

'She is quite right,' he said. 'There is a well, and it is as she says sealed up. I suppose it may have been dangerous. I don't think it was ever a wishing well. I think that's Mrs

Goodbody's own bit of fancy talk. There's a wishing tree, or there was once. A beech tree half-way up the hillside that I believe people did go round three times backwards and wished.'

'What's happened to that? Don't they go round it any more?'

'No. I believe it was struck by lightning about six years ago. Split in two. So that pretty story's gone west.'

'Have you told Miranda about that?'

'No. I thought I'd rather leave her with her well. A blasted beech wouldn't be much fun for her, would it?'

'I must go on my way,' said Poirot.

'Going back to your police friend?'

'Yes.'

'You look tired.'

'I am tired,' said Hercule Poirot. 'I am extremely tired.'

'You'd be more comfortable in canvas shoes or sandals.'

'Ah, *ça, non.*'

'I see. You are sartorially ambitious.' He looked at Poirot. 'The *tout ensemble*, it is very good and especially, if I may mention it, your superb moustache.'

'I am gratified,' said Poirot, 'that you have noticed it.'

'The point is rather, could anyone not notice it?'

Poirot put his head on one side. Then he said:

'You spoke of the drawing you are doing because you wish to remember the young Miranda. Does that mean you're going away from here?'

'I have thought of it, yes.'

'Yet you are, it seems to me, *bien placé ici.*'

'Oh yes, eminently so. I have a house to live in, a house small but designed by myself, and I have my work, but that is less satisfactory than it used to be. So restlessness is coming over me.'

'Why is your work less satisfactory?'

'Because people wish me to do the most atrocious things. People who want to improve their gardens, people who bought some land and they're building a house and want the garden designed.'

'Are you not doing her garden for Mrs Drake?'

'She wants me to, yes. I made suggestions for it and she seemed to agree with them. I don't think, though,' he added thoughtfully, 'that I really trust her.'

'You mean that she would not let you have what you wanted?'

'I mean that she would certainly have what *she* wanted herself and that though she is attracted by the ideas I have set out, she would suddenly demand something quite different. Something utilitarian, expensive and showy, perhaps. She would bully me, I think. She would insist on her ideas being carried out. I would not agree, and we should quarrel. So on the whole it is better I leave here before I quarrel. And not only with Mrs Drake but many other neighbours. I am quite well known. I don't need to stay in one spot. I could go and find some other corner of England, or it could be some corner of Normandy or Brittany.'

'Somewhere where you can improve, or help, nature? Somewhere where you can experiment or you can put strange things where they have never grown before, where neither sun will blister nor frost destroy? Some good stretch of barren land where you can have the fun of playing at being Adam all over again? Have you always been restless?'

'I never stayed anywhere very long.'

'You have been to Greece?'

'Yes. I should like to go to Greece again. Yes, you have something there. A garden on a Greek hillside. There may be cypresses there, not much else. A barren rock. But if you wished, what could there not be?'

'A garden for gods to walk –'

'Yes. You're quite a mind reader, aren't you, Mr Poirot?'

'I wish I were. There are so many things I would like to know and do not know.'

'You are talking now of something quite prosaic, are you not?'

'Unfortunately so.'

180

'Arson, murder and sudden death?'

'More or less. I do not know that I was considering arson. Tell me, Mr Garfield, you have been here some considerable time, did you know a young man called Lesley Ferrier?'

'Yes, I remember him. He was in a Medchester solicitor's office, wasn't he? Fullerton, Harrison and Leadbetter. Junior clerk, something of that kind. Good-looking chap.'

'He came to a sudden end, did he not?'

'Yes. Got himself knifed one evening. Woman trouble, I gather. Everyone seems to think that the police know quite well who did it, but they can't get the evidence they want. He was more or less tied up with a woman called Sandra – can't remember her name for the moment – Sandra Somebody, yes. Her husband kept the local pub. She and young Lesley were running an affair, and then Lesley took up with another girl. Or that was the story.'

'And Sandra did not like it?'

'No, she did not like it at all. Mind you, he was a great one for the girls. There were two or three that he went around with.'

'Were they all English girls?'

'Why do you ask that, I wonder? No, I don't think he confined himself to English girls, so long as they could speak enough English to understand more or less what he said to them, and he could understand what they said to him.'

'There are doubtless from time to time foreign girls in this neighbourhood?'

'Of course there are. Is there any neighbourhood where there aren't? *Au pair* girls – they're a part of daily life. Ugly ones, pretty ones, honest ones, dishonest ones, ones that do some good to distracted mothers and some who are no use at all and some who walk out of the house.'

'Like the girl Olga did?'

'As you say, like the girl Olga did.'

'Was Lesley a friend of Olga's?'

181

'Oh, that's the way your mind is running. Yes, he was. I don't think Mrs Llewellyn-Smythe knew much about it. Olga was rather careful, I think. She spoke gravely of someone she hoped to marry some day in her own country. I don't know whether that was true or whether she made it up. Young Lesley was an attractive young man, as I said. I don't know what he saw in Olga – she wasn't very beautiful. Still –' he considered a minute or two ' – she had a kind of intensity about her. A young Englishman might have found that attractive, I think. Anyway, Lesley did all right, and his other girl friends weren't pleased.'

'That is very interesting,' said Poirot. 'I thought you might give me information that I wanted.'

Michael Garfield looked at him curiously.

'Why? What's it all about? Where does Lesley come in? Why this raking up of the past?'

'Well, there are things one wants to know. One wants to know how things come into being. I am even looking farther back still. Before the time that those two, Olga Seminoff and Lesley Ferrier, met secretly without Mrs Llewellyn-Smythe knowing about it.'

'Well, I'm not sure about that. That's only my – well, it's only my idea. I did come across them fairly frequently but Olga never confided in me. As for Lesley Ferrier, I hardly knew him.'

'I want to go back behind that. He had, I gather, certain disadvantages in his past.'

'I believe so. Yes, well, anyway it's been said here locally. Mr Fullerton took him on and hoped to make an honest man of him. He's a good chap, old Fullerton.'

'His offence had been, I believe, forgery?'

'Yes.'

'It was a first offence, and there were said to be extenuating circumstances. He had a sick mother or drunken father or something of that kind. Anyway, he got off lightly.'

'I never heard any of the details. It was something that he

seemed to have got away with to begin with, then accountants came along and found him out. I'm very vague. It's only hearsay. Forgery. Yes, that was the charge. Forgery.'

'And when Mrs Llewellyn-Smythe died and her Will was to be admitted to probate, it was found the Will was forged.'

'Yes, I see the way your mind's working. You're fitting those two things as having a connection with each other.'

'A man who was up to a point successful in forging. A man who became friends with the girl, a girl who, if a Will had been accepted when submitted to probate, would have inherited the larger part of a vast fortune.'

'Yes, yes, that's the way it goes.'

'And this girl and the man who had committed forgery were great friends. He had given up his own girl and he'd tied up with the foreign girl instead.'

'What you're suggesting is that that forged Will was forged by Lesley Ferrier.'

'There seems a likelihood of it, does there not?'

'Olga was supposed to have been able to copy Mrs Llewellyn-Smythe's handwriting fairly well, but it seemed to me always that that was rather a doubtful point. She wrote handwritten letters for Mrs Llewellyn-Smythe but I don't suppose that they were really particularly similar. Not enough to pass muster. But if she and Lesley were in it together, that's different. I daresay he could pass off a good enough job and he was probably quite cocksure that it would go through. But then he must have been sure of that when he committed his original offence, and he was wrong there, and I suppose he was wrong this time. I suppose that when the balloon went up, when the lawyers began making trouble and difficulties, and experts were called in to examine things and started asking questions, it could be that she lost her nerve, and had a row with Lesley. And then she cleared out, hoping he'd carry the can.'

He gave his head a sharp shake. 'Why do you come and talk to me about things like that here, in my beautiful wood?'

'I wanted to know.'

'It's better not to know. It's better never to know. Better to leave things as they are. Not push and pry and poke.'

'You want beauty,' said Hercule Poirot. 'Beauty at any price. For me, it is truth I want. Always truth.'

Michael Garfield laughed. 'Go on home to your police friends and leave me here in my local paradise. Get thee beyond me, Satan.'

CHAPTER 21

Poirot went on up the hill. Suddenly he no longer felt the pain of his feet. Something had come to him. The fitting together of the things he had thought and felt, had known they were connected, but had not seen how they were connected. He was conscious now of danger – danger that might come to someone any minute now unless steps were taken to prevent it. Serious danger.

Elspeth MacKay came out to the door to meet him. 'You look fagged out,' she said. 'Come and sit down.'

'Your brother is here?'

'No. He's gone down to the station. Something's happened, I believe.'

'Something has happened?' He was startled. 'So soon? Not possible.'

'Eh?' said Elspeth. 'What do you mean?'

'Nothing. Nothing. Something has happened to somebody, do you mean?'

'Yes, but I don't know who exactly. Anyway, Tim Raglan rang up and asked for him to go down there. I'll get you a cup of tea, shall I?'

'No,' said Poirot, 'thank you very much, but I think – I think I will go home.' He could not face the prospect of black bitter tea. He thought of a good excuse that would mask any signs of bad manners. 'My feet,' he explained. 'My feet. I am not very suitably attired as to footwear for the country. A change of shoes would be desirable.'

Elspeth McKay looked down at them. 'No,' she said. 'I can see they're not. Patent leather draws the feet. There's a letter for you, by the way. Foreign stamps on it. Come from abroad – c/o Superintendent Spence, Pine Crest. I'll bring it to you.'

She came back in a minute or two, and handed it to him.

'If you don't want the envelope, I'd like it for one of my nephews – he collects stamps.'

'Of course.' Poirot opened the letter and handed her the envelope. She thanked him and went back into the house.

Poirot unfolded the sheet and read.

Mr Goby's foreign service was run with the same competence that he showed in his English one. He spared no expense and got his results quickly.

True, the results did not amount to much – Poirot had not thought that they would.

Olga Seminoff had not returned to her home town. She had had no family still living. She had had a friend, an elderly woman, with whom she had corresponded intermittently, giving news of her life in England. She had been on good terms with her employer who had been occasionally exacting, but had also been generous.

The last letters received from Olga had been dated about a year and a half ago. In them there had been mention of a young man. There were hints that they were considering marriage, but the young man, whose name she did not mention, had, she said, his way to make, so nothing could be settled as yet. In her last letter she spoke happily of their prospects being good. When no more letters came, the elderly friend assumed that Olga had married her Englishman and changed her address. Such things happened frequently when girls went to England. If they were happily married they often never wrote again.

She had not worried.

It fitted, Poirot thought. Lesley had spoken of marriage, but might not have meant it. Mrs Llewellyn-Smythe had been spoken of as 'generous'. Lesley had been given money by someone, Olga perhaps (money originally given her by her employers), to induce him to do forgery on her behalf.

Elspeth McKay came out on the terrace again. Poirot consulted her as to his surmises about a partnership between Olga and Lesley.

She considered a moment. Then the oracle spoke.

'Kept very quiet about it, if so. Never any rumours about those two. There usually is in a place like this if there's anything in it.'

'Young Ferrier was tied up to a married woman. He might have warned the girl not to say anything about him to her employer.'

'Likely enough. Mrs Smythe would probably know that Lesley Ferrier was a bad character, and would warn the girl to have nothing to do with him.'

Poirot folded up the letter and put it into his pocket.

'I wish you'd let me get you a pot of tea.'

'No, no – I must go back to my guest house and change my shoes. You do not know when your brother will be back?'

'I've no idea. They didn't say what they wanted him for.'

Poirot walked along the road to his guest house. It was only a few hundred yards. As he walked up to the front door it was opened and his landlady, a cheerful lady of thirty odd, came out to him.

'There's a lady here to see you,' she said. 'Been waiting some time. I told her I didn't know where you'd gone exactly or when you'd be back, but she said she'd wait.' She added, 'It's Mrs Drake. She's in a state, I'd say. She's usually so calm about everything, but really I think she's had a shock of some kind. She's in the sitting-room. Shall I bring you in some tea and something?'

'No,' said Poirot, 'I think it will be better not. I will hear first what she has to say.'

He opened the door and went into the sitting-room. Rowena Drake had been standing by the window. It was not the window overlooking the front path so she had not seen his approach. She turned abruptly as she heard the sound of the door.

'Monsieur Poirot. At last. It seemed so long.'

'I am sorry, Madame. I have been in the Quarry Wood and also talking to my friend, Mrs Oliver. And then I have been talking to two boys. To Nicholas and Desmond.'

'Nicholas and Desmond? Yes, I know. I wonder – oh! one thinks all sorts of things.'

'You are upset,' said Poirot gently.

It was not a thing he thought he would ever see. Rowena Drake upset, no longer mistress of events, no longer arranging everything, and enforcing her decisions on others.'

'You've heard, haven't you?' she asked. 'Oh well, perhaps you haven't.'

'What should I have heard?'

'Something dreadful. He's – he's dead. Somebody killed him.'

'Who is dead, Madame?'

'Then you haven't really heard. And he's only a child, too, and I thought – oh, what a fool I've been. I should have told you. I should have told you when you asked me. It makes me feel terrible – terribly guilty for thinking I knew best and thinking – but I did mean it for the best, Monsieur Poirot, indeed I did.'

'Sit down, Madame, sit down. Calm yourself and tell me. There is a child dead – another child?'

'Her brother,' said Mrs Drake. 'Leopold.'

'Leopold Reynolds?'

'Yes. They found his body on one of the field paths. He must have been coming back from school and gone out of his way to play in the brook near here. Somebody held him down in the brook – held his head under water.'

'The same kind of thing as they did to the child Joyce?'

'Yes, yes. I can see it must be – it must be madness of some kind. And one doesn't know *who*, that's what's so awful. One hasn't the least idea. And I thought I knew. I really thought – I suppose, yes, it was a very wicked thing.'

'You must tell me, Madame.'

'Yes, I want to tell you. I came here to tell you. Because, you see, you came to me after you'd talked to Elizabeth Whittaker. After she'd told you that something had startled me. That I'd seen something. Something in the hall of the house, my house. I said that I hadn't seen anything and that nothing had startled me because, you see, I thought –' she stopped.

'What *did* you see?'

'I ought to have told you then. I saw the door of the library open, open rather carefully and – then he came out. At least, he didn't come right out. He just stood in the doorway and then pulled the door back quickly and went back inside.'

'Who was this?'

'Leopold. Leopold, the child that's been killed now. And you see, I thought I – oh, what a mistake, what an awful mistake. If I'd told you, perhaps – perhaps you'd have got at what was behind it.'

'You thought?' Poirot said. 'You thought that Leopold had killed his sister. Is that what you thought?'

'Yes, that's what I thought. Not then, of course, because I didn't know she was dead. But he had a queer look on his face. He's always been a queer child. In a way you're a little afraid of him because you feel he's not – not quite right. Very clever and a high I.Q., but all the same not all there.

'And I thought "Why is Leopold coming out of there instead of being at the Snapdragon?" and I thought "What's he been doing – he looks so queer?" And then, well then I didn't think of it again after that, but I suppose, the way he looked upset me. And that's why I dropped the vase. Elizabeth helped me to pick up the glass pieces, and I went back to the Snapdragon and I didn't think of it again. Until we found Joyce. And that's when I thought –'

'You thought that Leopold had done it?'

'Yes. Yes, I did think that. I thought it explained the way he'd looked. I thought I knew. I always think – I've thought too much all my life that I know things, that I'm right about things. And I can be very wrong. Because, you see, his being killed must mean something quite different.

He must have gone in there, and he must have found her there – dead – and it gave *him* a terrible shock and he was frightened. And so he wanted to come out of the room without anyone seeing him and I suppose he looked up and saw me and he got back into the room and shut the door and waited until the hall was empty before coming out. But *not* because he'd killed her. No. Just the shock of finding her dead.'

'And yet you said nothing? You didn't mention who it was you'd seen, even after the death was discovered?'

'No. I – oh, I couldn't. He's – you see, he's so young – *was* so young, I suppose I ought to say now. Ten. Ten – eleven at most and I mean – I felt he couldn't have known what he was doing, it couldn't have been his fault exactly. He must have been morally not responsible. He's always been rather queer, and I thought one could get treatment for him. Not leave it all to the police. Not send him to approved places. I thought one could get special psychological teatment for him, if necessary. I – I meant well. You must believe that, I meant well.'

Such sad words, Poirot thought, some of the saddest words in the world. Mrs Drake seemed to know what he was thinking.

'Yes,' she said, '"I did it for the best." "I meant well." One always thinks one knows what is best to do for other people, but one *doesn't*. Because, you see, the reason he looked so taken aback must have been that he either saw who the murderer was, or saw something that would give a clue to who the murderer might be. Something that made the murderer feel that he himself wasn't safe. And so – and so he's waited until he got the boy alone and then drowned him in the brook so that he shouldn't speak, so that he shouldn't tell. If I'd only spoken out, if I'd told you, or told the police, or told someone, but I thought I knew best.'

'Only today,' said Poirot, after he had sat silent for a moment or two, watching Mrs Drake where she sat controlling her sobs, 'I was told that Leopold had been very flush of money lately. Somebody must have been paying him to keep silent.'

'But who – who?'

'We shall find out,' said Poirot. 'It will not be long now.'

CHAPTER 22

It was not very characteristic of Hercule Poirot to ask the opinions of others. He was usually quite satisfied with his own opinions. Nevertheless, there were times when he made exceptions. This was one of them. He and Spence had had a brief conversation together and then Poirot had got in touch with a car hire service and after another short conversation with his friend and with Inspector Raglan, he drove off. He had arranged with the car to drive him back to London but he had made one halt on the way there. He drove to The Elms. He told the driver of the car that he would not be long – a quarter of an hour at most – and then he sought audience with Miss Emlyn.

'I am sorry to disturb you at this hour. It is no doubt the hour of your supper or dinner.'

'Well, I do you at least the compliment, Monsieur Poirot, to think you would not disturb me at either supper or dinner unless you have a valid reason for so doing.'

'You are very kind. To be frank, I want your advice.'

'Indeed?'

Miss Emlyn looked slightly surprised. She looked more than surprised, she looked sceptical.

'That does not seem very characteristic of you, Monsieur Poirot. Are you not usually satisfied with your own opinions?'

'Yes, I am satisfied with my own opinions, but it would give me solace and support if someone whose opinion I respected agreed with them.'

She did not speak, merely looked at him inquiringly.

'I know the killer of Joyce Reynolds,' he said. 'It is my belief that you know it also.'

'I have not said so,' said Miss Emlyn.

'No. You have not said so. And that might lead me to believe that it is on your part an opinion only.'

'A hunch?' inquired Miss Emlyn, and her tone was colder than ever.

'I would prefer not to use that word. I would prefer to say that you had a definite opinion.'

'Very well then. I will admit that I have a definite opinion. That does not mean that I shall repeat to you what my opinion is.'

'What I should like to do, Mademoiselle, is to write down four words on a piece of paper. I will ask you if you agree with the four words I have written.'

Miss Emlyn rose. She crossed the room to her desk, took a piece of writing paper and came across to Poirot with it.

'You interest me,' she said. 'Four words.'

Poirot had taken a pen from his pocket. He wrote on the paper, folded it and handed it to her. She took it, straightened out the paper and held it in her hand, looking at it.

'Well?' said Poirot.

'As to two of the words on that paper, I agree, yes. The other two, that is more difficult. I have no evidence and, indeed, the ideas had not entered my head.'

'But in the case of the first two words, you *have* definite evidence?'

'I consider so, yes.'

'Water,' said Poirot, thoughtfully. 'As soon as you heard that, you knew. As soon as I heard that I knew. You are sure, and I am sure. And now,' said Poirot, 'a boy has been drowned in a brook. You have heard that?'

'Yes. Someone rang me up on the telephone and told me. Joyce's brother. How was he concerned?'

'He wanted money,' said Poirot. 'He got it. And so, at a suitable opportunity, he was drowned in a brook.'

His voice did not change. It had, if anything, not a softened, but a harsher note,

'The person who told me,' he said, 'was riddled with compassion. Upset emotionally. But I am not like that. He

193

was young, this second child who died, but his death was not an accident. It was, as so many things in life, a result of his actions. He wanted money and he took a risk. He was clever enough, astute enough to know he was taking a risk, but he wanted the money. He was ten years old but cause and effect is much the same at that age as it would be at thirty or fifty or ninety. Do you know what I think of first in such a case?'

'I should say,' said Miss Emlyn, 'that you are more concerned with justice than with compassion.'

'Compassion,' said Poirot, 'on my part would do nothing to help Leopold. He is beyond help. Justice, if we obtain justice, you and I, for I think you are of my way of thinking over this – justice, one could say, will also not help Leopold. But it might help some other Leopold, it might help to keep some other child alive, if we can reach justice soon enough. It is not a safe thing, a killer who has killed more than once, to whom killing has appealed as a way of security. I am now on my way to London where I am meeting with certain people to discuss a way of approach. To convert them, perhaps, to my own certainty in this case.'

'You may find that difficult,' said Miss Emlyn.

'No, I do not think so. The ways and means to it may be difficult but I think I can convert them to my knowledge of what has happened. Because they have minds that understand the criminal mind. There is one thing more I would ask you. I want your opinion. Your opinion only this time, not evidence. Your opinion of the character of Nicholas Ransom and Desmond Holland. Would you advise me to trust them?'

'I should say that both of them were thoroughly trustworthy. That is my opinion. They are in many ways extremely foolish, but that is only in the ephemeral things of life. Fundamentally, they are sound. Sound as an apple without maggots in it.'

'One always comes back to apples,' said Hercle Poirot sadly. 'I must go now. My car is waiting. I have one more call still to pay.'

CHAPTER 23

'Have you heard what's on at Quarry Wood?' said Mrs Cartwright, putting a packet of Fluffy Flakelets and Wonder White into her shopping bag.

'Quarry Wood?' said Elspeth McKay, to whom she was talking. 'No, I haven't heard anything particular.' She selected a packet of cereal. The two women were in the recently opened supermarket making their morning purchases.

'They're saying the trees are dangerous there. Couple of forestry men arrived this morning. It's there on the side of the hill where there's a steep slope and a tree leaning sideways. Could be I suppose, that a tree could come down there. One of them was struck by lightning last winter but that was farther over, I think. Anyway, they're digging round the roots of the trees a bit, and a bit farther down too. Pity. They'll make an awful mess of the place.'

'Oh well,' said Elspeth McKay, 'I suppose they know what they're doing. Somebody's called them in, I suppose.'

'They've got a couple of the police there, too, seeing that people don't come near. Making sure they keep away from things. They say something about finding out which the diseased trees are first.'

'I see,' said Elspeth McKay.

Possibly she did. Not that anyone had told her but then Elspeth never needed telling.

2

Ariadne Oliver smoothed out a telegram she had just taken as delivered to her at the door. She was so used to getting telegrams through the telephone, making frenzied hunts for a pencil to take them down, insisting firmly that she wanted a confirmatory copy sent to her, that she was quite startled to receive what she called to herself a 'real telegram' again.

'PLEASE BRING MRS BUTLER AND MIRANDA TO YOUR FLAT AT ONCE. NO TIME TO LOSE. IMPORTANT SEE DOCTOR FOR OPERATION.'

She went into the kitchen where Judith Butler was making quince jelly.

'Judy,' said Mrs Oliver, 'go and pack a few things. I m going back to London and you're coming with me and Miranda, too.'

'It's very nice of you, Ariadne, but I've got a lot of things on here. Anyway, you needn't rush away today, need you?'

'Yes, I need to, I've been told to,' said Mrs Oliver.

'Who's told you – your housekeeper?'

'No,' said Mrs Oliver. 'Somebody else. One of the few people I obey. Come on. Hurry up.'

'I don't want to leave home just now. I can't.'

'You've got to come,' said Mrs Oliver. 'The car is ready. I brought it round to the front door. We can go at once.'

'I don't think I want to take Miranda. I could leave her here with someone, with the Reynolds or Rowena Drake.'

'Miranda's coming, too,' Mrs Oliver interrupted definitely. 'Don't make difficulties, Judy. This is serious. I don't see how you can even consider leaving her with the Reynolds. Two of the Reynolds children have been killed, haven't they?'

'Yes, yes, that's true enough. You think there's something wrong with that house. I mean there's someone there who – oh, what do I mean?'

'We're talking too much,' said Mrs Oliver. 'Anyway,' she added, 'if anyone is going to be killed, it seems to me that probably the most likely one would be Ann Reynolds.'

'What's the matter with the family? Why should they all get killed, one after another? Oh, Ariadne, it's *frightening*!'

'Yes,' said Mrs Oliver, 'but there are times when it's quite right to be frightened. I've just had a telegram and I'm acting upon it.'

'Oh, I didn't hear the telephone.'

'It didn't come through the telephone. It came to the door.'

She hesitated a moment, then she held it out to her friend.

'What's this mean? Operation?'

'Tonsils, probably,' said Mrs Oliver. 'Miranda had a bad throat last week, hadn't she? Well, what more likely than that she should be taken to consult a throat specialist in London?'

'Are you quite mad, Ariadne?'

'Probably,' said Mrs Oliver, 'raving mad. Come on. Miranda will enjoy being in London. You needn't worry. She's not going to have any operation. That's what's called "cover" in spy stories. We'll take her to a theatre, or an opera or the ballet, whichever way her tastes lie. On the whole I think it would be best to take her to the ballet.'

'I'm frightened,' said Judith.

Ariadne Oliver looked at her friend. She was trembling slightly. She looked more than ever, Mrs Oliver thought, like Undine. She looked divorced from reality.

'Come on,' said Mrs Oliver, 'I promised Hercule Poirot I'd bring you when he gave me the word. Well, he's given me the word.'

'What's going on in this place?' said Judith. 'I can't think why I ever came here.'

'I sometimes wondered why you did,' said Mrs Oliver, 'but there's no accounting for where people go to live. A friend of mine went to live in Moreton-in-the-Marsh the other day. I asked him why he wanted to go and live there. He said he'd always wanted to and thought about it. Whenever he retired he meant to go there. I said that I hadn't been to it myself but it sounded to me bound to be damp. What was it actually like? He said he didn't know what it was like because he'd never been there himself. But he had always wanted to live there. He was quite sane, too.'

'Did he go?'

'Yes.'

'Did he like it when he got there?'

'Well, I haven't heard that yet,' said Mrs Oliver. 'But people are very odd, aren't they? The things they want to do, the things they simply *have* to do . . .' She went to the garden and called, 'Miranda, we're going to London.'

Miranda came slowly towards them.

'Going to London?'

'Ariadne's going to drive us there,' said her mother. 'We'll go and see a theatre there. Mrs Oliver thinks perhaps she can get tickets for the ballet. Would you like to go to the ballet?'

'I'd love it,' said Miranda. Her eyes lighted up. 'I must go and say goodbye to one of my friends first.'

'We're going practically at once.'

'Oh, I shan't be as long as that, but I must explain. There are things I promised to do.'

She ran down the garden and disappeared through the gate.

'Who are Miranda's friends?' asked Mrs Oliver, with some curiosity.'

'I never really know,' said Judith. 'She never tells one things, you know. Sometimes I think that the only things that she really feels are her friends are the birds she looks at in the woods. Or squirrels or things like that. I think everybody likes her but I don't know that she has any particular friends. I mean, she doesn't bring back girls to tea and things like that. Not as much as other girls do. I think her best friend really was Joyce Reynolds.' She added vaguely: 'Joyce used to tell her fantastic things about elephants and tigers.' She roused herself. 'Well, I must go up and pack, I suppose, as you insist. But I don't want to leave here. There are lots of things I'm in the middle of doing, like this jelly and –'

'You've got to come,' said Mrs Oliver. She was quite firm about it.

Judith came downstairs again with a couple of suitcases just as Miranda ran in through the side door, somewhat out of breath.

'Aren't we going to have lunch first?' she demanded.

In spite of her elfin woodland appearance, she was a healthy child who liked her food.

'We'll stop for lunch on the way,' said Mrs Oliver. 'We'll stop at The Black Boy at Haversham. That would be about right. It's about three-quarters of an hour from here and they give you quite a good meal. Come on, Miranda, we're going to start now.'

'I shan't have time to tell Cathie I can't go to the pictures with her tomorrow. Oh, perhaps I could ring her up.'

'Well, hurry up,' said her mother.

Miranda ran into the sitting-room where the telephone was situated. Judith and Mrs Oliver put suitcases into the car. Miranda came out of the sitting-room.

'I left a message,' she said breathlessly. 'That's all right now.'

'I think you're mad, Ariadne,' said Judith, as they got into the car. 'Quite mad. What's it all *about*?'

'We shall know in due course, I suppose,' said Mrs Oliver. 'I don't know if I'm mad or he is.'

'He? Who?'

'Hercule Poirot,' said Mrs Oliver.

3

In London Hercule Poirot was sitting in a room with four other men. One was Inspector Timothy Raglan, looking respectful and poker-faced as was his invariable habit when in the presence of his superiors; the second was Superintendent Spence. The third was Alfred Richmond, Chief Constable of the County and the fourth was a man with a sharp, legal face from the Public Prosecutor's office. They looked at Hercule Poirot with varying expressions, or what one might describe as non-expressions.

'You seem quite sure, Monsieur Poirot.'

'I *am* quite sure,' said Hercule Poirot. 'When a thing arranges itself so, one realizes that it must be so, one only looks for reasons why it should not be so. If one does not find the reasons why it should not be so, then one is strengthened in one's opinion.'

'The motives seem somewhat complex, if I may say so.'

'No,' said Poirot, 'not complex really. But so simple that they are very difficult to see clearly.'

The legal gentleman looked sceptical.

'We shall have one piece of definite evidence very soon now,' said Inspector Raglan. 'Of course, if there has been a mistake on that point . . .'

'Ding dong dell, no pussy in the well?' said Hercule Poirot. 'That is what you mean?'

'Well, you must agree it is only a surmise on your part.'

'The evidence pointed to it all along. When a girl disappears, there are not many reasons. The first is that she has gone away with a man. The second is that she is dead. Anything else is very far-fetched and practically never happens.'

'There are no special points that you can bring to our attention, Monsieur Poirot?'

'Yes. I have been in touch with a well-known firm of estate agents. Friends of mine, who specialize in real estate in the West Indies, the Aegean, the Adriatic, the Mediterranean and other places. They specialize in sunshine and their clients are usually wealthy. Here is a recent purchase that might interest you.'

He handed over a folded paper.

'You think this ties up?'

'I'm sure it does.'

'I thought the sale of islands was prohibited by that particular government?'

'Money can usually find a way.'

'There is nothing else that you would care to dwell upon?'

'It is possible that within twenty-four hours I shall have for you something that will more or less clinch matters.'

'And what is that?'

'An eye-witness.'

'You mean –'

'An eye-witness to a crime.'

The legal man looked at Poirot with mounting disbelief.

'Where is this eye-witness now?'

'On the way to London, I hope and trust.'

'You sound – disturbed.'

'That is true. I have done what I can to take care of things, but I will admit to you that I am frightened. Yes, I am frightened in spite of the protective measure I have taken. Because, you see, we are – how shall I describe it? – we are up against ruthlessness, quick reactions, greed pushed beyond an expectable human limit and perhaps – I am not sure but I think it possible – a touch, shall we say, of madness? Not there originally, but cultivated. A seed that took root and grows fast. And now perhaps has taken charge, inspiring an inhuman rather than a human attitude to life.'

'We'll have to have a few extra opinions on this,' said the legal man. 'We can't rush into things. Of course, a lot depends on the – er – forestry business. If that's positive, we'd have to think again.'

Hercule Poirot rose to his feet.

'I will take my leave. I have told you all that I know and all that I fear and envisage as possible. I shall remain in touch with you.'

He shook hands all round with foreign precision, and went out.

'The man's a bit of a mountebank,' said the legal man. 'You don't think he's a bit touched, do you? Touched in the head himself, I mean? Anyway, he's a pretty good age. I don't know that one can rely on the faculties of a man of that age.'

'I think you can rely upon him, said the Chief Constable. 'At least, that is *my* impression. Spence, I've known you a good many years. You're a friend of his. Do you think he's become a little senile?'

'No, I don't,' said Superintendent Spence. 'What's your opinion, Raglan?'

'I've only met him recently, sir. At first I thought his – well, his way of talking, his ideas, might be fantastic. But on the whole I'm converted. I think he's going to be proved right.'

CHAPTER 24

Mrs Oliver had ensconced herself at a table in the window of The Black Boy. It was still fairly early, so the dining-room was not very full. Presently, Judith Butler returned from powdering her nose and sat down opposite her and examined the menu.

'What does Miranda like?' asked Mrs Oliver. 'We might as well order for her as well. I suppose she'll be back in a minute.'

'She likes roast chicken.'

'Well, that's easy then. What about you?'

'I'll have the same.'

'Three roast chickens,' Mrs Oliver ordered.

She leaned back, studying her friend.

'Why are you staring at me in that way?'

'I was thinking,' said Mrs Oliver.

'Thinking what?'

'Thinking really how very little I knew about you.'

'Well, that's the same with everybody, isn't it?'

'You mean, one never knows all about anyone.'

'I shouldn't think so.'

'Perhaps you're right,' said Mrs Oliver.

Both women were silent for some time.

'They're rather slow serving things here.'

'It's coming now, I think,' said Mrs Oliver.

A waitress arrived with a tray full of dishes.

'Miranda's a long time. Does she know where the dining-room is?'

'Yes, of course she does. We looked in on the way.' Judith got up impatiently. 'I'll have to go and fetch her.'

'I wonder if perhaps she gets car sick.'

'She used to when she was younger.'

She returned some four or five minutes later.

'She's not in the Ladies',' she said. 'There's a door outside it into the garden. Perhaps she went out that way to look at a bird or something. She's like that.'

'No time to look at birds today,' said Mrs Oliver. 'Go and call her or something. We want to get on.'

2

Elspeth McKay pricked some sausages with a fork, laid them on a baking dish, put it in the Frigidair and started to peel potatoes.

The telephone rang.

'Mrs McKay? Sergeant Goodwin here. Is your brother there?'

'No. He's in London today.'

'I've rung him there – he's left. When he gets back, tell him we've had a positive result.'

'You mean you've found a body in the well?'

'Not much use clamming up about it. The word's got around already.'

'Who is it? The *au pair* girl?'

'Seems like it.'

'Poor girl,' said Elspeth. 'Did she throw herself in – or what?'

'It wasn't suicide – she was knifed. It was murder all right.'

3

After her mother had left the Ladies' Room, Miranda waited for a minute or two. Then she opened the door, cautiously peered out, opened the side door to the garden which was close at hand and ran down the garden path that led round to the back yard of what had once been a coaching inn and was now a garage. She went out at a small door that enabled pedestrians to get into a lane outside. A little farther down the lane a car was parked. A man with beetling grey eyebrows and a grey beard was sitting in it reading a news-paper. Miranda opened the door and climbed in beside the driving-seat. She laughed.

'You do look funny.'

'Have a hearty laugh, there's nothing to stop you.'

The car started, went down the lane, turned right, turned left, turned right again and came out on a secondary road.

'We're all right for time,' said the grey-bearded man. 'At the right moment you'll see the double axe as it ought to be seen. And Kilterbury Down, too. Wonderful view.'

A car dashed past them so closely that they were almost forced into the hedge.

'Young idiots,' said the grey-bearded man.

One of the young men had long hair reaching over his shoulders and large, owlish spectacles. The other one affected a more Spanish appearance with side-burns.

'You don't think Mummy will worry about me?' asked Miranda.

'She won't have time to worry about you. By the time she worries about you, you'll have got where you want to be.'

4

In London, Hercule Poirot picked up the telephone. Mrs Oliver's voice came over.

'We've lost Miranda.'

'What do you mean, lost her?'

'We had lunch at The Black Boy. She went to the loo. She didn't come back. Somebody said they saw her driving away with an elderly man. But it mightn't have been her. It might have been someone else. It –'

'Someone should have stayed with her. Neither of you ought to have let her out of your sight. I told you there was danger. Is Mrs Butler very worried?'

'Of course she's worried. What do you think? She's fran-tic. She insists on ringing the police.'

'Yes, that would be the natural thing to do. I will ring them also.'

'But why should Miranda be in danger?'

'Don't you know? You ought to by now.' He added, 'The body's been found. I've just heard –'

'What body?'

'A body in a well.'

CHAPTER 25

'It's beautiful,' said Miranda, looking round her.

Kilterbury Ring was a local beauty spot though its remains were not particularly famous. They had been dismantled many hundreds of years ago. Yet here and there a tall megalithic stone still stood, upright, telling of a long past ritual worship. Miranda asked questions.

'Why did they have all these stones here?'

'For ritual. Ritual worship. Ritual sacrifice. You understand about sacrifice, don't you, Miranda?'

'I think so.'

'It has to be, you see. It's important.'

'You mean, it's *not* a sort of punishment? It's something else?'

'Yes, it's something else. You die so that others should live. You die so that beauty should live. Should come into being. That's the important thing.'

'I thought perhaps –'

'Yes, Miranda?'

'I thought perhaps you ought to die because what you've done has killed someone else.'

'What put that into your head?'

'I was thinking of Joyce. If I hadn't told her about something, she wouldn't have died, would she?'

'Perhaps not.'

'I've felt worried since Joyce died. I needn't have told her, need I? I told her because I wanted to have something worth while telling her. She'd been to India and she kept talking about it – about the tigers and about the elephants and their gold hangings and decorations and their trappings. And I think, too – suddenly I wanted somebody else to know, because you see I hadn't really thought about it before.' She added: 'Was – was *that* a sacrifice, too?'

'In a way.'

Miranda remained contemplative, then she said, 'Isn't it time yet?'

'The sun is not quite right yet. Another five minutes, perhaps, and then it will fall directly on the stone.'

Again they sat silent, beside the car.

'*Now*, I think,' said Miranda's companion, looking up at the sky where the sun was dipping towards the horizon. 'Now is a wonderful moment. No one here. Nobody comes up at this time of day and walks up to the top of Kilterbury Down to see Kilterbury Ring. Too cold in November and the blackberries are over. I'll show you the double axe first. The double axe on the stone. Carved there when they came from Mycenae or from Crete hundreds of years ago. It's wonderful, Miranda, isn't it?'

'Yes, it's very wonderful,' said Miranda. 'Show it me.'

They walked up to the topmost stone. Beside it lay a fallen one and a little farther down the slope a slightly inclined one leant as though bent with the weariness of years.

'Are you happy, Miranda?'

'Yes, I'm very happy.'

'There's the sign *here*.'

'Is that really the double axe?'

'Yes, it's worn with time but that's it. That's the symbol. Put your hand on it. And now – now we will drink to the past and the future and to beauty.'

'Oh, how lovely,' said Miranda.

A golden cup was put into her hand, and from a flask her companion poured a golden liquid into it.

'It tastes of fruit, of peaches. Drink it, Miranda, and you will be happier still.'

Miranda took the gilt cup. She sniffed at it.

'Yes. Yes, it does smell of peaches. Oh look, there's the sun. Really red gold – looking as though it was lying on the edge of the world.'

He turned her towards it.

'Hold the cup and *drink*.'

She turned obediently. One hand was still on the megalithic stone and its semi-erased sign. Her companion now was standing behind her. From below the inclined stone down the hill, two figures slipped out, bent half double. Those on the summit had their backs to them, and did not even notice them. Quickly but stealthily they ran up the hill.

'Drink to beauty, Miranda.'

'*Like hell she does!*' said a voice behind them.

A rose velvet coat shot over a head, a knife was knocked from the hand that was slowly rising. Nicholas Ransom caught hold of Miranda, clasping her tightly and dragging her away from the other two who were struggling.

'You bloody little idiot,' said Nicholas Ransom. 'Coming up here with a barmy murderer. You should have known what you were doing.'

'I did in a way,' said Miranda. 'I was going to be a sacrifice, I think, because you see it was all my fault. It was because of me that Joyce was killed. So it was right for me to be a sacrifice, wasn't it? It would be a kind of ritual killing.'

'Don't start talking nonsense about ritual killings. They've found that other girl. You know, the *au pair* girl who has been missing so long. A couple of years or something like that. They all thought she'd run away because she'd forged a Will. She hadn't run away. Her body was found in the well.'

Oh!' Miranda gave a sudden cry of anguish. 'Not in the wishing well? Not in the wishing well that I wanted to find so badly? Oh, I don't want her to be in the wishing well. Who – who put her there?'

'The same person who brought you here.'

CHAPTER 26

Once again four men sat looking at Poirot. Timothy Raglan, Superintendent Spence and the Chief Constable had the pleased expectant look of a cat who is counting on a saucer of cream to materialize at any moment. The fourth man still had the expression of one who suspends belief.

'Well, Monsieur Poirot,' said the Chief Constable, taking charge of the proceedings and leaving the D.P.P. man to hold a watching brief. 'We're all here –'

Poirot made a motion with his hand. Inspector Raglan left the room and returned ushering in a woman of thirty odd, a girl, and two adolescent young men.

He introduced them to the Chief Constable. 'Mrs Butler, Miss Miranda Butler, Mr Nicholas Ransom and Mr Desmond Holland.'

Poirot got up and took Miranda's hand. 'Sit here by your mother, Miranda – Mr Richmond here who is what is called a Chief Constable, wants to ask you some questions. He wants you to answer them. It concerns something you saw – over a year ago now, nearer two years. You mentioned this to one person, and, so I understand, to one person only. Is that correct?'

'I told Joyce.'

'And what exactly did you tell Joyce?'

'That I'd seen a murder.'

'Did you tell anyone else?'

'No. But I think Leopold guessed. He listens, you know. At doors. That sort of thing. He likes knowing people's secrets.'

'You have heard that Joyce Reynolds, on the afternoon before the Hallowe'en party, claimed that she herself had seen a murder committed. Was that true?'

'No. She was just repeating what I'd told her – but pretending that it had happened to her.'

'Will you tell us now just what you did see.'

'I didn't know at first that it was a murder. I thought there had been an accident. I thought she'd fallen from up above somewhere.'

'Where was this?'

'In the Quarry Garden – in the hollow where the fountain used to be. I was up in the branches of a tree. I'd been looking at a squirrel and one has to keep very quiet, or they rush away. Squirrels are very quick.'

'Tell us what you saw.'

'A man and a woman lifted her up and were carrying her up the path. I thought they were taking her to a hospital or to the Quarry House. Then the woman stopped suddenly and said, "Someone is watching us," and stared at my tree. Somehow it made me feel frightened. I kept very still. The man said "Nonsense," and they went on. I saw there was blood on a scarf and there was a knife with blood on that – and I thought perhaps someone had tried to kill themselves – and I went on keeping very still.'

'Because you were frightened?'

'Yes, but I don't know why.'

'You didn't tell your mother?'

'No. I thought perhaps I oughtn't to have been there watching. And then the next day nobody said anything about an accident, so I forgot about it. I never thought about it again until –'

She stopped suddenly. The Chief Constable opened his mouth – then shut it. He looked at Poirot and made a very slight gesture.

'Yes, Miranda,' said Poirot, 'until what?'

'It was as though it was happening all over again. It was a green woodpecker this time, and I was being very still, watching it from behind some bushes. And those two were sitting there talking – about an island – a Greek island. She said something like, "It's all signed up. It's ours, we can go to it whenever we like. But we'd better go slow still – not rush things." And then the woodpecker flew away, and I moved. And she said – "Hush – be quiet – somebody's watching us." It was just the way she'd said it before, and she had just the same look on her face, and I was frightened again, and I remembered. And this time I *knew*. I knew it had been a murder I had seen and it had been a dead body they were carrying away to hide somewhere. You see, I wasn't a child any more. I *knew* – things and what they must mean – the blood and the knife and the dead body all limp –'

'When was this?' asked the Chief Constable. 'How long ago?'

Miranda thought for a moment.

'Last March – just after Easter.'

'Can you say definitely who these people were, Miranda?'

'Of course I can.' Miranda looked bewildered.

'You saw their faces?'

'Of course.'

'Who were they?'

'*Mrs Drake and Michael . . .*'

It was not a dramatic denunciation. Her voice was quiet, with something in it like wonder, but it carried conviction.

The Chief Constable said, 'You did not tell anyone. Why not?'

'I thought – I thought it might have been a sacrifice.'

'Who told you that?'

'Michael told me – he said sacrifices were necessary.'

Poirot said gently, 'You loved Michael?'

'Oh yes,' said Miranda, 'I loved him very much.'

CHAPTER 27

'Now I've got you here at last,' said Mrs Oliver, 'I want to know all about *everything*.'

She looked at Poirot with determination and asked severely:

'Why haven't you come sooner?'

'My excuses, Madame, I have been much occupied assisting the police with their inquiries.'

'It's criminals who do that. What on earth made you think of Rowena Drake being mixed up in a murder? Nobody else would have dreamed of it?'

'It was simple as soon as I got the vital clue.'

'What do you call the vital clue?'

'Water. I wanted someone who was at the party and who was *wet*, and who shouldn't have been wet. Whoever killed Joyce Reynolds would necessarily have got wet. You hold down a vigorous child with its head in a full bucket of water, and there will be struggling and splashing and you are bound to be wet. So something has got to happen to provide an innocent explanation of how you got wet. When everyone crowded into the dining-room for the Snapdragon, Mrs Drake took Joyce with her to the library. If your hostess asks you to come with her, naturally you go. And certainly Joyce had no suspicion of Mrs Drake. All Miranda had told her was that she had once seen a murder committed. And so Joyce was killed and her murderer was fairly well soaked with water. There must be a reason for that and she set about creating a reason. She had to get a witness as to *how* she got wet. She waited on the landing with an enormous vase of flowers filled with water. In due course Miss Whittaker came out from the Snapdragon room – it was hot in there. Mrs Drake pretended to start nervously, and let

213

the vase go, taking care that it flooded her person as it crashed down to the hall below. She ran down the stairs and she and Miss Whittaker picked up the pieces and the flowers while Mrs Drake complained at the loss of her beautiful vase. She managed to give Miss Whittaker the impression that she had seen something or someone coming out of the room where a murder had been committed. Miss Whittaker took the statement at its face value, but when she mentioned it to Miss Emlyn, Miss Emlyn realized the really interesting thing about it. And so she urged Miss Whittaker to tell me the story.'

'And *so*,' said Poirot, twirling his moustaches, 'I, too, knew who the murderer of Joyce was.'

'And all the time Joyce had never seen any murder committed at all!'

'Mrs Drake did not know that. But she had always suspected that someone had been there in the Quarry Wood when she and Michael Garfield had killed Olga Seminoff, and might have seen it happen.'

'When did *you* know it had been Miranda and not Joyce?'

'As soon as common sense forced me to accept the universal verdict that Joyce was a liar. Then Miranda was clearly indicated. She was frequently in the Quarry Wood, observing birds and squirrels. Joyce was, as Miranda told me, her best friend. She said: "We tell each other everything." Miranda was not at the party, so the compulsive liar Joyce could use the story her friend had told her of having once seen a murder committed – probably in order to impress *you*, Madame, the well-known crime writer.'

'That's right, blame it all on me.'

'No, no.'

'Rowena Drake,' mused Mrs Oliver. 'I still can't believe it of her.'

'She had all the qualities necessary. I have always wondered,' he added, 'exactly what sort of woman Lady Macbeth was. What would she be like if you met her in real life? Well, I think I *have* met her.'

'And Michael Garfield? They seem such an unlikely pair.'

'Interesting – Lady Macbeth and Narcissus, an unusual combination.'

'Lady Macbeth,' Mrs Oliver murmured thoughtfully.

'She was a handsome woman – efficient and competent – a born administrator – an unexpectedly good actress. You should have heard her lamenting over the death of the little boy Leopold and weeping large sobs into a dry handkerchief.'

'Disgusting.'

'You remember I asked you who, in your opinion, were or were not nice people.'

'Was Michael Garfield in love with her?'

'I doubt if Michael Garfield has ever loved anyone but himself. He wanted money – a lot of money. Perhaps he believed at first he could influence Mrs Llewellyn-Smythe to dote upon him to the extent of making a Will in his favour – but Mrs Llewellyn-Smythe was not that kind of woman.'

'What about the forgery? I still don't understand that. What was the point of it all?'

'It was confusing at first. Too much forgery, one might say. But if one considered it, the purpose of it was clear. You had only to consider what actually happened.

'Mrs Llewellyn-Smythe's fortune all went to Rowena Drake. The codicil produced was so obviously forged that any lawyer would spot it. It would be contested, and the evidence of experts would result in its being upset, and the original Will would stand. As Rowena Drake's husband had recently died she would inherit everything.'

'But what about the codicil that the cleaning woman witnessed?'

'My surmise is that Mrs Llewellyn-Smythe discovered that Michael Garfield and Rowena Drake were having an affair – probably before her husband died. In her anger Mrs Llewellyn-Smythe made a codicil to her Will leaving everything to her *au pair* girl. Probably the girl told Michael about this – she was hoping to marry him.'

'I thought it was young Ferrier?'

'That was a plausible tale told me by Michael. There was no confirmation of it.'

'Then if he knew there was a real codicil why didn't he marry Olga and get hold of the money that way?'

'Because he doubted whether she really *would* get the money. There is such a thing as undue influence. Mrs Llewellyn-Smythe was an elderly woman and a sick woman also. All her preceeding Wills had been in favour of her own kith and kin – good sensible Wills such as law courts approve of. This girl from foreign parts had been known to her only a year – and had no kind of claim upon her. That codicil even though genuine *could* have been upset. Besides, I doubt if Olga could have put through the purchase of a Greek island – or would even have been willing to do so. She had no influential friends, or contacts in business circles. She was attracted to Michael, but she looked upon him as a good prospect matrimonially, who would enable her to live in England – which is what she wanted to do.'

'And Rowena Drake?'

'She was infatuated. Her husband had been for many years a crippled invalid. She was middle-aged but she was a passionate woman, and into her orbit came a young man of unusual beauty. Women fell for him easily – but he wanted – not the beauty of women – but the exercise of his own creative urge to make beauty. For that he wanted money – a lot of money. As for love – he only loved himself. He was Narcissus. There is an old French song I heard many years ago –'

He hummed softly.

'Regarde, Narcisse
Regarde dans l'eau
Regarde, Narcisse, que tu es beau
Il n'y a au monde
Que la Beauté
Et la Jeunesse,
Hélas! Et la Jeunesse . . .
Regarde, Narcisse . . .
Regarde dans l'eau . . .'

'I can't believe – I simply can't believe that anyone would do murder just to make a garden on a Greek island,' said Mrs Oliver unbelievingly.

'Can't you? Can't you visualize how he held it in his mind? Bare rock, perhaps, but so shaped as to hold possibilities. Earth, cargoes of fertile earth to clothe the bare bones of the rocks – and then plants, seeds shrubs, trees. Perhaps he read in the paper of a shipping millionaire who had created an island garden for the woman he loved. And so it came to him – *he* would make a garden, not for a woman, but – for himself.'

'It still seems to me quite mad.'

'Yes. That happens. I doubt if he even thought of his motive as sordid. He thought of it only as necessary for the creation of more beauty. He'd gone mad on creation. The beauty of the Quarry Wood, the beauty of other gardens he'd laid out and made – and now he envisaged even more – a whole island of beauty. And there was Rowena Drake, infatuated with him. What did she mean to him but the source of money with which he could create beauty. Yes – he had become mad, perhaps. Whom the gods destroy, they first drive mad.'

'He really wanted his island so much? Even with Rowena Drake tied round his neck as well? Bossing him the whole time?'

'Accidents can happen. I think one might possibly have happened to Mrs Drake in due course.'

'One more murder?'

'Yes. It started simply. Olga had to be removed because she knew about the codicil – and she was also to be the scapegoat, branded as a forger. Mrs Llewellyn-Smythe had hidden the original document, so I think that young Ferrier was given money to produce a similar forged document. So obviously forged that it would arouse suspicion at once. That sealed *his* death warrant. Lesley Ferrier, I soon decided, had had no arrangement or love affair with Olga. That was a suggestion made to me by Michael Garfield, but

I think it was Michael who paid money to Lesley. It was Michael Garfield who was laying siege to the *au pair* girl's affections, warning her to keep quiet about this and not tell her employer, speaking of possible marriage in the future but at the same time marking her down cold-bloodedly as the victim whom he and Rowena Drake would need if the money was to come to them. It was not necessary for Olga Seminoff to be accused of forgery, or prosecuted. She needed only to be *suspected* of it. The forgery appeared to benefit her. It could have been done by her very easily, there was evidence to the effect that she did copy her employer's handwriting and if she was suddenly to disappear, it would be assumed that she had been not only a forger, but quite possibly might have assisted her employer to die suddenly. So on a suitable occasion Olga Seminoff died. Lesley Ferrier was killed in what is purported to have been a gang knifing or a knifing by a jealous woman. But the knife that was found in the well corresponds very closely with the knife wounds that he suffered. I knew that Olga's body must be hidden somewhere in this neighbourhood, but I had no idea where until I heard Miranda one day inquiring about a wishing well, urging Michael Garfield to take her there. And he was refusing. Shortly afterwards when I was talking to Mrs Goodbody, I said I wondered where that girl had disappeared to, and she said "Ding dong dell, pussy's in the well" and then I was quite sure the girl's body was in the wishing well. I discovered it was in the wood, in the Quarry Wood, on an incline not far from Michael Garfield's cottage and I thought that Miranda could have seen either the actual murder or the disposal of the body later. Mrs Drake and Michael feared that someone had been a witness – but they had no idea who it was – and as nothing happened they were lulled into security. They made their plans – they were in no hurry, but they set things in motion. She talked about buying land abroad – gave people the idea she wanted to get away from Woodleigh Common. Too many sad associations, referring always to her grief over her husband's death. Everything was nicely in train and then came the shock of Hallowe'en and Joyce's sudden assertion of having witnessed a murder. So now Rowena knew, or thought she knew, who it had been in the wood that day. So she acted quickly. But there was more to come. Young Leopold asked for money – there were things he wanted to buy, he said. What he guessed or knew is uncertain, but he was Joyce's brother, and so they probably thought he knew far more than he really did. And so – he, too, died.'

'You suspected her because of the water clue,' said Mrs Oliver. 'How did you come to suspect Michael Garfield?'

'He fitted,' said Poirot simply. 'And then – the last time I spoke to Michael Garfield, I was sure. He said to me, laughing – "Get thee beyond me, Satan. Go and join your police friends." And I knew then, quite certainly. *It was the other way round*. I said to myself: "*I* am leaving *you behind* me, Satan." A Satan so young and beautiful as Lucifer can appear to mortals . . .'

There was another woman in the room – until now she had not spoken, but now she stirred in her chair.

'Lucifer,' she said. 'Yes, I see now. He was always that.'

'He was very beautiful,' said Poirot, 'and he loved beauty. The beauty that he made with his brain and his imagination and his hands. To it he would sacrifice everything. In his own way, I think, he loved the child Miranda – but he was ready to sacrifice her – to save himself. He planned her death very carefully – he made of it a ritual and, as one might put it, indoctrinated her with the idea. She was to let him know if she were leaving Woodleigh Common – he instructed her to meet him at the Inn where you and Mrs Oliver lunched. She was to have been found on Kilterbury Ring – there by the sign of the double axe, with a golden goblet by her side – a ritual sacrifice.'

'Mad,' said Judith Butler. 'He must have been mad.'

'Madame, your daughter is safe – but there is something I would like to know very much.'

'I think you deserve to know anything I can tell you, Monsieur Poirot.'

'She is your daughter – *was she also Michael Garfield's daughter?*'

Judith was silent for a moment, and then she said, 'Yes.'

'But she doesn't know that?'

'No. She has no idea. Meeting him here was a pure coincidence. I knew him when I was a young girl. I fell wildly in love with him and then – and then I got afraid.'

'Afraid?'

'Yes. I don't know why. Not of anything he would do or that sort of thing, just afraid of his nature. His gentleness, but behind it, a coldness and a ruthlessness. I was even afraid of his passion for beauty and for creation in his work. I didn't tell him I was going to have a child. I left him – I went away and the baby was born. I invented the story of a pilot husband who had had a crash. I moved about rather restlessly. I came to Woodleigh Common more or less by chance. I had got contacts in Medchester where I could find secretarial work.

'And then one day Michael Garfield came here to work in the Quarry Wood. I don't think I minded. Nor did he. All that was over long ago, but later, although I didn't realize how often Miranda went there to the Wood, I *did* worry –'

'Yes,' said Poirot, 'there was a bond between them. A natural affinity. I saw the likeness between them – only Michael Garfield, the follower of Lucifer the beautiful, was evil, and your daughter has innocence and wisdom, and there is no evil in her.'

He went over to his desk and brought back an envelope. Out of it he drew a delicate pencil drawing.

'Your daughter,' he said.

Judith looked at it. It was signed 'Michael Garfield.'

'He was drawing her by the stream,' said Poirot, 'in the Quarry Wood. He drew it, he said, so that he should not forget. He was afraid of forgetting. It wouldn't have stopped him killing her, though.'

Then he pointed to a pencilled word across the top left hand corner.

'Can you read that?'

She spelt it out slowly.

'Iphigenia.'

'Yes,' said Poirot, 'Iphigenia. Agamemnon sacrificed his daughter, so that he should get a wind to take his ships to Troy. Michael would have sacrificed his daughter so that he should have a new Garden of Eden.'

'He knew what he was doing,' said Judith. 'I wonder – if he would ever have had regrets?'

Poirot did not answer. A picture was forming in his mind of a young man of singular beauty lying by the megalithic stone marked with a double axe, and still clasping in his dead fingers the golden goblet he had seized and drained when retribution had come suddenly to save his victim and to deliver him to justice.

It was so that Michael Garfield had died – a fitting death, Poirot thought – but, alas, there would be no garden blossoming on an island in the Grecian Seas . . .

Instead there would be Miranda – alive and young and beautiful.

He raised Judith's hand and kissed it.

'Goodbye, Madame, and remember me to your daughter.'

'She ought always to remember you and what she owes you.'

'Better not – some memories are better buried.'

He went on to Mrs Oliver.

'Good night, chère Madame. Lady Macbeth and Narcissus. It has been remarkably interesting. I have to thank you for bringing it to my notice –'

'That's right,' said Mrs Oliver in an exasperated voice, 'blame it all on me as usual!'